Dating Daniel

Book Four in the Cloverleaf Series
Tales from Birch Valley

By Gloria Herrmann

Dating Daniel

Limitless Publishing, LLC
Kailua, HI 96734
www.limitlesspublishing.com

Formatting: Limitless Publishing

ISBN-13: 978-1-68058-770-8
ISBN-10: 1-68058-770-6

Dedications

This book is dedicated to siblings—our very first enemies, our very first friends. They know the real you, all your secrets, all your fears, and all your dreams. Having a sibling means compromise, learning to share, and protecting and loving one another, all important things we need to be able to do in life. Siblings can drive you crazy, make you laugh until your sides hurt, and be there when no one else is. They understand you and your crazy family. They simply get you.

Then there are the siblings who marry into the family, those in-laws who become like a sister or brother in every sense of the word. They are there with you, sharing in adult moments, like parenthood or watching our parents age.

Brothers and sisters are special, unique, irritating, annoying, and one of the best parts of growing up. If you have one, go hug him or her and tell them just how much they mean to you.

I have several sibling in-laws. I love them, their spouses, and their children dearly.

But there are not enough words to describe my brother, my true partner in crime growing up. I'm proud of everything he is accomplishing in life, and thankful for all the support and grief he has given me over the years. I love his beautiful children, and I love him for being one helluva guy. Thank you, Alex, for being the best baby brother EVER!

Chapter One

Daniel

"Watch out, Daniel!" Patrick shouted.

But it was too late. Daniel collapsed against the cold, wet surface, making a loud thud. Cement, freshly poured for a brand new driveway. The culprit behind the fall? A white plastic bucket which had been hiding behind him. He remained in the thick goo for a moment before he started to laugh.

The expression on his oldest brother Patrick's face was priceless. Was he panicked? Afraid? Angry? Daniel wasn't sure. Patrick had changed quite a bit over the last month. He had been without Beth for over four years, but when Amber showed up, Patrick became completely different but in a very good way. Daniel was thrilled to have the happier version of his older brother around.

"Here, let me help you." Patrick offered his hand to Daniel. "We need to get back to the shop so you can clean up before that cement sets."

"I'll be fine. Let's fix this mess I made." Daniel

could see the large imprint he had left and quickly felt embarrassed.

He felt Patrick put a hand on his shoulder as they both surveyed the damage. "It's okay. We can fix this."

Daniel nodded. He appreciated Patrick being nice and calm about his clumsiness. If this had happened a couple months ago, he knew Patrick would have freaked out.

"Well, let's see if we can smooth this out and then we'll get back to the shop. Sound good?" Patrick smiled at Daniel and turned to go to the work truck.

Daniel could hear Patrick's cell phone ring. As soon as his older brother answered the call, he knew it was Amber. A bite of loneliness hit Daniel unexpectedly. Maybe he should call Nina? They'd last gone out about a week ago. He enjoyed her company for the most part, and she was beyond gorgeous, but there was something, almost like an itch you just couldn't quite reach, something that he couldn't explain but definitely felt.

***

"Oh good, you guys are back. Geez, Daniel, what happened?" Maggie asked from her desk as they walked into the shop. She rose slowly out of her chair, carefully balancing as she righted herself. Daniel almost laughed. His sister looked as though she had swallowed a beach ball. Her hands supported her lower back as she waddled over to them. "You're a mess."

"I know. I tripped on a dang bucket. I just wasn't watching where I was going." Daniel could feel his cheeks grow warm.

"But you're okay?" Her green eyes were bright with concern.

"He's fine," Patrick interjected, patting Daniel's back as he headed toward his office.

Daniel nodded. He was fine. It was more his ego that was bruised. "I'm okay, Mags."

"Good." Maggie looked into his eyes searchingly, almost as if she didn't quite believe him.

He offered her a stiff smile. "I'm fine, really."

Maggie's brilliant and famed O'Brien eyes suddenly grew wide. "Ouch." She pressed her hand to her round, protruding belly.

"Maggie, is something wrong?" Daniel could feel panic surging through him.

"I think so. Gosh, that was the weirdest pain. I don't think the baby was kicking." She steadied herself against the counter.

"Well, what was it doing?" Daniel moved around to the other side of the counter and gingerly started to pat Maggie's back. He bent down toward her belly and whispered, "This is your Uncle Daniel. Listen here, you, you adorable little baby in there, be nice to your mom."

Maggie let out a deep laugh. "You'd better listen to your uncle." She looked at him and offered a grateful smile as she grasped his arm. "Thanks."

"I don't know how you do it. I mean, that's got to be the scariest thing."

"What, being pregnant? It's a little nerve-wracking, but I kind of signed up for this." Maggie cradled her belly and ran her hands along the sides, smiling the entire time. There was not a doubt in Daniel's mind that his sister was happy. "When you meet the right girl and finally settle down, you are going to make an awesome dad, Daniel."

He swallowed. Finding the right girl to settle down with was proving far more difficult than he had ever imagined. Growing up he'd thought he would have worked the family construction business, met a great girl, and had kids by now. He was almost thirty and it was looking less and less like a real possibility, but there was Nina.

***

Daniel was stretched out on the leather couch in the living room of his childhood home. Heck, it was still his home. He had never moved out.

"I think we should float the river tomorrow," Daniel suggested to his brother, Patrick. He rearranged the throw pillows and burrowed himself into a more comfortable position.

Patrick sat across from him on the opposite couch, his eyes closed, and he grunted a reply.

"Why not?"

"I don't know. Maybe Amber and Dylan would like to go. I can see if Mom will watch Finn and Connor," Patrick relented as he exhaled loudly.

"I thought it would be fun. You know, summer is almost gone."

"Daniel, it's only August. I think it's going to hang around for a while," Patrick added. He attempted to stifle a yawn.

"Yeah, but the river will be lower and I don't like getting caught up on those rocks." Daniel could recall his fair share of getting stuck on the nasty rocks which were hidden under the flowing water. As far back as Daniel could remember, he and all of his siblings would take their giant inner tubes and make their way down the river, basking in the warmth of the summer sun while enjoying a leisurely float. At the start of the season, right after spring, the snow runoff from the surrounding mountains would cause small rapids, which only added to the thrill. Hanging out with friends and family down on the river was a popular thing to do during the summer. As you floated from the best starting point, you would pass little kids splashing and building sandcastles. There was a key point where you had to exit the river, right before a nasty gorge, which was formed from years of the mighty water carving deep grooves into the sides of the mountain. Was floating dangerous? Hell yes. Was floating awesome, especially if you strung an ice chest to your inner tube? Hell yes. As far as Daniel was concerned, it was his favorite part of summer and he felt like he had missed out this year. First there was his brother Liam's wedding, then Patrick had fallen in love and was now making Daniel pick up more hours at work. As for Maggie, well, she was already married and had Melanie, but things had gotten a little rocky in her marriage at the start of spring. But Daniel knew things would work out. They always sort of did with the O'Brien family. That's why he couldn't make any sense of why he was still single.

"You know, Daniel, you're right. We can float the river tomorrow."

Daniel blinked rapidly. His usually argumentative, moody brother was being far too agreeable. Daniel was still surprised at how well Patrick reacted to him falling into the driveway they had been putting in earlier that day. "You sure?"

"I mean, I'll run it by Amber, but I'm sure she'd love for us to go and it'd be fun for Dylan." Patrick shrugged lightly when their mother, Mary, rounded the archway of the living room.

"What are you boys up to?" Her hands were on her plump hips, a cheerful apron draped across her front. She eyed them suspiciously.

"Nothing. Daniel suggested we float the river tomorrow. Would you mind watching the boys, Mom?" Patrick asked.

"Float the river? Oh dear, that's so dangerous." Her eyes turned stormy with worry. "Dinner is ready if you guys are."

Daniel looked up at her. His stomach gurgled. The thought of dinner was enticing. His mother's cooking was amazing; it was one of the reasons he was so reluctant to leave home. "What's for dinner, Mom?"

Mary smiled at him. "Well, those little boys insisted on my mac n' cheese and I just couldn't say no."

Patrick and Daniel both laughed as they slowly rose from their couches. Mary turned her attention to Patrick. "Is Amber coming by for dinner?"

"I'm not sure. I know she was working at the diner today. I'll call her and double-check," Patrick answered. He fished his cell phone out of his back jean pocket.

"Tell her she can bring her lovely boy as well. I made plenty of food," Mary added as she started to retreat back to her favorite part of their home, the kitchen.

Daniel watched as Patrick started to call Amber. It felt so strange that his brother was dating again after four years of being widowed. Daniel was happy that he had found someone, but he couldn't help but feel almost lonely. A vibration tingled through him as his own cell phone buzzed unexpectedly. He pulled it out and answered.

"Hello?"

"Hi, Daniel," he heard Nina's sugary voice reply. He was a caught a little off guard. They'd gone out a couple times over the summer, but he wasn't sure he really felt a deep connection with her, at least not in the way that his brothers all seemed to be connected with their significant others. Liam was beyond in love with Rachel. Watching the two of them together was almost unbearable. Patrick and Amber seemed like they had always been together. They were completely comfortable with one another, and Amber sort of fit right into the family. Where did that leave Daniel? Alone.

"What's up, Nina?" Daniel felt Patrick's eyes on him, but he tried to ignore the curious stare and decided to take this call into his bedroom.

There was a long pause. "I don't know. I was kind of bored. What are you doing right now?"

"I'm about to eat dinner with my family."

"You want to take me out instead?" Her tone

shifted from sweet to sultry. She certainly didn't beat around the bush.

Daniel let out a sigh. He could hear the loud chattering of the family gathering around the table for dinner. They wouldn't mind if he went out; it wasn't as though he were a child. But Daniel enjoyed spending time with his family, and he loved that on every Sunday they would all get together and share a meal. They would catch up on everything that had happened during the week, and the kids would play. It was Daniel's favorite day of the week. He looked forward to the noise, the bickering, and the memories that were made. The only thing that was difficult about the family dinners were was he didn't have a significant other seated next to him. Nope, he usually sat next to one of the twins. That got him thinking. How was he ever going to finally bring someone home or have someone special sitting next to him if he didn't get out there and start really dating? It was high time he did.

"Nina, want me to come and get you?"

There was another pause. "What do you have in mind?"

Daniel didn't really know. He was sort of just winging it. Digging up false confidence from some unknown place, Daniel said, "How about we just see where the night takes us?"

"Now you're talking." She hung up.

He couldn't help but feel a little nervous. What was he going to do to entertain this girl? His stomach let rumbled loudly. He knew there was homemade mac and cheese being gobbled up right at that very moment. Maybe he could sneak a couple bites of that cheesy goodness before he had to get ready.

He had the large serving spoon dipped into the gooey cheddar-infused concoction when Patrick appeared next to him.

"So why was Nina calling?" his older brother asked quietly. He held his plate out to Daniel and nodded toward the food.

Daniel sighed and scooped a large portion onto Patrick's plate. "She wanted to get together tonight."

Patrick frowned. "Man, don't get involved with her."

"Why not?" Daniel glared at Patrick. Didn't he deserve to meet someone, to have a shot at happiness?

Patrick's brow softened and he held Daniel's gaze for a moment. He sported the same famed O'Brien eyes. Patrick finally looked down. "She's just not the right type of girl for you. You need someone…" He stopped as they both saw their mother approach.

"Daniel, dear, do you want to come sit down and join the family?" She wore a broad smile, and her eyes twinkled under the bright lights of the kitchen.

"Yeah, Mom. I'm just making a plate."

Mary grabbed the cobalt blue dinner plate from him and ordered, "You go sit. You worked today and from the sounds of it had a rough time of things. Let me make your plate, dear."

Patrick held his plate and led the way into the dining room. Daniel took an empty seat next to

Connor, the boy's chubby four-year-old face covered in cheese sauce. He had even managed to land a rogue noodle in his curly blonde hair. Connor looked up at Daniel, his blue eyes, his mother's eyes, filled with joy.

"Uncle Daniel, this is the bestest meal ever." Connor happily shoveled more noodles into his mouth. The kid was right. This was the best mac and cheese, and no one could argue that.

Grandpa Paddy sat at one end of the long table. He eyed Daniel and cleared his throat to speak. "Heard you had yourself a wee bit of trouble today, son."

Daniel hung his head before facing his grandfather's curious and playful stare. "Yeah, I wasn't looking where I was going."

His father, Pat, seated at the other end of the table, looked over at Daniel. "Son, you need to be more aware of your surroundings. It's a good thing it was only cement."

Daniel couldn't help but feel a mixture of irritation blended with embarrassment. "I know, Dad. It was an accident."

"I understand that accidents happen, but you can prevent them by being more careful," Pat spoke slowly, clearly trying to drum his point into Daniel.

Patrick glanced over at him, a tight-lipped frown on his face. "It was honest mistake, Dad," Patrick said in an attempt to defend Daniel.

Their father, with his graying dark hair and piercing emerald green eyes—both of which Patrick had inherited—turned his focus on his oldest child. "Patrick, I don't recall having to tell you to be careful. You have some sense about you. Your brother, Daniel, he could do better with paying attention and being a little more like you. The job site is a dangerous place."

Daniel's cheeks were growing warm. He felt like a child. This wasn't the first time their father had compared him to his oldest brother. He had been told on more than one occasion to be more serious like Patrick, to be more helpful like Liam, so this was hardly anything new, but that didn't take away the sting.

"That's quite enough now," Mary interrupted as she gave Pat a stern look. Daniel knew his mother would be discussing this in private with their father later. He almost felt pity for him.

Pat exhaled loudly and set his fork a little too loudly down on the plate. "Just be more aware of your surroundings. You need to start paying attention. Your mind is always elsewhere. Treat the business like a real job. Respect the job, and you won't find yourself in a puddle of cement."

"Pat, enough," Mary grumbled quietly, her hand wrapped tightly around a cloth napkin.

"Aye, your father is right, lad. The site is mighty dangerous, but you're smart and you do a good job." Grandpa Paddy gave Daniel a sympathetic look before shooting a warning stare to Pat.

Daniel simply nodded and found he had lost his appetite. He pushed his plate forward and rose from his seat. "I'm actually expected elsewhere."

"Where are you going, dear?" Mary asked. She glared at her husband.

"Don't act like that. Sit back down and eat your

dinner. Can't someone say anything to you without you throwing a fit?"

"I already had plans. But I also don't appreciate being spoken to like I'm some kind of screw up either, Dad," Daniel answered defensively.

As the two men squared off, everyone grew quiet and kept their gazes on their plates. Daniel stood and looked down at his father, who kept his eyes on his plate, a tiny muscle in his jaw ticking away in irritation. "You know what? Just go," Pat spat angrily.

Daniel loved his father, but their relationship often broke down in a series of arguments and belittling comments. It was a source of frustration for both of them at times. Daniel was not a fighter. He used his jovial nature to get him through tough situations and cherished the close relationship he had with his mother, who he took after. Daniel had always felt as though their father favored Patrick and Liam. And Maggie, being the only girl and the apple of Pat's eye, had a special place in his heart. Where did that leave Daniel, the middle child? He often tried to find refuge behind a joke, trying to pass it off as not a big deal when it really did cut him deeply.

Daniel eyed everyone. When he spoke, his voice shattered the uncomfortable tension which hung thick in the room. "I'm sorry, everyone." He looked back at his father, who avoided his gaze. Daniel squeezed his father's shoulder as he exited the room. He loved his father, but he wasn't certain just how many more of these arguments he could take. As Daniel got into his truck, he felt more eager to see

Nina. After the rough day he'd had, it was time to see if he could turn this night into a win.

Chapter Two

Summer evenings were incredible in Birch Valley. Granted, it wasn't as though Daniel knew anything different. He'd spent his entire life in this rural, close-knit town. He only knew that when the hot day was done sizzling, the evenings were the reward. The sky would stay bright until well after ten at night, and the temperature would lower to a comfortable coolness which made sitting outside a pleasure.

Daniel drummed his fingers against the steering wheel, and he turned up the volume on the radio, making the music louder. He needed to banish these feelings. He still reeled from the argument with his father, but he was on his way out to the Belsky farm to pick up Nina. What he was going to do with her after he got her, God only knew. Daniel couldn't explain how lost he felt when he was in her company.

He rolled the window down and inhaled the sweet fragrance of the summer air—a mixture of freshly cut grass and sun-baked pine trees, with a smoky tinge from BBQ cookouts. These were the scents of Birch Valley in late August, the tail end of one of Daniel's favorite seasons. It was the cusp before vibrant yellows and burnt orange colors masked the trees, before the leaves browned and littered the ground. Everyone savored these last days before the autumn chill started to nip at their faces. Summer was so short, and all of the residents of Birch Valley made the most of the warm weather.

Daniel was deep in thought, but he paid attention his surroundings as he passed several streets lined with similar-looking homes, homes that belonged to friends, kids he grew up and played with. The abodes were a wide variety of colors. All of them had neatly trimmed hedges and lawns which were brilliant shades of green and shaded by large trees. These homes belonged to people who practically raised him. This town, so close-knit and interconnected, felt like one large family.

When Daniel pulled onto the road that led toward the Belsky home, he remembered that was part of Nina's appeal. Her whole family lived on the outskirts of town, distancing themselves from the heart of the Birch Valley. They weren't interested in the town gossip, though they were sometimes the center of many ridiculous tales and rumors. They were the famed *Russians*, after all. Daniel grew up knowing very little about those people, other than their thick accents and their strange but simple clothing. He did know one thing: his mother had always reminded him stories were just that, only stories, and they weren't always fact. He was to show them the same kindness as anyone in town.

His truck cruised smoothly down the quiet highway leading out to Nina's family's farm. The sky was beginning to turn a shade of violet, with a thick colorful streak of tangerine closer to the horizon. There was not a cloud to be seen for miles. Singing along to a one of his favorite songs he hadn't heard on the radio for a long time, Daniel was starting to feel the anger from the earlier fight with his father dissipate. He was more at ease. It didn't take much to pull him out of a rotten mood. Some good music and riding around in his truck outside of town pretty much healed any sour feelings.

Daniel found himself pulling slowly into a gravel driveway sooner than he expected. He had been so enthralled with the tunes, he had sort of been on autopilot. He parked the truck near the tall two-story home, which was painted a faded apricot with white trim on the eaves.

As Daniel exited his truck, a small flock of speckled chickens scattered wildly. A goat was in the yard, grazing on the lawn and staring at him with little interest. He shook his head and laughed. He wasn't a city boy by any means, but he certainly hadn't been raised on a farm either. The O'Brien family had owned a dog once, and Daniel had a couple of goldfish growing up, but he couldn't imagine his mother putting up with much more. He stared at the rolling hills which sheltered the vast fields the Belsky family worked and farmed. It wasn't Daniel's first time out to the farm. He and Patrick had completed several jobs for Mr. Belsky, but Daniel had been so focused on the work he hadn't taken too much notice of how gorgeous their property was. Maybe someday he'd own a piece of land outside of town. His brother, Liam, had purchased a cabin, which came with some land and a lake. It was in the opposite direction of the farm and was a little more elevated and far more mountainous, whereas this land was flat, perfect for farming—at least that's what he thought. What did he know?

Daniel walked up to a porch in desperate need of paint. It was peeled, chipping, weathered, and had certainly seen better days. He knocked on the white front door, and as he waited he began to feel a little nervous. Where was he going to take Nina?

He was about to knock again when he saw Nina's older sister, Hannah, open the door slowly.

"Hi." Her voice was quiet. She looked away, but a small smile remained on her lips.

"Hey, Hannah. How are you doing?" Daniel asked as Hannah motioned for him to come inside.

"I'm good. How are you?" she responded as she started to lead him inside.

The first thing Daniel noticed was the strong citrus smell; it permeated the air, a crisp, clean scent. The dark wood floors gleamed, even in the dim lighting. Daniel looked around as Hannah ushered him toward the dining room. A massive table swallowed up the room, and an enormous hutch stood against one wall, its shelves covered in delicate-looking dishes.

Hannah smiled at him again. "Have a seat. Nina's not quite ready. Can I get you something to drink? I just made some lemonade."

Daniel did feel a little parched, and he was not about to refuse homemade lemonade. "That would be great, Hannah, only if you don't mind."

Her cheeks turned a simple shade of pink. She nodded and left him there. The house was eerily quiet, so completely different than the O'Brien home. Daniel's family home was either filled with the sounds of his rambunctious niece and nephews, or the noise of Grandpa Paddy yelling at the TV as he watched a soccer game from his home country of Ireland. Silence was not something he was used to, which suited him fine. He enjoyed noise, especially when the family gathered around the table. There was always an array of conversations, with everyone chiming in on each others' talks, adding bits here and there and then going back to their own. If nothing else being an O'Brien was entertaining. Daniel never really remembered a time when he felt bored with his family. In fact, standing there in that dining room, with everything silent, started to make Daniel a tad more nervous and a little uncomfortable.

He shoved his hands in the front pockets of his jeans and stretched, trying to dismiss his unease as Hannah appeared. She carried a tray with two glasses and a small plate piled with cookies. As she sat the tray down on the table, she smiled again. Daniel could sense her shyness. He suddenly felt the overwhelming desire to crack a joke, something to break the ice.

"I know you guys are going out, but I thought, since it might be awhile, maybe you were hungry?" she asked as she shrugged.

"Nah, me? I'm on a strict diet. I can't be having cookies."

Daniel watched as the color drained from her face. He knew she didn't get his joke. "Oh no, I'm kidding. Obviously I like cookies a lot." He patted his stomach.

She let out a slight laugh and rolled her eyes. "You had me there for a minute." She removed the glasses from the tray and took a seat. "You might as well sit. It's going to be a while."

"Gosh, really?" Daniel scowled as he glanced down at his watch. It had been almost two hours since he'd spoken with Nina.

Hannah nodded. "That's Nina for ya."

Daniel slowly took a seat as Hannah offered the plate of cookies to him. "I know they aren't probably nearly as good as your mother's, but these are pretty darn tasty." She grabbed one for herself and took a bite.

Hannah's earlier awkwardness was now gone. He felt better about that and started to relax as he bit into a cookie. Shortbread—the light buttery flavor filled his mouth. He didn't dare say it, but this cookie might just be better than his mom's shortbread. "These are awesome," Daniel said as he put the rest of the cookie in his mouth and reached for another.

"I told you." She winked at him.

"So what's keeping Nina?" His patience was wearing a little thin.

Hannah laughed again and her whole body shook with the sound. Daniel loved it. "Oh, Daniel, you poor thing. This is Nina we're talking about. She takes *forever* to get ready."

The words "high maintenance" rang out in Daniel's mind. Not that he should be surprised, because she always looked flawless. His gaze drifted up toward Hannah. She was the complete opposite of her sister. She reminded him a lot of himself. He had two brothers, who were well known for being the town hunks, and he often felt as though he was overlooked. He imagined Hannah must feel that way too. She was pretty, but not a knockout like her sister. Nina had long, pale blonde hair, and Hannah's was golden. Nina's makeup was always impeccable, and Daniel wasn't sure that Hannah even had any on, but he didn't think she needed it. He would have to say she won when it came to her eyes; they were gorgeous. They were a funny blue with flecks of amber he hadn't really noticed before. Hannah's eyes were stunning.

Daniel took a leisurely sip of the lemonade, which was some of the most refreshing he'd ever had. The sourness matched the sweetness and wasn't overpowering. It was, well, perfect.

"Think we'll have a long summer?" Hannah asked, lifting her glass to her lips for a drink.

"I'm not sure. I love this time of the year though. I'm not really ready for winter to come back yet."

Hannah's eyes twinkled, a faraway expression softening her face. "Yeah, I love this time of the year best. But fall is beyond the most beautiful time of the year. God, the colors." She let out a heavy sigh of appreciation.

She was right; Daniel had to agree. Fall was gorgeous in Birch Valley.

The distant sound of someone clearing their throat caught them both off guard. Nina stood at the entrance of the dining room, hands on her hips in a sassy pose, almost as if she were waiting for the compliments to start.

"Hi, Daniel." Nina cooed.

He rose from his chair, his gaze briefly meeting Hannah's. He almost missed the flicker of disappointment which passed through her eyes.

"Hey, Nina." He moved toward her. "Hannah, thanks again for the lemonade and cookies."

Without looking up she politely but quietly answered, "You're very welcome."

***

"So, where to?" Daniel asked after he got Nina inside the truck and was slowly pulling away from her house.

Nina grinned. "Wanna go to Spokane?"

Daniel crinkled his nose. "Now?" He caught a glimpse of the time on his radio. It was already almost nine, though it looked more like early evening with the bright sky.

"Why not? There's nothing else to do in this crummy town." Her voice was laced with apparent irritation and mild disgust.

He pulled the truck out onto the highway and started in the direction of town. He really had no desire to drive over an hour away, and for what? To deal with traffic and hoards of people? He'd much rather them just do something in Birch Valley. They could catch a late movie or eat somewhere, just anything besides going to Spokane.

"Nina, why don't we just grab something to eat and maybe go for a drive? Or…"

She cut him off before he could finish his suggestion. "Daniel, that's boring."

"Boring?" He was a little surprised by her quick dismissal. What was he doing with a girl like this? How could he possibly keep her entertained?

"Yes, because that's, like, normal everyday stuff to do here. Let's go to some bars in Spokane, experience a little nightlife." She wiggled her eyebrows playfully and sent him a sexy, yet sinister smile. "Let's go have fun."

"But it's already sort of late," Daniel countered as they rolled slowly through town. He spotted Herrick's and wished they could just go and eat there.

Nina rolled her eyes. "Don't act like such an old man. Geez, it's only, like, nine." She turned her pretty face to him and pouted. "You haven't really taken me anywhere, like, ever."

"Fine," he relented. There was no way he could argue with her, and she quickly rewarded him with a kiss to his cheek, her tongue tracing down the side of his neck. He felt her hand on his thigh, and he tried to focus as he navigated them out of Birch Valley.

The drive to Spokane seem to take far longer than he hoped. As they followed the single-lane highway, Daniel scanned the road for any deer that may decide to dart across. He started to grow anxious. Nina was cuddled next to him. She wasn't much for talking tonight, which surprised Daniel as she was usually more chatty. Granted, it was usually about topics that interested her, not that he minded. He just didn't care for uncomfortable silence. He applied a little more pressure to the gas pedal. He needed to get them to Spokane soon, and Daniel felt the urge to get out of this truck.

Some miles had passed and the sky grew darker, the cab of the truck still quiet. "Everything okay?"

"Yeah," she said, her hand squeezed his thigh, sending a zing further up his body, something that he had been fighting the entire ride. This girl had him in nervous knots, and he was finding it hard to concentrate. "You know, we should spend the night in Spokane. Get a room after we go bar hopping." She nipped at his earlobe, tugging it gently with her teeth. He heard himself groan.

"Yeah, I don't think your father would appreciate that." Daniel focused on the road, willing all his blood flow to stay in his brain. He had to remain in control and not allow the flood of thoughts to cloud his reasoning.

"Ah, don't be like that. It would be fun." Another squeeze of his thigh, and this time she dug her nails into his jeans. He could almost swear they were piercing through the denim material. This girl was sending him over the edge. Daniel grew more eager to get to Spokane and have a drink, just so he could get a little breathing room.

"I'm still not so sure it's a good idea. Let's just get into Spokane and kind of see where the night takes us, okay?" He sighed with relief as they were welcomed by the bright lights of the largest city on their side of the state.

"Thank God." He heard her mutter quietly as she turned her attention to the array of buildings and cars on either side of them.

"Want to grab a bite to eat?" Daniel suggested as they passed an endless variety of fast food options. His stomach started to growl.

"Is that all you think about?" Nina curled her top lip slightly. "Head downtown, we're about to have a good time." She moved back over to the passenger seat away from him. He instantly missed her warmth.

Daniel swallowed. He wasn't so sure her idea and his idea of a good time matched up so well. He snuck a glance at her. Even in the darkness her beauty was obvious. She had started to touch up her makeup and fuss with her hair, paying no attention to him.

"Nina, you're beautiful. You don't need to do anymore." Daniel was hoping to reassure her.

She rolled her eyes at him again, obviously annoyed. "I know, but I need to look good. We're not in Birch Valley anymore. You never know who you might meet." She winked and smiled slyly.

They continued down Division Street, the main stretch of road that led them through the enormous and busy city.

"Ooh, stop at that one." Nina pointed right by his face. He could smell her heady fruity scent. It came from expensive lotion, and she had just slathered her tan arms in the stuff.

He pulled into a spot in front of a street corner bar. Patrons crowded inside. What did he expect? It was a Friday. But the place was almost full to bursting with people, and Daniel instantly knew he was out of his element. When they walked into the bar, he didn't know how to describe how he felt. Shell-shocked, that was it. Daniel loved noise but this was too much. He could feel people staring at them, well, staring at Nina. He felt judged by the looks, like why was a girl of her caliber there with him? Nina though, she reveled in the attention. She wore a black tank top, with silky thin straps hanging precariously on her tan shoulders. Her gold necklace and earrings sparkled and reflected the lights from inside the bar. Her tight, dark-wash jeans clung to what curves she did have. Nina wanted to be noticed and as she swayed her hips to the blasting music, the two of them sauntered over to the bar. Daniel could feel the lustful glances gobbling her up. *Mission accomplished, Nina.* He moved his hand to the small of her back to show some kind of command, but she was the one leading them to the front of the bar. A young guy was tending bar. He sported a hip beard and hair that was far too pretty for a guy, in Daniel's opinion. It was purposely kept long and was parted in a fashion that seemed like it would get in his face. He had thick earrings embedded in his lobes, and tattoos covered his exposed arms. Daniel knew there were probably dozens more under the white dress shirt he sported. The bartender wore black skinny jeans, something Daniel still didn't quite get. Why did these guys want to make their legs look like sticks? He knew he was judging this guy solely based on his appearance, and Daniel was a little ticked at himself. That wasn't the kind of person he was and that's why it was best for him not to be a place like this.

"What can I get you?" the bartender asked Nina. His eyes glinted with interest as he looked her up and down appreciatively.

Nina batted her lashes. "What do you suggest?" Her voice became sugary. Daniel watched the two interact. It was obvious they were flirting. It was as though Nina had completely forgotten about Daniel.

"I have just the thing for someone as hot as you." He winked at her and grinned as he grabbed a small glass, then a bottled filled with red liquid. After splashing in a little of this and that and God knows what else to the mixture, he passed her the drink.

"Mmm, that's yummy." Nina turned up her charm. Daniel slid onto the bar stool, but neither the bartender or Nina took notice of him.

Daniel coughed. "I'll take a beer, please."

"Sure thing, buddy." The bartender replied with a quick nod, then threw a lusty stare back at Nina. "Is that drink any good?"

Nina nodded. "So good. I think I need a couple more," she said, her voice sing-song with delight.

Daniel was finally given the beer he ordered. Nina braced herself against the wooden counter of the bar. The bartender brought her another drink and let his fingers linger on her wrist. Daniel took a long swig of his beer. He didn't have any claim on Nina. It's not like they were a couple, but didn't it go without saying that when you were out with someone, that you didn't flirt with other people?

After another beer down and several drinks in, Nina loudly said, "We need to make this more fun."

Daniel wasn't so certain he could put up with much more. His head was pounding slightly from the loud music and lack of food. The bartender was still sending Nina sexy smiles and winks, and a couple of people approached her as they worked on their drinks. The invitation for free drinks was unreal to Daniel. Everyone wanted to buy his beautiful date something, *his date*. Somehow Nina seem to forget she was there with him. Her laughter rang out as others told her how incredible she looked, and had she considered modeling? The compliments just went on and on. She devoured all their words and rewarded them with a killer smile or a gentle pat, and even a couple hugs. Was there no end in sight? Daniel wasn't so sure, and they had only been in the bar for an hour or so.

Daniel tried to get her attention but was finding it increasingly difficult. Enough was enough. Maybe it was time for him to take charge. He rose up from his stool and pinned her gently against the counter, his hands taking hold of her narrow hips. He eliminated any space between them. Daniel stared at her mouth, her glossy pink rosebud lips pouty and begging to be kissed. Daniel pulled her close to him and claimed her mouth with his. He could hear her moan softly. He had never kissed her before. He expected a spark, some kind of jolt, but where was it? He leaned back, giving her a little space. Nina's eyes were filled with a thick mixture of lust, intrigue, and confusion. He could see she was trying to figure this out in her mind. She had challenged Daniel, flaunted herself enough to make him so terribly jealous that he'd acted like an animal. That wasn't him. He hadn't been raised to treat a woman that way, especially one he might want to bring home to meet the family, to become a part of the family.

"Let's go have some fun."

Daniel grabbed his dark ale and swallowed the remaining contents. He was growing a little dizzy, and he knew he was getting in over his head with Nina. "What did you have in mind?"

Nina smiled and brought herself closer to him. She splayed her hands across his broad chest, and in a sexy slur Nina whispered, "I think you know."

Yes, Daniel was way in over his head.

Chapter Three

"Come on, Nina, please just get inside the truck." Daniel grabbed at her, but she pulled away.

She shook her head, her normally perfect blonde hair messy and in her face. Her mascara and eyeliner were smudged, creating dark streaks. "No, let's go to one more bar."

"No, we're good. It's time to go home now." Daniel wasn't used to dealing with someone who was drunk, let alone a wild girl like Nina. They had visited several bars, and Daniel was done. He wanted to get them home, but Nina was making it nearly impossible.

"You're no fun," she shouted.

Fun. Yeah, she had promised him there would be more fun in store, but apparently that translated into more bars, more drinking, her dancing, and her having fun. Daniel had anything but.

He had hit his breaking point, and she was beginning to make a scene in the parking lot. A police cruiser rolled by slowly, the officer insider eyeing Daniel as he tried to get her inside the truck.

29

Running his hands through his hair, he felt himself growing more irritated by the second.

"Just get inside the damn truck. We need to head home," Daniel commanded with a little more bite in his voice.

"Whatever." Nina stumbled to the opened passenger side door. Daniel practically shoved her inside and slammed the door with frustration.

He inhaled deeply as he got around to the driver's side. Once inside the cab he started the truck. He let the engine warm up and watched some cars move down the now quiet street. It was as though everyone had vanished. It was a little after one in the morning, and it was eerily quiet. They were surrounded by tall buildings, ancient and weathered, mixed in with modern works of art. The architectural giants stood silent, shadowing the downtown area, masking the traffic lights and street lamps. Daniel could almost hear the rumble of the Spokane river running through Riverfront Park. He sighed and started to work his way to the north, exhausted from babysitting Nina for the last couple hours, enduring her whiny demands. Daniel was more than ready to be home. He wasn't looking forward to the drive ahead, and as they ventured further up Division Street, they finally rolled into the darkness of the single-lane highway that would lead them home.

The late-night darkness surrounded them, and Daniel tiredly watched for deer or any other wildlife that might try to dart across the road. Nina laid her head on Daniel, snorting gently. He softened toward her, his irritation vanishing as he let his thoughts run wild. The weight of her sleeping body leaning on him felt nice. Maybe tonight was a fluke; he sure hoped so. Bar hopping in Spokane, as Daniel came to realize, was not something he wanted to do again anytime soon, or rather, ever again. If he could just find a way to keep Nina content and happy, find things to entertain her in Birch Valley, maybe they could make this into something. Not that Daniel was desperate, but in some ways he kind of was. He wanted what his brothers and sister had, what his parents had. Was that too much to ask for? He didn't think so.

He yawned as they continued to drive, the hum of the truck almost lulling Daniel to sleep. He stretched his eyelids high and turned the radio on low, then turned on the air conditioner to help him wake up. A thought popped into his mind, and he began to formulate a plan to show Nina how he liked spending his time. Well, it was worth a shot.

***

Sunlight filtered into Daniel's bedroom, causing him to peel his tired eyes open. He flipped his pillow over, relishing the cool material, and he closed his eyes again, praying he could catch a little more sleep. Unfortunately he could hear noise coming from the kitchen, undoubtedly caused by two four-year-old boys he loved tremendously. The ceiling fan hummed as it cut through the warmth entering the room. Today was going to be hot, which only made going to the river that much more perfect.

Daniel managed to leave the comfort of his bed. He could smell the scents of breakfast and his stomach growled. Bacon and coffee, just what he needed to shake the headache punching his brain and pounding behind his eyes. His eyeballs felt like they were dry and shriveled up. He hadn't drunk much, and he'd been completely sober by the time he'd managed to get Nina in the truck. Dehydrated was more like it. Daniel shuffled down the hall to the kitchen.

"Morning, dear," Mary's cheery voice welcomed him as she stood in front of the stove.

Daniel grabbed his favorite mug, an overly large one with a moose silhouette on it, and headed straight for the coffee pot. He inhaled the rich aroma and watched the dark liquid fill his mug. It had been a gift from Finn and Connor. "Morning, Ma."

"What time did you get in last night?" Mary asked as she moved the eggs around in the large skillet.

Daniel groaned. "More like this morning."

"Oh dear, I knew it was late. Maybe you should go back to bed."

"Nah, I'm going to float the river today." Daniel let the coffee work its magic and took several sips, burning his mouth each time. "Is Patrick around? I thought I heard the boys."

"Yes, Patrick dropped them off a little bit ago. He went to pick up Amber and Dylan. I guess they are all going to the river too. Maggie mentioned that she and Rachel were going to come over for a visit."

"Michael and Melanie going to go to the river too?" Daniel asked as he moved over to the dining room and took a seat. He practically inhaled his coffee.

"Let me get you some breakfast, my precious boy," Mary said in a sing-song voice as she scooped eggs onto a plate. Daniel watched as small billows of steam escaped from the pile. His stomach let out a loud growl, making both of them laugh.

"Thanks, Mom."

"Let me grab my tea and we can eat together." Mary hurried back into the kitchen. Daniel watched as she retrieved toast and quickly buttered it. "Here, sweetie, you should have some toast." She handed him the warm and buttery bread, and Daniel smiled in appreciation.

"You're too good to me."

"You're my boy. This is what moms do." Mary planted a kiss on his cheek.

***

The truck was loaded with several neon-colored tubes for floating down the river. Daniel wiped the sweat from his brow after hefting the overly full ice chest into the back of the bed. As he slammed the tailgate closed, he knew it was going to be a scorcher. The metal of the handle was hot to the touch. Daniel was even more grateful for the cool relief he was about to feel from the Columbia River.

The drive to the tube launch was only a thirty-minute drive from the house. Daniel drove a little faster than normal. He already had been in touch with his brothers, and they were already there hanging out on the sandy shore waiting on him. His mother had insisted on making sandwiches for everyone and he hadn't been able to sneak away quick enough, not without her loading that ice chest with enough food and drinks to feed several O'Brien families.

Daniel followed the highway, making a right at the turn which would lead him to a gravel and primitive road. He was thankful he had a four-by-four. The rain ruts were deep and the sandy mix of gravel was slippery under even the best tires, but Daniel maneuvered carefully and grew excited as he saw the sun bouncing off the cold blue body of the river.

When he parked his overly large truck next to Liam's smaller red pickup, he got out of the cab and noticed Liam and Patrick heading in his direction.

Liam waved as he climbed up a small sandy hill. "Hey, Daniel," he called out. Daniel raised his hand and went to the bed of his truck. The sun was beating down hard. He could feel it biting through his loose t-shirt.

"You finally made it," Patrick announced as he and Liam stood to the side of the truck. They began removing the ties which secured all the brightly colored tubes. Liam grabbed a pink and green tube and stood waiting as Patrick helped Daniel remove the ice chest. "God, what's in here?"

"Mom packed us lunch." Daniel laughed. They carefully climbed down to the shore, where the rest of the group gathered, and found a small section of shade under a tree. Michael was in the water with

Melanie, splashing around as she giggled loudly. Amber and her son, Dylan, were stretched out on towels absorbing the sun's rays.

"Weren't you bringing Nina?" Liam asked as he dropped the tubes to the ground and started back up the hill to retrieve more. Daniel and Patrick placed the cooler under the tree, and Daniel jogged to catch up. Liam and Daniel couldn't look more different. Liam was tall and made of lean muscle, sharing a similar build with Patrick. In contrast, Daniel was stout and noticeably shorter than his over six-foot-tall brothers.

"She was still pretty tired when I called her this morning. She said that she and Hannah will come by a little later," Daniel explained, but failed to mention how terribly cranky and extremely hung over Nina had been when he phoned her earlier.

"Well, that's cool. You guys have a good time last night?" Liam asked, fishing out an enormous blue tube out of the back of the truck.

Daniel considered that for a moment. He could tell Liam just about anything, and he knew it wasn't going to get back to the rest of the family. Liam was the best when it came to talking to about problems and seeking advice. He never betrayed anyone's trust and always had other people's back. He didn't like confrontation or drama. Liam preferred his life to be simple, easygoing, and mellow, but that all had changed when he'd met Rachel. With a new bride and twins on the way, life couldn't be any further than simple, but Liam was handling it all pretty darn well.

"Well, you know, I picked her up and she had us

go to Spokane," Daniel said, starting to tell the story of the night before, but he saw Patrick heading their direction. "Maybe we should talk later."

Liam nodded, but Patrick had already heard Daniel. "So what happened last night?"

Daniel rolled his eyes. As close as he was with Patrick, he didn't feel like he could open up to him, at least without any kind of judgment. "Nothing really."

"Nah, I'm not buying that. You were about to tell one helluva story. I could tell when I heard you talk." Patrick placed his hand on Daniel's shoulder and gave it a squeeze. "Go on."

"There's really not a lot to tell," Daniel lied. He had planned on explaining to Liam how Nina had acted: partially seductive but craving attention from anyone and everyone.

"Come on, don't be like that. How was the date?" Patrick insisted, taking his hand off Daniel. He leaned against the side of the truck. "Damn, that's hot." He hissed as the scorching metal burned his naked torso.

"Why don't we grab a cool drink and get in that water? I'm burning up just standing here," Liam said, winking at Daniel.

"Fine." Patrick reached for another tube, this one neon orange. He started to lead them back down the sandy slope.

Daniel and Liam trailed behind. "Hey, thanks. It's not like anything major happened, but you know." Daniel nodded in Patrick's direction.

"I do. But you know, Daniel, he just wants to be there for you too."

"Well, yeah, I get that, but either he'll run and tell Mom or he'll give me crap. I guess I'm just not in the mood today."

Liam shifted the tube he was carrying and grinned. "We all have days like that, trust me. But maybe include him. He's a little different now." Daniel watched as Liam's eyes, the same deep green as his own, focused on Amber.

"I'm glad. I really am. He has been a lot cooler," Daniel admitted as they inched closer to everyone. "But he's still Patrick."

Liam laughed. "True, very true."

***

The water was frigid, but it was a good kind of cold—the kind that instantly chilled him from the wicked heat. Daniel released a huff as felt the water lick up his waist. Okay, it was a little more than cold. The snow runoff which fed this wild river helped keep the temperature cool.

"Ah, get in there. It's not that bad," Patrick insisted as he easily plopped himself inside a tube. Daniel's older brother had already helped Amber and Dylan, and he now floated next to them. They had tied some thin white rope between the tubes, tethering all of them together. Liam and Michael had tied themselves to Melanie's fluorescent pink tube. Michael was tightening the straps of her lifejacket, a mixture of fear and concern present in his eyes and face.

"It'll be okay, Michael," Daniel heard Liam try to assure Michael and Melanie. "We float the river all the time. This will be a lot of fun, Mel, Uncle Liam promises." Daniel saw Liam pat Melanie's head, her rust-colored tresses wet and sparkling in the sunlight. She looked up at him with complete trust and then turned to look at Daniel. He sent her a silly smile and stuck his tongue out at her as he crossed his eyes. He heard Melanie erupt in loud giggles.

Daniel waded out further. He was getting used to the water's temp or growing numb. Either way, he was enjoying himself. He felt the sun on his back, the thick sand sliding between his toes as he got closer to Melanie and Michael, securing his tube to theirs.

They all started to float along the surface of the dark water, their little groups bumping into one another as they passed giant granite mountainsides which had been carved out by the river. They acted as a wall, trapping the O'Briens on this wild ride they were venturing on. They would occasionally hit some slightly angry rapids, which made Melanie squeal and sometimes plead for them to get out of the water. Then the river would right itself, become smooth, and gently send them to the next stretch of bumpy rapids. Daniel closed his eyes, letting the water carry his tube, relishing the serenity surrounding them. The sound of the river and the slight breeze which whispered between them as they bobbed in their tubes made Daniel feel the most relaxed he had felt in a very long time. He reluctantly opened his eyes and caught a glimpse of a bald eagle circling overhead. This is why he loved living here. He couldn't find that kind of nature and solitude in a big city. *Nina.* He had almost forgotten about her.

He closed his eyes again, letting his arms dangle in the water, allowing his body to move with the fluid motion of the river.

"Uncle Daniel, this is so much fun," Melanie cried as they approached curling white waves, the water dousing them as they hit the torrent of wild water. "Never mind!" Melanie screamed as her eyes went wide with fear.

Michael grabbed her protectively, but the smile on his face told Daniel that he was enjoying this local thrill. The rapids ceased, and they were soon sailing smoothly as the current took them to the small beach, where all the floaters got out of the river. The trick was getting back up to the launch point. Luckily, Patrick had parked his SUV. They would drive back up to their original spot and float again.

The group trudged through the hot sand, burning the bottoms of their feet. They carried their tubes and headed for Patrick's SUV.

"Let's make two trips. I can't fit everyone, but we can bring a car back for the next float," Patrick announced, his arm linked behind Amber's naked waist. She smiled at him. Daniel could see the richness of their new, budding relationship. A little stab of jealousy pricked at him.

After the group divided, Daniel stood alone with Liam. He plopped himself on the sand and Liam joined him. They stared out at the other floaters on the water.

"So you want to talk about last night?" Liam

asked as he tossed a small rock toward the water's edge.

Daniel felt his back grow warm as the sun baked his already sun burnt skin. He sighed. "Well, you know it was okay, I guess."

"Hmm," Liam responded without making eye contact.

Daniel knew Liam wouldn't push him, unlike Patrick. He would just leave it if Daniel didn't want to talk. But Daniel did—he needed advice, especially before Nina arrived. "We went into Spokane, as I mentioned earlier. She wanted to check out the bars there," Daniel began to explain, fiddling with a smooth piece of wood and poking the sand with it.

"Okay, you guys are young and Spokane has a lot to do. Especially nightlife stuff."

"I know, but I really hate going into Spokane. I love being here."

"Daniel, compromise, buddy. It's all about compromise. Trust me on this." Liam laughed as he turned to look at Daniel.

"I know. I took her to Spokane, didn't I?" Daniel countered, but he couldn't erase the frustration which seemed to crawl around inside of him.

"Well, you did, but I take it you had a miserable time?"

Daniel released another pent-up sigh. "It was more how she acted and how everyone around her responded. But I would love to make it work."

"Look, I'm not trying to sound like a jerk, but do you and her even have anything in common? I mean, I know she's hot, but like interests and stuff? You know beauty fades, brother." The serious scowl on Liam's face worried Daniel a little. Did he really have anything in common with her? Was he just trying to make something out of nothing?

***

The sun was beginning to set, creating an orange tint across the sky. The river grew more quiet as families started to leave, and Daniel could feel the pleasant soreness of a fun day deep in his muscles as he loaded up the tubes back inside the bed of his truck. They had floated the river several times, splashed around in the water with Melanie, and ate their fill all thanks to his mother. Daniel had helped his precious niece build a lopsided sandcastle, and even allowed her to feebly attempt to bury him. River sand wasn't exactly the best for burying an uncle, Daniel had tried to explain, but she spent a good while trying to cover him up and proving him wrong, and he loved every minute of it.

Earlier that day, Daniel had received a message from Nina, saying she wasn't going to be coming to the river, as she was more than a little hung over. He couldn't dismiss the relief he felt after reading her text. It was odd that he wasn't anxious to see her, but the time he was having with his family somehow outweighed anything a pretty girl could offer. Today just felt right in every way, and if he were truly honest with himself, adding Nina to the mix would taint that. Why was he so desperate to make this relationship with her work?

***

Maggie

"Mom, seriously?" Maggie asked as Mary filled her glass with a second serving of lemonade.

Mary nodded before filling Rachel's glass.

"Thanks, Mary." Rachel smiled.

They were all seated outside on the deck enjoying an early lunch. Most of the family was at the river with plans to float down it and play all day in the sand. Maggie was now eight months pregnant, and Rachel was nearly seven months along but looked like she was going to pop any day. Maggie knew how cramped she felt being pregnant with one baby. She could only imagine Rachel's discomfort being pregnant with twins.

"Honey, I don't know what to tell you. Daniel asked if she could join us tomorrow for Sunday dinner. I couldn't tell him no."

"But it's Nina Belsky, Mom. He really shouldn't even be seeing her." Maggie exhaled loudly. She couldn't stand Nina. At first she didn't pay her much mind, but a couple of weeks ago, when she went to talk to Nina's older sister, Hannah, about having some curtains made for the nursery, she saw Nina for what she was. While chatting with Hannah Maggie caught Nina flirting with a farmhand. If this girl was so interested in her brother, why was she batting her fake lashes at some guy who was very much not Daniel?

Rachel looked perplexed. "They're dating? Is it getting serious?"

"It better not be," Maggie quickly said, taking a long sip of the cold drink to cool her temper.

"Dear, your brother is just trying to search for what you have, and what Liam found." Mary smiled at Rachel. "We have been lucky so far. Maybe Nina isn't that bad." Mary shrugged as she took a seat and grabbed her own glass.

"She is, Mom," Maggie quickly countered. "I just went over to her family's farm. I needed to see Hannah. Now, she is a nice girl, but anyway, I went there to talk to Hannah about some curtains and stuff for the nursery." Maggie huffed as she continued, a little steely spark of anger surging through her. She was protective of her family, especially Daniel. He just seemed to wear blinders when it came to Nina. "Anyway, long story short, Nina was flirting with a farmhand."

"Oh no." The cheerful expression her mother wore faded quickly.

Rachel's blues eyes flickered with a quiet rage, something that Maggie had not witnessed before. "Are you serious? What nerve!" Rachel rolled her eyes.

"Oh yeah, and she totally saw me too." This only fueled Maggie's annoyance further.

Mary frowned, but sticking true to her sweet-natured self, much like Daniel, she smiled. "Well, we can only pray then, right? I'm sure it will all work out."

"I just wish he wasn't inviting her to our house," Maggie stated. She looked away from her mother, knowing she would disapprove of her attitude.

"Maggie, love…"

43

Maggie cut Mary off. "I know, Mom. I just don't want to see him get hurt."

"I have to agree with Maggie on this, Mary," Rachel added, her hand moving in slow circles on her round abdomen. "I would hate to see Daniel wind up with someone who didn't truly care about him. He's a good guy and deserves the best."

Mary patted Rachel's arm from across the glass patio table. "I appreciate you caring so much about my boy. You both are right. Daniel needs a good girl. We just need to have a little faith." Mary smiled brightly at both of them, the famous all-knowing Mary O'Brien smile, which really meant that she would find a way to make everything right. Maggie took another sip of her sweet lemonade and felt a little more at peace.

Chapter Four

Daniel

Maybe it hadn't been such bright idea to invite Nina over for Sunday dinner. The looks on Maggie and Rachel's faces confirmed that. He had barely walked inside the kitchen with Nina in tow when the room grew quiet. Tension quickly formed a thick cloud. *Awkward.* Daniel said a silent prayer and hoped his mother could help make Nina feel comfortable. His mother always had a way of making everyone feel welcomed. Nina stood stiffly next to Daniel, almost pouting. It was apparent she would rather be anywhere but there, in that kitchen, with several O'Brien females. For her, it was basically a lethal lions' den.

"Mom, this is Nina Belsky." It felt odd introducing her. Of course his mother knew who she was, the whole family did, but he felt the need to use the formality to cut through the storm of tension that was brewing.

Nina made no motion to reach out to his mother.

Daniel nudged her slightly. She whipped her pretty face toward him, her eyes sending a warning. She was not pleased.

"Nina, why don't you come in and join us ladies? We are just getting ready to set the table." Mary, in her favorite floral apron, whisked Nina away. Nina spun her head back to look at Daniel. She looked helpless and a tad angry, but Daniel knew she was in good hands. He glanced over at Maggie and Rachel, who were both wearing sour expressions, their large pregnant bellies matching under their aprons. Neither of them looked happy with him. What did he do? Women.

"Well, I'm going to join the guys if you don't need anything, Mom," Daniel informed his mother. He avoided the piercing stares from the other women. He caught a slight glimpse of Amber, but she kept her expression neutral. She was, after all, still fairly new to this family. She and Patrick had only been dating for a couple months, and it was too soon to tell where their relationship would go. Daniel guessed they would get married eventually, but for now they were content just as they were.

"That's fine, son. We're all good here." Mary beamed at him, the look a mix of reassurance and love. She knew he was beyond nervous, and it was her job as his mother to rid him of those fears.

Daniel moved out of the kitchen swiftly and made his way outside to the backyard, where the rest of the men were. Michael was in the yard playing with Melanie and the twins. Even Dylan, an awkward pre-teen, was out there tossing a bright red Frisbee to Michael. Liam was getting up from his seat to join Michael in the game with the kids. Grandpa Paddy and Pat were lounging under the shade of the porch roof, Patrick next to them, looking every bit like his namesakes. It would have made a fantastic picture: the eldest Patrick, Grandpa Paddy, was the original version, and then there was his son, Pat, a slightly older version, with a salt and pepper mix of gray hair, versus Grandpa Paddy's shock of white. Then there was the youngest Patrick, his dark hair and black Irish features matching those of his father and grandfather. They all had the same long legs. Liam had inherited those as well, but not Daniel. The older men were a little softer than Patrick, who had clearly defined muscle which showed through his dark t-shirt. But seeing them all seated next to each other, to witness the genetic strength that passed from generation to generation, was really quite remarkable. Carbon copies.

"Hey, Daniel," said Patrick. The older versions of Patrick all looked in Daniel's direction, their sets of famed green O'Brien eyes glittering as they each welcomed him. There was no question they were happy to see him, but they were eager to know more about the guest he had brought along.

"So where's the gorgeous lass?" Grandpa Paddy asked as Daniel sat down in a spot across from him.

"She's in the kitchen with the girls."

"Oh, Lord help her." Pat laughed. "Do you think it was wise to throw her to the wolves so soon?"

"Mom will protect her."

"Mom's the leader of the pack," Patrick added quickly. "God love her, but Mom's the ring leader."

Daniel didn't agree with that statement at all.

"Nah, Mom's kind to everyone. If anything, I figure she will protect Nina from Maggie and Rachel. You should have seen the evil eye they were giving me."

"What about Amber?" Patrick's stare grew curious.

"She played it cool."

Patrick smiled. He was pleased. "Well, Amber doesn't like drama, and she honestly likes everyone. She's just amazing that way." As he spoke about her, his face softened and his eyes lit up. Yes, Daniel was right, those two were bound to get married.

"Amber's cool. I like her."

Grandpa Paddy puffed on his pipe and as a sweet tobacco scent wafted through the air, he said, "Amber is a great gal. She'd be a good one for you to settle down with Patrick, my boy."

"I agree. She's been fitting in real well with the rest of ladies," Pat added, grabbing the brown beer bottle in front of him and taking a swig.

Patrick grinned and replied, "I know. She's really special. It's just so soon."

Grandpa Paddy's thick white eyebrows lowered into a stubborn line on his wrinkled face. "Lad, we've been over this, me and you. Time is a funny thing. Sometimes it seems as though there is far too much, then suddenly there isn't nearly enough."

"I know. Well, let's just give it a little more time. Things are good now, and I'm sure they will only get better."

Daniel envied Patrick's position. He desperately wanted to be in a relationship with someone he thought he had a future with. Bringing Nina here was a huge step in that direction. He just worried she wasn't walking with him.

***

Maggie

Maggie eyed Nina as the young woman stood there uncomfortably. She was reserved and cold, so it wasn't possible for Maggie to feel sympathy.

"So, Nina, dear, how are your parents?" Mary asked as she plunged a wooden spoon into the large mixing bowl.

"They're well, thank you," Nina responded in muted politeness.

Maggie sat on a barstool next to the counter, her swollen calves and ankles begging for relief. "Nina, I'm getting some amazing curtains from Hannah. Do you sew too?" Mary tossed her a warning look. Maggie responded with an innocent smile.

"Well, that's just how Hannah is. She's a homebody. She doesn't enjoy going out and living life. I prefer to actually do things besides sewing. It's all she ever does."

"Well, she's darn good at it." Her mother raised her eyebrows and shot Maggie another glare. Okay, she'd best cool it before she really upset her mother. She did not want to get on Mary O'Brien's bad side.

"I'm actually having two baby blankets being made by Hannah," Rachel chimed in, shooting Maggie a sister-like glance from under her blonde bangs, which kept sweeping across her eyes.

Nina scrunched up her face. "Two blankets?"

"Yes, we're having twins. Well, not us, but Liam and I." Rachel had reached out to Maggie and started laughing. "Maggie already got an amazing blanket when you guys had the booth at the fair earlier this summer."

Nina nodded and twirled her long blonde hair around her slender fingers. It was easy to see how out of place she seemed in this company of women. Rachel and Maggie were basically a pregnant duo, a tag team waiting to start a little trouble. Mary was watchful. Maggie saw her mother taking Nina in, not so much sizing her up, but watching and waiting to be impressed. So far, that wasn't happening. Amber stood quietly next to the kitchen counter, as if she were still making her decision about whether or not to like Nina. "Mary, did you want me to put this in the oven?" Amber pointed to a large glass dish. It would seem that Amber was trying to redirect the conversation and just wanted to simply keep the peace.

"Do you enjoy cooking?" Mary asked as she opened the oven door for Amber. She turned her attention to the supermodel-esque Russian who was standing in her kitchen.

"No, not really. That's how you get fat and ugly."

Everyone's eyebrows raised, and Maggie heard herself gasp. Did she really just say that? Wow, that was brave or utterly stupid. Maggie caught a glimpse from Amber, who was naturally curvy. She knew Amber had been offended.

"Well, how about we move outside and see what the guys are up to?" Mary wore a cheery facade that

Maggie saw right through.

***

Daniel

The sun had begun to set, drifting a little lower behind the neighboring hills. The temperature was cooling slightly, and Daniel felt the grip of fall trying to take hold. The days of summer were numbered, and that meant fewer opportunities to go to the river. Daniel was glad they had gone yesterday; they might not get another chance. He looked out at the stretch of green grass, watching the twins rolling around on the ground. Melanie was being taught how to properly throw a Frisbee by Liam, and Michael was standing next to Dylan, laughing at something the pre-teen had just said. Daniel inhaled deeply, taking in the scents of the evening, feeling blessed and thankful for family gatherings like this. This is what made him happy: being surrounded by everyone and sharing in good times.

"You know, Daniel, you need to really think about the type of woman you will want to settle down with," Daniel heard his father say, breaking into his thoughts.

Grandpa Paddy nodded in agreement and commented, "He's right, lad. You are getting on in age, and you'll be wanting children soon."

Daniel sat with his back to the house and continued to listen to the unwanted words of wisdom from his father and grandfather. He heard the back door close and noticed the expression on his father and grandfather's faces change. Patrick's look changed to one of complete admiration, so Daniel instantly knew Amber was near.

"Dinner will be ready soon," Mary announced as she moved to stand beside Pat, planting a kiss on top of his head. Pat looked up lovingly and clasped Mary's arm. The simple act of affection wasn't missed by Daniel. He wanted what his parents had—that long-standing love.

Daniel swiveled in his seat and looked at Nina. Her gaze met his briefly, but then she quickly focused on Patrick. His brother was completely oblivious. His gaze seemed far away, as if Amber, who had staked her claim in a manner of speaking, had him in a trance. She was behind him, looping her arms around his neck, whispering something in his ear. Patrick smiled and turned to look up at her. Daniel wanted that too—that new kind of love.

As the kids continued to play in the yard, their shouts of joy could probably be heard throughout the neighborhood. Liam and Michael laughed as they raced over to where the rest of the adults were, happy expressions on their faces.

But then Maggie gave Michael an interesting look, one that Daniel couldn't quite make out, but it appeared as though they were exchanging information telepathically. Michael looked quickly at Nina, then at Daniel. So that is what that was about. No surprise. Daniel could feel Maggie's chilly reception when Nina had entered the kitchen. His sister usually took a little while to warm up to newcomers. She had been aloof with Rachel, well, for like ten minutes, then they became the best of friends and only kept growing closer. Then with Amber, Maggie had shown very little hesitation in accepting Patrick's new girlfriend.

Nina moved to an empty seat that was near Daniel, but close enough to Patrick. Daniel noticed her pale blue eyes had not quite broken eye contact with him. This was something that Daniel was fairly used to: always playing second fiddle to his handsome brothers. But for Nina to so blatantly do this in front of him and his family? It made his stomach sour. He could feel his mother looking at him. That woman didn't miss a thing, but she offered him a sympathetic and kind smile.

"Nina, is it?" Grandpa Paddy asked slowly, taking her all in. Daniel wondered what thoughts were rolling around in the old man's mind. Did he approve? Did he think Daniel was being foolish trying to make this girl his? Grandpa Paddy hadn't steered any of Daniel's siblings wrong, and now it was his turn.

Nina smiled and reluctantly looked away from Patrick. Daniel saw the relief wash over Amber's face, but her sea-green eyes continued to look daggers in Nina's direction.

Everyone had turned their attention to Nina. Liam offered her an encouraging grin as he wrapped his arms around Rachel, pulling her protectively to him.

"Ycs," Nina answered quietly.

"So your folks own that farm on the outskirts of town," Pat stated, rather than asked. Grandpa Paddy and Pat continued to take turns attempting to engage

Nina in conversation. Daniel groaned. This was not really going well. Nina was hardly making an effort; she was only answering in clipped sentences. Her annoyance and lack of patience was growing as each question was handed to her. They were simply trying to get to know her, to break the ice, and find room for her.

"Well, why don't we all head inside to eat? Us ladies will go and get everything served up. You men grab those kiddos," Mary ordered as she led the way back into the house. Maggie followed but tossed back a look at Daniel that said it all. She did not like Nina. Both Rachel and Amber gave him tight-lipped smiles that spoke volumes. They were offering him some sort of an apology. Nina remain seated, not even looking in the direction of the women that were filing back inside this house. The evening had not gone well and it was only going to get worse. Maybe Daniel could pull Nina aside and try to explain how things sort of worked in the O'Brien family. To some it may appear slightly old-fashioned, that the women enjoyed their time together primarily in the kitchen, where he knew so many secrets were shared and plans were hatched, but he wanted Nina to be included, and as she sat there with a bored expression, he saw that the only interest that danced in her eyes was when she would sneak glimpses at his brothers or Michael. The more Daniel saw from her, the less he wanted to see. This was not how he imagined this dinner going.

***

Maggie

"I don't like her. And I was right."

"Maggie, that's enough. She could walk in her any moment," Mary scolded her.

Amber sighed loudly as she retrieved the glass casserole dish out of the oven. Rachel released a huff as she grabbed dishes to set the table.

"Why aren't either of you saying anything?" Maggie asked angrily. She stood looking at them ignoring the obvious issue at hand.

"It's not my place," Amber quickly answered.

"Uh, did you not see the way she was looking at Patrick? That was so not cool," Maggie explained as she was handed glasses by Mary to take to the table.

"Go set these over there. You need to stop. We can discuss this after she goes home. It isn't good to stand here and gossip about her when she's just beyond this wall." Mary motioned toward the kitchen wall near the backyard.

Maggie didn't care if Nina walked in. After the short time they had spent with her, and then seeing her practically devour her brothers with her eyes, it was confirmed in her mind that she didn't like Nina Belsky one bit. All Maggie could think was, *Poor Daniel.*

***

Daniel

He couldn't mistake the uncomfortable glances

from around the table. It was also an eerily quiet for a Sunday dinner at the O'Brien household. He knew why, he wasn't stupid, and he actually didn't blame his family all that much. Nina was pushing bits of lettuce around on her plate, obviously completely uninterested in the food in front of her or the people around her. This wasn't what Daniel had anticipated. He figured that since Nina had come from a fairly large family, she would be as family oriented as he was. Maybe they were too different.

Somehow they managed to get through dinner, and Mary politely suggested that Daniel take Nina home before it got too late. He was a little surprised she hadn't offered dessert, but seeing how Nina hadn't eaten much, she probably figured there was no point to continuing their suffering.

Nina said goodbye to the family and practically ran out the door. Daniel helped her into his truck and then got inside.

"God, I'm so glad that is over." She exhaled loudly, keeping her gaze out the window.

"I'm sorry. I just really wanted you to meet my family. We do so much cool stuff together. I just wanted to be able to include you."

"Daniel…" Her voice trailed off, and she refused to meet his eyes.

"What?"

"I just want to keep whatever this is between me and you just fun. I don't want us making it all serious, like involving our families," Nina explained, twirling her blonde tresses through her fingers.

Daniel swallowed. "I wasn't trying to rush things. Hell, I don't even really know what we are even doing."

"That's the thing. This should just be fun. We're so young. I can't even begin to think of marriage or any of that right now. I have so many things I want to do and it certainly doesn't involve staying here in Birch Valley."

"So what now?" Daniel asked. He could hear the disappointment in his own voice. He couldn't hide it. He didn't know what he had expected, especially from someone like Nina.

Nina slid over closer to him. She raked her nails gently up his thigh and kissed his neck. "Fun."

He swallowed again. Fun. She had offered fun on Friday, which ended up her being drunk and more than a handful, to say the least. It had been anything but *fun*. Daniel shifted nervously in his seat and started up the truck. If only she knew exactly why he was nervous, she might not want anything to do with him.

Chapter Five

Patrick

"So what did you guys end up doing after you left?" Patrick asked as he sorted the mail at the counter.

The inside of the shop was a little warm. Daniel fussed with a fan and looked in Patrick's direction. Maggie hadn't come into work today due to a doctor's appointment, and Daniel was slightly relieved. He was already dreading the countless questions he knew Patrick was going to unleash on him. It had been obvious that Maggie was not a fan of Nina, so he knew it was a matter of time before she pummeled him with her advice. Everyone always wanted to add their two cents, as if Daniel were completely unable to handle a relationship or anything in his life.

"I pretty much dropped her off at home." He didn't feel like being probed for more details, but knew trying to change the subject was futile.

Patrick rolled his eyes. "Oh, come on. You can't

be serious? Man, here you got this gorgeous chick, and you're just taking her home?"

"What else do expect me to do?" Daniel felt his face grow hot. He stood up from the crouching position he was in. He turned on the fan in hopes to cool his warming cheeks.

"Daniel, seriously?" Patrick's brow raised in confusion.

He knew what his brother was hinting at, and it was something he would just rather not discuss. He turned his attention away from Patrick, praying that his brother would just leave well enough alone.

"Daniel." Patrick's tone was curious and before Daniel realized, Patrick was standing next to him.

"What?"

Patrick exhaled hard. "Come on."

"There's nothing to discuss. I'm not even really sure what you're asking or wanting to know," Daniel stated as he bent down and rummaged through the toolbox, pretending to be busy searching for something.

"You need me to come right out and ask?" Patrick was relentless. Daniel ignored him and grabbed a screwdriver to tighten a blade on another fan he was working on. "So you haven't slept with Nina?"

There. His brother had said it. Instantly, Daniel was flooded with naive embarrassment. "No, I haven't." He kept his answer vague and hoped it would suffice, but with Patrick it probably wouldn't.

"Damn. I'm kind of surprised. I mean, not to sound rude or anything, but I sort of figured that was why you were tolerating her. If you aren't getting laid, why do you put up with her?" Patrick's face scrunched in annoyance.

"She's not that bad, jeez," Daniel lied. Nina was kind of difficult to be around though. He found they literally had nothing in common or discussed anything worthwhile. He sort of felt like she might be using him for a good time, just someone to help pass the summer boredom that a lot of people got in Birch Valley.

Neither of them heard the bell on the door ring, but they suddenly noticed Hannah was standing only feet away. She wore a perplexed and troubled look on her face. God, he hoped she hadn't heard them.

"Hey, Hannah." Daniel said, wiping his hands on the back of his jeans.

"Hi, I didn't mean to drop in or anything, but I'm in a bit of a pickle, and, well, you were the closest one who I thought could help me," Hannah rambled, shifting her weight from foot to foot as she sent him a pleading look.

Patrick eyed her with interest. "Aren't you Nina's sister?"

"Uh, yes, I am. I'm really sorry to bother you guys. But my car just broke down a couple blocks away and I wanted to see if perhaps you could maybe drive me back out to the farm. I figure I can tell one of my dad's farmhands and they can come help tow it back." Her pink bottom lip quivered. "Gosh, I'm so sorry to ask."

"Oh, Hannah, it's fine. Sorry to hear about your trouble. Daniel would be more than happy to run you back home," Patrick quickly replied. Of course

Daniel didn't mind taking Hannah home, but leave it to Patrick—the man who hated when others meddled in his own life—to get involved.

"Sure, I'd be happy to." Daniel offered her a smile and was happy to see her face soften.

***

It was midday, and the sun made Birch Valley swelteringly hot in the last days before fall overthrew summer. Daniel turned up the air conditioning—not that it really helped much.

"So what do you think happened to your car?" Daniel asked as he steered down the bustling main street. Tourists crowded the sidewalks as they window shopped. Children were riding their bikes, enjoying their last days of freedom before school started the following week.

"Well, it's hard to say. I'm not really all that good at car stuff, but I know that smoke coming out from under the hood is not a good sign." Hannah laughed nervously.

"Nope, it's usually not. I'm sure it'll all work out."

Daniel peeked at his gauges and noticed he needed gas. "Do you mind if I fill up real quick?"

"Oh God, no. I'd be happy if you'd let me pay."

Daniel shook his head. "Nah, I don't mind taking you back home. You never know. I might need you to return the favor. My truck isn't exactly brand new," he teased as he drove in the direction of the single gas station in town. It had a little market, a car wash, and only six gas pumps.

"So, how's your sister? I'm just about done with some curtains for her nursery," Hannah said, seemingly trying to make small talk.

"Maggie's good. Her and Rachel are nearing the finish line."

"How fun must that be, to be pregnant with your sister-in-law. They seem like such great friends."

"Yeah, they are quite a pair." Daniel laughed and slowed as the traffic light changed to yellow then red. "You like kids?"

"I love them. I hope to have a ton when I get married. I have no nieces or nephews, but a couple very young cousins." She had a happy grin on her face as she continued to describe how adorable her cousins were.

"They are the cutest things and are so silly."

He was enjoying their conversation and listened as she described their little personalities. Daniel loved his nephews and niece and was thrilled about more little ones being added to the family. He only hoped someday he could add to the O'Brien name. The light switched to green, and Daniel pulled into the gas station to the side of the intersection. He spotted another truck. The driver was a guy he'd gone to school with. Granted, who had he *not* gone to school with in Birch Valley?

As he found an empty pump to park next to, he noticed her: Nina. She was sitting happily in the passenger side of that truck, giggling at something and toying with her long blonde hair. Daniel grunted, and Hannah peered over to have a look through his window.

"Oh," Hannah said and leaned back against her

seat.

Daniel got out of the truck, removed his wallet, and fished out his credit card. As he undid the gas cap, he pretended not to notice her. Why in the hell was Nina hanging out in that guy's truck? He swiped his card, removed the nozzle of the gas pump, and slammed it into his gas tank opening a little harder than he should have. He felt someone watching him, but he tried to keep his attention on the task at hand, keeping his back to Nina.

"Daniel?"

Crap. He clicked the safety on the pump to let it fill by itself and turned around slowly.

She stood there with her hands on her narrow hips, wearing some of the shortest white shorts he had ever laid eyes on. Nina's pale robin egg-blue tank top accented her perfectly golden skin, and she had thrown her blonde hair into a sloppy twist on the top of her head. He looked down, not wanting to meet her eyes, but he noticed her dainty toes were painted pale pink. Patrick was right; she was gorgeous, but she wasn't his. He lifted his gaze and noticed an irritated look in her eyes.

"Why is my sister in your truck?" she asked, her voice sharp. She was angry, but did she really have a right to be upset? Couldn't Daniel ask her the same thing? Why was she in that guy's truck?

"Her car broke down and I was taking her home. You?" He met her annoyed stare, almost challenging her to come up with a better excuse.

"I was just hanging out with my friend." Nina sounded nervous as she quickly turned around, as if to see if anyone else had heard her.

"Hey, it's fine. You didn't want anything serious, remember?" Daniel was wounded inside, not much, but he could feel the sting of her thoughtlessness, especially to his pride.

"Daniel, I'm sorry." Nina pouted. She was used to getting everything she wanted and she liked being the one in control. Daniel had switched it up on her, and she didn't know how to react.

"It's completely fine, trust me. Saves me a lot of trouble actually, so thanks." The machine beeped and the pump clicked off. Perfect timing. "Have a good rest of your day, Nina. I need to get Hannah back home." He grabbed his receipt and got into the driver's side of his truck without another word.

As he pulled out of the gas station, Hannah seemed awkwardly quiet, as if deciding when she should say something. Daniel decided to confront it head-on.

"Hey, it's okay."

Hannah quickly responded, "Gosh, I'm so sorry, Daniel. I know you guys were kind of seeing each other."

"She didn't want anything serious, so no harm, no foul." Daniel smiled and turned onto the highway leading them out to her farm.

"Yeah, but that's not really cool. You don't treat people like they are disposable. You're a really nice guy, Daniel. You don't deserve that."

"Well, thanks." He felt himself blush unexpectedly.

"I'm serious. Nina always does this. She doesn't respect anything or anyone. I'm tired of seeing her hurt people." Hannah crossed her arms over her

64

chest in a huff.

As Daniel drove, sitting opposite Hannah, he couldn't help but wonder if God was showing him something.

"I appreciate your concern. It's very sweet." Daniel turned to see her cheeks turn a lovely shade of rose as a half-smile blossomed on her lips. It would appear they both wore their true feelings on their faces. For Daniel, sometimes it was torture knowing that his face gave everything away. He was not a good poker player. Any of his pals would agree. He would bet that Hannah wasn't so great either.

***

Maggie

"God, I'm huge," Maggie stated as she stood in front of the full-length mirror on her bedroom wall.

Michael wrapped his arms around her from behind and began to nuzzle her neck. "Stop. I find you to be quite gorgeous."

"It's all your fault, you know." Maggie laughed. She pulled his hands to her large stomach, stretched and full. "You feel that little one? Oh, there's a big one," she said as the baby kicked.

"Wow. It doesn't hurt when he kicks you?" Michael's eyes glowed in astonishment.

"No, but how do you know it's a boy? Could be another little girl in there," Maggie replied, basking in the warmth of their embrace. To think earlier that year, in the beginnings of spring, they had almost lost this—this closeness, this love, this marriage.

"This pregnancy just seems different, so I'm going purely on scientific facts here. Well, and my terrible and desperate need for a son." Michael kissed her neck, sending pleasant shivers down her spine.

"So you do care about what we're having! You are such a liar, Michael. You've been telling me you don't care." Maggie spun around, only to be captured in her husband's arms and to see a devilishly sexy grin on his handsome face.

"I don't, but is it too much to hope to equal out the testosterone and estrogen in this household?" He raised a dark eyebrow, then quickly planted his mouth on hers.

She moaned into his mouth. Her husband still had the ability to make lightning travel through to her core, even if she felt like an enormous cow.

"Let me show you how gorgeous I think you are." He pulled her tighter against him, her belly keeping them from being as close as normal. Maggie giggled. "What's so funny?" He pressed his forehead against hers, and he stared at her like she was the most delicious thing he'd ever seen.

"This." She bumped her belly against his naked and firm abs.

"Baby, trust me, that makes you even that much hotter."

Maggie rolled her eyes. "Oh please! Now you have some weird pregnant lady fetish?"

Michael knelt down in front of her. He lifted the enormously over-sized t-shirt and kissed her belly. He whispered, "You be good in there. I'm about to show your mother how sexy I think she is."

She swatted him playfully and scolded, "Don't tell him that. Geez, he'll need therapy before he's even born."

He looked up at her, desire shining brightly in his chocolate-colored eyes, a sinister smirk on his lips. "So you agree it's a boy?"

***

After an incredible late morning love session with Michael, Maggie was on her way to visit her doctor. She felt complete, content, but every bit ready for this baby to be born. Only another short month—she was now on the countdown. She was eager to get the nursery finished once school started back up next week, and she would have a little more quiet time on her hands. Maggie had decided to walk to her appointment. The day was warm but pleasant, and the clinic was only a couple blocks away from home. She knew the exercise would do her some good, even though Michael was not so keen on her walking that far. He had insisted she allow him to drop her off, but he had a client in the next town over. Otherwise he would have accompanied her to do their favorite thing: listening to the baby's heartbeat. There was always that split second of anxiety when she lay on that table, belly exposed as they rubbed the Doppler over it; that moment of fear that they wouldn't be able to find the baby's heartbeat; and that wave of happy relief when the fluttering sound echoed in the room.

She opened the glass door to the clinic and

noticed only a couple of people sitting in the waiting room. Maggie smiled as soon as she saw Rachel was reading a magazine, completely oblivious to the world around her. After checking in at the front desk, Maggie waddled over to where Rachel was seated.

"Hey, you."

Rachel dropped the magazine to the floor, obviously startled. "Geez, Maggie." She started to laugh, her hand clutching her chest as bent down to grab the magazine. "You scared me."

"Must be a really good article," Maggie teased.

Rachel's cheeks turned a soft pink. "It is."

"Let me see." Maggie snatched the magazine from Rachel. "Oh my.

Rachel raised her eyebrows and she smiled in embarrassment. "I know."

"Okay, so are you guys, like, not, you know…anymore?" Maggie tried to ask delicately. She didn't want to make Rachel any more uncomfortable. Granted, at this point in their friendship they should be able to talk about anything, but some topics were sort of off limits.

"Well, I mean, we have and we kind of do, but not like before. He's just scared and worried. It's driving me crazy, to be perfectly honest."

"That's normal. I remember Michael was the same way when I was pregnant with Melanie. Once he realized that not only was it awesome during pregnancy, but that it's supposed to help a little. He was all for being a team player," Maggie explained. She understood how Rachel was feeling. It happened to almost every couple she knew when they were going through their first pregnancy.

"That's sort of a relief to hear. I was a little worried it was me. That maybe…"

Maggie raised her hand to stop Rachel. "Nope. It has nothing to do with that. Liam loves you and is still attracted to you. You just wait. Trust me on this. I can barely keep Michael's hands off of me, not that I'm complaining. Why he wants anything to do with a fat cow is beyond me. Maybe it's a pregnancy fetish. I don't know."

"Maggie, you're stunning," Rachel stated seriously as she patted her friend's arm. "I'm the one who looks like a cow. I'm not even due until November. It's only the end of August."

Maggie looked at Rachel's enormous belly. She had a point. "But you have two in there."

"You are due at the end of next month and you look fabulous, and here I am, with nearly three months to go, and I look like I could pop them out any day." Maggie could see Rachel's frustration. Sometimes there was just no arguing with a woman, especially a pregnant one.

"So why are you here?" Maggie asked, shifting the conversation as she started flipping through a magazine nonchalantly. The glossy images of skinny women looking back up at her were not helping her mood.

"They wanted me to take another glucose test or something. Plus, my blood pressure was a little elevated last time I was in," Rachel explained.

"Well, I'm sure everything is fine. Babies love to give us trouble even before they're born. You want to grab lunch after our appointments?"

"Yes, I'm starving." Rachel quickly covered her mouth. "See? That's why I'm huge. It has nothing to do with me having twins. It's me just wanting to eat everything in sight."

"That's the fun part of pregnancy. Trust me, once we get these kiddos out, the fun of losing the baby weight comes next." Maggie rubbed her belly in exaggerated circles. She actually cherished this time, to be able to eat whatever she wanted. During the first couple months of pregnancy she could barely keep anything down.

A nurse entered the waiting room and called for Rachel to follow her. Maggie reached for her hand. "It'll be okay." Rachel nodded and followed the nurse, who wore the palest pink scrubs Maggie had ever seen.

She skimmed through another couple magazines before her name was called and she went back to a small room. She knew the drill all too well: disrobe and then wait forever for the doctor while barely covered in a paper gown. They kept these tiny rooms almost unbearably cold. Good times.

There was a knock at the door, and Maggie's doctor entered. After meeting Rachel's doctor, Maggie knew she had to switch. Dr. Salinger just had a soothing presence about her.

"Maggie." Dr. Salinger immediately hugged her. She released her, quickly mounted a small rolling stool, and scooted back over to Maggie. "So how have you been feeling? Any worries, concerns?" Dr. Salinger asked, her large blue eyes scanning Maggie curiously.

"I feel good," Maggie answered truthfully.

"Not tired? In any kind of pain?" Dr. Salinger rose from her stool, yanking the stethoscope which hung around her neck. "Let me listen. Deep breaths," she ordered. Maggie inhaled and exhaled. She repeated the exercise again. "Okay, sounds good."

Dr. Salinger went over to the small sink against the wall and proceeded to wash her hands. "So, any contractions?"

"I get some of those Braxton Hicks, but for the most part it's not too bad."

"They might increase as we start getting a little closer to delivery. How about movement? How's our lil guy?"

"Lil guy?" Maggie laughed. "Michael and I were just discussing this. He's convinced it's a boy." Dr. Salinger immediately looked away, guilt covering her face. Instantly, Maggie knew their surprise was now no longer a surprise. They were having a little boy. Her heart leaped happily inside her chest. She had expected to be upset or feel a pang of disappointment if she learned the baby's gender early. Life offered so few surprises. That's why they had chosen not to know the gender, but now Maggie could concentrate on more of a theme for the nursery, and she knew Michael would be thrilled.

"I'm so sorry. I didn't mean for that to slip," Dr. Salinger apologized as she approached Maggie again.

"Oh, it's fine. I'm actually really happy and a little relieved," Maggie said, trying to reassure her.

"I know, but you guys wanted it to be a surprise. I just ruined it." Tears pooled in her eyes. With her black hair in its usual tight knot, her eyes stood out, watery and filled with regret.

"Dr. Salinger, please don't feel bad. I'm even more excited now that I know our lil guy is actually a guy. It's great news."

"Well, I am sorry. He presented all his assets proudly in the last several ultrasounds. I have it in the charts, but I've been trying to so hard not to slip up." She used her sleeve to catch a tear that rolled from her cheek.

Maggie carefully gathered her flimsy paper gown and hopped off the examine table. She gathered Dr. Salinger into a tight hug. Maggie whispered as they stood together in the quiet sterile room, with its awful beige wallpaper and bright light, "It's the best news. Thank you."

After getting measured and enjoying the rest of her visit with Dr. Salinger, Maggie headed for the front counter to make another appointment. She was now in the final stretch, and the visits were to be weekly until delivery. Surprised that Rachel wasn't already in the waiting room, Maggie went in search for some of the other magazines that were spread around the different chairs and end tables. She started to grow a little concerned as she eyed the clock. She had already gone through all of her reading material by the time Rachel emerged into the waiting room.

"So, how did your appointment go?" Maggie asked her friend.

"It was fine, I guess. I had to drink this awful thick concoction. Then I had to wait and wait some more. They did a bunch of blood work and made me pee in a cup. I'm so over that. I can barely keep my balance," Rachel said, her voice tense with frustration. "How did yours go?"

Maggie couldn't help but smile. "Really great, actually."

Rachel scrunched her face in confusion. "Do tell?"

"How about we grab some lunch? I know you and I are both starving."

***

Daniel

"Do you want to come inside for some iced tea or maybe a slice of pie?" Hannah asked after they arrived at her home.

"Sure, why not?" If her pie was anything like those cookies he had last week, he'd be a fool to say no. There were things he just shouldn't pass up. Besides, he had enjoyed their drive out to the farm. He found Hannah to actually be quite funny, good natured, and such a breath of fresh air compared to her sister.

"Great."

Daniel hopped out of truck quickly and raced to her side to open the door, but she was already halfway out by the time he got there. "Thanks." She smiled nervously, and Daniel could see the sunlight dance off her light spray of freckles, her eyes squinting from the brightness of the sun. Standing this close he could see she had very little makeup on, if any. Her skin looked soft, her lashes natural, not thick with black paste like Nina's. Hannah had a simple beauty about her. Daniel had noticed it last time he'd seen her, but with Nina freshly out of his mind, he was more aware of how truly pretty Hannah was. Maybe it was the late summer sun illuminating something he had missed before, but either way, he was enjoying the view.

Chapter Six

Hannah

What a strange turn of events, sitting there in her family's dining room with Daniel O'Brien, laughing until their sides hurt. She sure hadn't seen her afternoon going in this direction, especially after her car practically blew up on her, leaving her stranded and helpless. Hannah hadn't been quite sure where else to go for assistance, but after chatting with Daniel last week, she knew one thing: he was friendly and seemed like someone who could help.

"Stop. Ah, you're killing me, Hannah." Daniel wiped the corners of his eyes. Those eyes, she just couldn't stop looking into them. Their piercing green color, the joy and the goodness, they all seemed to draw her in.

She could understand why her sister had thought he was attractive. Daniel was handsome, and he had a light beard which enhanced his gorgeous and happy smile. The sound of his laugh, genuine and full, was almost like music to her. It was a real laugh and she loved it. Daniel had a jovial personality, which Hannah had noticed when Daniel and Patrick had first come to the farm to do work for her father. She had been immediately interested, but then Nina swooped in, as she always did, and captured him. Was it wrong that she had been saying a silent prayer that they had run into Nina today? Hannah just hoped that Daniel wanting to hang out for a bit wasn't in retaliation for his wounded pride from her sister being caught with another guy.

"No, you're the funny one." On her plate, Hannah moved around a piece of leftover crust from the blueberry pie she had served them.

"Okay, let's face it. We're both funny as hell."

She hardly considered herself comical. She just liked telling stories and people usually laughed. She had figured it was because she was annoying; Nina constantly reminded her that she was. Daniel was the first person who said he thought she was actually funny, and it made her feel special somehow. That was not a feeling she was used to.

"I better head out. I really enjoyed that pie. Don't tell my mom, but I think you could give her a run for her money," Daniel teased as he started to rise from his chair. He grabbed the spotless plate and started for the kitchen.

"Oh here, let me take that," Hannah said quickly.

"Nope, my mom raised me the right way. If you cooked it, the least I could do is take the dish to the sink." He quickly took the dish into the kitchen and returned.

Hannah's heart sank a little. She missed her

mom. Hannah could bet she would have enjoyed meeting Daniel. He would have made her laugh as well.

"You okay, Hannah?" Daniel asked softly, concern darkening the green of his eyes.

"Sorry, was just thinking about my mom," she admitted. "She's been gone a long time, but it's still hard sometimes."

"I'm really sorry. I didn't mean anything…"

Hannah stopped him. "Oh, it's okay. It wasn't what you said."

"Still, I'm sure it has to be hard." He frowned with sympathy, but she could see he really didn't understand what the loss of a parent was like. She didn't wish that on anyone.

They stood there quietly, both lost in their own thoughts for a brief moment. Daniel suddenly spoke, "Well, I better head home. Thanks again for the slice of pie and the conversation."

"Thanks again for the ride, and sorry for the trouble."

"No trouble at all. I really enjoyed myself." They were both being polite, as if a sudden change had swept over them, neither knowing how to properly say goodbye. Maybe neither of them really wanted to.

"I had a great time visiting with you too. I'm sorry again about Nina." Hannah felt terribly guilty that her heart was singing with joy. It was a confusing mixture of feelings.

"Not a big deal. We weren't even dating or anything." She could see Daniel trying to play off his hurt.

Hannah watched his gaze drop to the wooden floor. He was hesitating, something lingering on his tongue. Hannah could tell a lot about people. She just had this uncanny ability to read them. Nina had been the one who had always gotten all the attention, and maybe Hannah had developed her ability by watching people and not being noticed.

"Hannah…"

"Yeah?" She waited as she saw him battle inside his own mind.

"Would you like to go out sometime? I mean, I know it's got to be kind of weird, considering everything, and…" Daniel rambled, not meeting her eyes.

Hannah grabbed his hand. She was shocked at her own bravery when she replied, "I'd love to."

***

Daniel

Giddiness—yes that's the word he would use to describe how he felt at that moment. As Daniel drove back into town, he felt downright giddy. He'd had no idea this afternoon would have changed so much, but it had. Spending the afternoon eating some of the best blueberry pie he had ever tasted, laughing so hard with someone who wasn't one of his siblings, was just so unexpected. Hannah turned out to be everything Nina wasn't. She was genuine, kind, and incredibly funny. Her eyes would twinkle as she laughed and giggled, and she'd even snorted once, which, oddly enough, he found to be quite adorable. His only regret was not remembering that her mother had passed away. He'd felt like the biggest idiot when he was going on about his mom. Daniel couldn't imagine losing her. She was one of the most important people in his life. Mary was the glue that held their family together, and she made the best muffins and pot roast in Birch Valley. Daniel loved her with all his heart, and if Hannah felt anything like he did about his mother, that poor girl must have been devastated when her own mother passed. But even with Daniel making mention of moms, Hannah had still been kind to him, so much so she agreed to go out with him. What had spurred him to ask, he still wasn't certain. It just felt right, not forced or complicated. After their chat that afternoon, he already had some ideas as to where he wanted to take her. Dating Hannah would hopefully prove to be a great deal easier than his attempts in dating Nina. God, what had he been thinking? *That was the problem,* he could almost hear his mother say, *you hadn't been thinking.* Instead, he went off on purely shallow desire, and the fact that this hot girl actually wanted to go somewhere with him sort of blew his mind. He had been overlooked for so long, and it felt nice to be noticed. But considering how awful everything had gone, especially after he had brought her home for dinner with his family, he knew he didn't want a repeat of that night. That had been a royal disaster. His mother was kind enough to discuss it with him as he had his breakfast that morning. Now, she hadn't been trying to sway Daniel from Nina, but she'd simply pointed out the facts. He knew it in his heart. It was just hard hearing it from his family, especially his mother.

Daniel pulled into the driveway and shut off his truck. Once inside the house, he was welcomed with the wonderful scents which only his mother could conjure. Well, maybe Hannah could too. He couldn't help but think of her and how she would act if invited into their home, into his mother's kitchen.

"Daniel, you're home. I was getting a little worried," Mary exclaimed as Daniel entered the kitchen. His mother was removing a tray from the oven. The distinct smell of toasted nuts, nutmeg, cinnamon, and banana hovered low in the air. Those golden little mounds of perfection were his mother's famous banana nut muffins.

"Those smell amazing, Mom." Daniel would steal one, but he knew the roof of his mouth would pay dearly.

"Thanks, dear. I felt the need to bake." She smiled up at him as she sat the tray on a cooling rack on the counter. "So Patrick came by a couple of hours ago to pick up the twins. He'd mentioned you helped Hannah. Something about car trouble?"

"Yeah, she needed a lift home." Daniel knew where this was headed. Maybe he should chance eating the scorching hot muffin.

"Well, that's nice of you, dear. I was just curious as to why you were getting back so late."

"I wasn't with Nina, Mom." Daniel knew that's what she was after. It was clear she was relieved.

"Good."

"Mom, we talked this morning. I know your

feelings about her. I agree with you. She's not the right one for me." Daniel decided to go for a muffin, but his mother beat him to it. She carefully grabbed a large one and sat it on a saucer.

"Butter?" she asked. He nodded as his mother quickly slid a pad of butter into the slit she had made in the muffin. "Be careful, it's hot."

"Thanks." The sweetness hit his mouth first, the flavors exploding all at once. Why wouldn't his mother sell these magnificent muffins? "So good," Daniel commented, his mouth full.

"So, how's Hannah?" Her hazel eyes sparkled and a funny grin appeared on her face. Well, that was quick. Daniel started to laugh as Mary O'Brien did what she did best—keep tabs on her children.

***

Hannah

She watched the tiny cluster of bubbles swirl down the drain. The citrus smell of the dish soap was strong but wonderful. This was Hannah's favorite part of the day, after dinner, when everyone had slipped away to different parts of the house. She was left to the quiet of her kitchen, her mother's kitchen. God, how she missed her. Could things have ended differently if they'd sought help earlier? Maybe, or perhaps it was simply God's plan.

Cancer. A sick and dirty word, foreign to their Russian ears when they'd finally gone to see a doctor. The man in the starched white coat, with the thick rimmed glasses and sullen expression, had said it was too far along to fight. The Belsky family rode home together that evening, quiet. Their lives were about to be forever changed, and Hannah had only been fourteen years old. As she lay in her bed that night, she could hear her mother and father crying through the wall. Her tears soaked her own pillow, and she didn't know just how much worse things were about to get. Nina had been young but old enough to understand. She was the favorite, the beautifully majestic child, with pale blonde hair and icy blue eyes. Hannah loved her sister, but there had always been a divide between them. That gap had only widened more after her mother passed away only two months later. They were prepared, but Hannah knew no one could be truly ready to see their mother waste away into virtually skin and bones, the sick smell of death hovering in the air. Hannah had been raised to know how to run a home. She'd learned cooking, cleaning, and mending, all while being homeschooled. Nina was naturally lazy and had no desire to learn any of those vital skills. Hannah would find herself not only taking the place of her mother, but having to try and raise her wild sister. Nina lashed out and hated Hannah, especially when Hannah would try to make Nina do anything, whether it be cooking or cleaning. Nina wanted to escape. Hell, they all did. Their father was never the same after their mother died, and he hadn't exactly been the warmest man to begin with. They knew he loved them, but he was denied sons, and it was under her mother's watch and insistence that he showed their daughters any affection. Hannah felt as though she had simply become a maid, cook, nanny, and runner of the household. She had never felt like she was his daughter. He did show more kindness to her sister. Perhaps he knew she was actually the weaker of the two, that she needed more love.

Hannah wiped away a lone tear. It had been almost fourteen years. Fourteen years of putting herself last, years spent just watching quietly and just being expected to keep the house. Hannah never experienced fun in the traditional sense, but Nina had enough for the both of them. So when she'd sat in their dining room with the charming Daniel O'Brien, their time together blindsided her. He made her feel like she was in one of those classic romance movies; the ones she liked to watch when she was alone. She knew nothing of dating, yet when Daniel asked her out she quickly jumped at the chance. What had she been thinking?

Hannah was lost in her thoughts as the warm water ran over her hands, rinsing the clean dish she held. Nina appeared at her side.

"So what was today all about?" Nina leaned against the counter, her eyes burning with a quiet rage.

"What do you mean?"

"Having Daniel get gas and seeing me. Geez, Hannah." Nina rolled her eyes, obviously annoyed.

Hannah sighed. Leave it to her sister to try and twist things, somehow making Hannah think it was her fault, when it was Nina's all along. Typical behavior. Nina always tried to toss the blame onto someone else, whether it be Hannah or a farmhand—literally anyone but herself.

"Well, why'd you do it?" Nina pestered more firmly, her hands on her hips and a little more aggression in her voice.

"I didn't do anything. He needed gas. Nina, there's only one gas station in town," Hannah explained with patience. She could feel her own temper starting to take hold.

"You didn't need to break the car, for starters."

Hannah laughed hard at the absurdity of her sister's remark. "Are you serious?"

"It's your fault, Hannah. If he wasn't having to give you a ride home, he wouldn't have seen me." The look on Nina's face, like she actually believed she was telling the truth, blew Hannah's mind.

"Nina, you have been stringing poor Daniel along. He doesn't deserve that."

Nina glared at Hannah with anger and quickly stomped away like a spoiled child, because that was truly what Nina was. She had never had to be responsible for anything in her entire life, not before their mother's death and certainly not after. In all honesty, it worried Hannah. How was Nina going to ever survive in the world? Would Hannah always have to raise her little sister?

Hannah turned off the sink and dried her hands on a nearby dishtowel. She pondered things for a moment. What if things went well between her and Daniel? What if they got serious? What if they got married or had kids? What would she do about her father and Nina? Who would take care of things here? Hannah knew it was a lot of what-ifs, but she needed to be prepared, because if she had learned anything from her mother's death, it was that life

took you on unexpected journeys, whether you were
ready, willing, or otherwise.

***

Daniel

Canadian geese flew overhead in a V formation
as Daniel carefully cast the line of his fishing pole
out into the still lake. The late evening swarm of
mosquitoes were nipping at his neck, but this was
the perfect time to fish: just as the sun was setting
behind the mountains, when the heat of the day was
cooling, and when the deer could be seen grazing in
the fields. Daniel loved this time of the day, this
brief period of calm with muted light, that lull
before night took over.

"So, Hannah, huh?" Liam asked as he reeled his
line back in.

Daniel was visiting his brother at his cabin for an
impromptu evening of fishing. It was the best stress
reliever in the world, as far as Daniel was concerned.
Not that he was stressed, but fishing seem to cure
all sorts of worries.

"Well, maybe." Daniel had opened up to Liam
about the day before, spending just those few hours
with Hannah, and even his run-in with Nina.

Liam paused and took a swig from his beer
bottle, then said, "Well, you did say you asked her
out."

"I know, but do you think it's too soon?" Daniel
asked. He was feeling a bit of remorse. He worried
that Hannah would think he was simply asking her

out because Nina had rejected him.

"Nah, I don't think so. I mean, look at it like this. Nina wasn't the right one. We all could have told you that, but you needed to figure that out on your own." Liam sat his bottle back down on the grassy shore and sent his line sailing through the air and into the water.

"You have a valid point. I guess I was just sort of excited that a girl that looked like that would want anything to do with a guy like me." Daniel looked away, focusing on the darkening surroundings, the quiet of nature encompassing them. He didn't want Liam to see the truth in his eyes.

"Daniel, you're a good guy, man. Any girl would be lucky to have you. It's about you finding one who deserves someone as decent and kind as you."

Daniel sighed. What Liam, or anyone in the family, didn't understand was that Daniel didn't see his value or worth. Girls had passed him over so many times that he was actually terrified of them. He didn't have to ask Nina out. She'd just sort of ordered him to pick her up and take her here or there. Sure, they kissed, but it didn't really do anything for Daniel.

"I'm serious. I'm not saying it because you're my brother. You are one of the best guys I know." Liam looked at Daniel, then bent down and retrieved his beer again. Daniel did the same, and they both took a long, leisurely sip. Daniel cherished moments like this with Liam, simple quiet activities like fishing. These were some of the best times. He could count on his brother to build him up when he was at his lowest, to give him sound advice, and to just be there without any kind of judgment. Liam was more than his brother; he was also Daniel's best friend.

Chapter Seven

Rachel

"Are you almost ready, babe?"

She could hear the slight irritation in Liam's voice from the other side of the bathroom door. Hell no, she wasn't ready. Today was the first day of school, and as she stood in front of the mirror, she couldn't believe how enormous she looked. Rachel had tried changing into various maternity shirts. Everything seemed so tight or made her look like a whale.

"Come on, Rachel. We need to leave or we'll be late." His tone turned a bit more authoritative.

"Just go ahead and go," Rachel shouted from the bathroom, tears of frustration starting to sting her eyes.

She heard him knock, then he entered. "What's wrong?"

Everything. She didn't dare tell him that. The poor guy was constantly worried about her. "I'm fine." The tears pushed past the corners of her eyes and streamed down her face.

"Oh, babe." Liam scooped her up into his strong arms, cradling her like she was the most precious thing.

"It's nothing. I'm fine. I promise." Her tears told a different story as she tried to convince him and herself that she was okay. Damn pregnancy hormones!

"I can call Karen and let her know we're running late," Liam offered as he kissed the top of her head.

"No, let's just go." Rachel ran her hands down her black maternity blouse and gray slacks. She grabbed some toilet paper and tried sopping up the mess her tears had caused.

He held her arms and looked at her, deep concern shining in his gorgeous eyes. "Are you sure?"

Rachel could only nod. If she even attempted to speak, she knew that it would only end in crying.

"It'll be okay," Liam tried to reassure her as he pulled her tightly against his chest. Rachel inhaled his scent: the same sexy mix of his aftershave and soap she had fallen in love with months ago.

***

They drove together in Rachel's silver BMW, the sun blinding them as they drove in the direction of town. The beginning of September still had the feeling of summer. It was warm and beautiful, but by the end of the month, when the students and teachers had gotten into the groove and settled in, the leaves would start to change and there would be a crispness in the air. Then fall would turn the leaves on the trees a bountiful array of colors, and the scents of summer would be forgotten and replaced with warm cups of cider and wood smoke from chimneys as the cold nights took hold of Birch Valley.

As they arrived in the heart of the small community, they saw children with their new shoes, backpacks, and clothes walking to school. The parking lot of Birch Valley Elementary was not full yet, and they easily found a place to park.

"You ready?" Liam asked as he undid his seat belt. *God, he's so handsome.* Rachel wanted to kiss him right there, well, amongst other things. Again, damn pregnancy hormones. The green button-down shirt he wore tucked into his dark wash jeans brought out all the hues of emerald in his eyes. His hair had been freshly cut at her insistence, and he had even shaved that sexy jawline she loved kissing. Yes, this man was all hers.

Liam got out of the car and went over to her side to help her out. All visions of sexiness were lost as she realized that she must look like a helpless cow. Unable to remove herself out of the low bucket seats, she felt frustrated. Liam extended his hand and practically yanked her out of the car. Straightening her blouse and inhaling deeply, Rachel waited as Liam gathered his backpack from the trunk. He swung it onto to one shoulder, took her hand, and led her to old brick building, where their love story began.

***

Liam

Once inside the school, as they crossed into the bright foyer, Liam spotted Karen, the school secretary, as she rounded the corner. "Oh my, look at you." Karen squealed in delight. "You're just glowing, you beautiful dear."

Rachel smiled, but Liam could see she was uncomfortable. He knew his wife was feeling anything but beautiful or radiant. Liam smiled to himself at the word *wife.*

They were approaching two months of wedded bliss, though he'd hardly call it that. He loved her, more than he ever thought possible, and that love continued to flourish and grow as each day passed. But they had met some challenges—one being her hormones. She was crying one minute, laughing another, and then right back at crying. Liam didn't know where the tears began or where they stopped sometimes. The latest marital issue, one that was weighing pretty heavily on Liam, was their intimacy. They shared this almost combustible type of passion. He missed it, but he was terrified of somehow hurting Rachel. He wasn't quite sure about how that factored in with pregnancy. She tried to reassure him, but he couldn't shake his fears. Unfortunately, he could see that it was taking its toll on both of them.

"Oh, Karen, please." Rachel shooed her away.

The bell buzzed and children started filing into the school. Liam bent down and gave Rachel a quick kiss. In the background he heard someone say, "Mr. O'Brien is kissing the principal." He couldn't help but laugh. Little did any of these students know that Ms. Montgomery was now Mrs. O'Brien. A happy little thrill surged through him. "Stay off your feet," Liam instructed before he jogged toward his classroom.

***

Rachel

"Worried about the wifey, I see," Karen teased as they both smiled and greeted the children.

"You could say that." Rachel could feel the smile on her lips as she watched her husband disappear in the sea of students.

"So, tell me. How's married life? How are you feeling?" Karen was not only her right-hand woman at work, she had also become almost a mother figure to Rachel when she had moved to Birch Valley.

"Well, married life is good. Pregnancy life, ugh," Rachel admitted reluctantly, feeling her smile drift away.

A concerned scowl appeared on Karen's softly wrinkled face. "How so?"

Another bell chimed, and the once-crowded foyer was now nearly empty of students. Rachel and Karen went back to Rachel's office to catch up. She plopped down in her comfortable office chair behind the large mahogany desk, kindly left to her by Mr. Anderson, the lovely man she'd replaced. Rachel noticed there was not nearly as much room, and she felt a little constricted in the limited space.

Karen noticed right away and started to move the desk forward.

"You have gotten quite a bit bigger since I saw you in July," Karen commented, taking a seat in front of the desk.

"I know. I'm huge," Rachel complained. "I'm not due until November, Karen. How much larger am I going to get?"

"Dear, don't worry about it. You're gorgeous." Karen paused briefly. "You know, we do need to think about your baby shower."

"Seriously? You can't even wait a full ten minutes. You and Mary are the same. She just hit me up last night at dinner."

"Can you blame her? I certainly don't. Rachel, these things need to be planned. I'm sure you would like to have your mother here for it, and maybe your lovely friend?" Karen asked firmly.

"I know. I just hate party planning."

"Trust me, I'm well aware. However, the beauty of a baby shower is that we get to do the planning. You just show up, play games, collect gifts, and be all adorably pregnant."

"Still sounds like a lot on my part," Rachel said sarcastically.

"Oh, you stop. You have been hanging around that stubborn O'Brien boy too long. I'll phone Mary later and start figuring stuff out so that you can let your folks know."

Rachel nodded as Karen rose from her seat and left the office. She sat there all by herself, with only her thoughts to keep her company. Well, that wasn't entirely true. Rachel had two people with her—little, tiny people who were taking turns kicking her as hard as they could. The twins seemed to be tag teaming her with an assault she hadn't quite felt before. As Rachel rubbed her belly, begging her babies to stop, she caught sight of the heart-shaped paperweight Liam had given her. Inscribed, it read, *You have my heart,* when, in truth, he had hers. She would be lost without that man. He had been so caring and gentle with her, patient almost to a fault. God love him. Liam was the best thing that ever happened to her. Rachel picked up the paperweight. The cold metal was heavy in her hands. It wasn't just the physical weight, but the words too. For him to have already felt that strong connection with her, to be so bold to leave something with such a powerful statement on her desk, that took guts and pure bravery. Nope, Rachel was a coward. She had struggled owning her own feelings for Liam. Only months later after he'd given her the paperweight, he'd become her husband and the father of her babies. Well, father first, then husband.

Rachel laid her head on her desk, feeling exhausted and almost overwhelmed at the thought of being back to work. She heard a knock on her door. "Come in."

Maggie poked her head in. "Did I catch you at a bad time?" She looked worried as she entered the small office.

"No, why?" Rachel sat up straight in her chair.

"I don't know. You look, well…"

"I know, like crap, right?" Rachel finished for her.

"No, just like you'd rather be anywhere but here.

I just dropped off Mel and wanted to pop in and say hi." Maggie took the same seat Karen had been in earlier. She wore a light sun dress, which glorified her perfectly round belly. A muu muu, now that was an idea. Why hadn't she thought of that before?

"I was just having a hard morning. I couldn't find anything that fit or was comfortable enough. I don't know. These hormones, they are just all over the place." Rachel felt frustration brewing again, and another set of tears was ready to pour.

"Rachel, trust me, I have so been there." Maggie offered her a sympathetic smile.

"I know." Rachel groaned. "Does it get better?"

Maggie seemed to be choosing her words carefully. "It does, eventually."

"Eventually?"

"Okay, here's the thing no one ever tells you. After you have the baby, it takes awhile for your hormones to go back to normal. Hell, they never really do. Maybe it's more like we adapt." Maggie started to laugh, but Rachel found nothing funny about this. She was being driven mad with her feelings fluctuating all the time. The very thought of these tidal waves of hormones never ending, well, that was more than she could bear right then.

Shaking her head and trying to keep from crying again, Rachel asked, "So how are you feeling? How's the lil guy?"

"Squirming around like he owns the place. I feel a little more tired now, but we have less than a month, so we're excited." Maggie's eyes shone with such happiness, it made Rachel's hormones kick into overdrive.

"I can't wait to meet him. He's going to be just the most adorable thing ever," Rachel commented as she wiped away some loose tears.

Maggie got up and went behind the desk to hug Rachel. "I can't wait to meet your precious babies. This is such a wonderful time, Rachel."

As they embraced, Rachel did feel better from being hugged by her sister-in-law and best friend. They chatted a little while longer, and Maggie confirmed dinner plans for them all in a couple days. She also asked Rachel to help with some final touches on the nursery, which got Rachel thinking. Her and Liam really needed to start thinking about their nursery. They had double the work to do.

***

Maggie

As Maggie made the short walk from the school to the O'Brien Construction shop, she couldn't but feel a bit concerned for Rachel. Granted, she herself hadn't been all that happy about being pregnant the first time, and not even that thrilled the second time around. She knew how Rachel felt. Maggie understood the worry of getting pregnant so soon in a new relationship and what others would think all too well. Oh yes, Maggie could sympathize big time. However, Maggie had been lucky. When she had gotten pregnant with Melanie she was living in Seattle, away from the small gossip and curious stares. Poor Rachel was not so lucky.

"Finally," Patrick shouted from his office as

Maggie entered the metal building. The business had been in their family since Grandpa Paddy opened it up so many years ago.

"Good morning to you too, Patrick," Maggie hollered back.

Daniel peeked out from his office. "What are you guys shouting about?"

"Morning, Daniel," Maggie said as she sat her purse down and turned on her computer. She had gone from working nearly full-time to only a couple of hours a day a few days a week. Maggie actually missed being there with her brothers full-time. There had been some tense times, but they always seem to manage to get through them.

Daniel and Patrick appeared by the counter which separated her work area from the shop's entrance.

"What?" Maggie playfully snapped at her brothers.

Daniel smiled broadly. "So, I think Daniel is a very nice name."

Patrick shook his head. "I disagree. Patrick is perfect. It would sort of stick with tradition, you know."

Maggie bit her lip and looked up at the ceiling. "Um, how do you figure that would stick with tradition? Patrick, you would have had to name one of your boys Patrick."

Daniel chimed in, "That would have been Finn. He's the oldest. So, yeah, how come you didn't?"

Patrick's expression soured. "Because that isn't what Beth wanted them to be named."

Maggie looked down. She had a feeling the very

mention of Beth's name would cause some sorrow for Patrick. It had been over four years since she'd died at the hands of a drunk driver. Patrick was barely beginning to heal, thanks to Amber.

Daniel swept his gaze away as well. "Hey, I didn't mean…"

Patrick stopped him. "It's okay, Daniel. If you had asked me a couple months ago, I wouldn't be." A crooked and goofy smile appeared on his face just as Maggie felt brave enough to let her gaze meet his. "I think I'm starting to fall in love in with Amber."

Maggie and Daniel both let out a laugh. A confused expression flashed across Patrick's face, which was quickly replaced by anger. Maggie cupped her mouth and fanned her hands at her eyes to stop the tears. Every time she looked over at Daniel, she broke out in another round of uncontrollable giggles. Daniel and Maggie had had this same problem when they were kids, but it was their closeness in age—they weren't even two years apart—which made them what some considered *Irish twins.*

"I don't see what's so funny. This is exactly why I never tell either of you anything." Patrick glared at them as they tried to compose themselves.

"Oh, big brother, it's just funny that you're barely admitting you think you love Amber. Come on, you guys are practically a married couple."

"Maggie, I'm not that transparent," Patrick said, defending himself.

"Oh yeah, you are," Daniel added as he caught his breath.

"Well, you two wait right there." Patrick jogged back to his office and quickly hurried back. Daniel was bent over the counter, and Maggie tried to stay focused on Patrick. She didn't dare look at Daniel or another eruption of laughter might start again.

Maggie moved to the counter. Daniel straightened up, and they both watched as Patrick revealed a small velvet box. "How transparent am I again?" Patrick asked.

Daniel raised his eyebrows in surprise. Maggie wasn't completely shocked, but at the same time she had a little bit of a hard time processing what it all meant. Patrick was going to ask Amber to marry him.

"Oh, Patrick." Maggie waddled to the other side of the dividing counter and grabbed Patrick. She wrapped her arms tightly around his waist. She felt Daniel join in the embrace. This tender moment would always stay lodged in her mind. Maggie felt tears roll down her cheeks. She had only wanted her brother to find happiness again. This meant Patrick had finally moved on and her prayers had been answered.

***

They all took Patrick's SUV to go to lunch at Herrick's. Maggie tried to encourage the guys to walk to the best place to eat in Birch Valley.

"You need to quit walking so much. Won't the baby, like, come out if you keep doing that?" Daniel asked from the backseat as they pulled into the full parking lot of the diner. It was just a little after one in the afternoon, but the lunch rush was still in full force.

"Is Amber working today?" Maggie asked. Amber's family had made this diner into what it was well known for—great food and great company.

Patrick parked and shut the car off. "Probably." He swiveled around to look at both Daniel and Maggie and leaned in closer, as if to tell a secret. "You better not breathe a word." He hissed, just like he always had when they were kids. He had always been taller than them and he was the oldest, so it went without saying that when Patrick told them something, they listened. Maggie, being the youngest and the only girl, enjoyed challenging her oldest brother. She responded with a smirk that left Patrick shaking his head as exited the SUV.

As they entered, the bell on the weathered yarn rung. The diner was filled with loud chatter of so many residents of Birch Valley enjoying lunch, mixed with the strong aroma of French fries and something else that Maggie couldn't quite place. But her stomach growled and her little baby boy squirmed.

"Hey, guys," Amber greeted them with a wide and happy smile. She had her dark hair pulled up into a ponytail, making her brilliant lagoon-colored eyes stand out. Immediately, Amber pulled Maggie into a hug. "I'm so happy for you."

News traveled fast, especially in this family. Michael had wanted to keep the gender a secret and do some grand stunt to tell everyone. The only other person Maggie had told was Rachel, and she had kept her mouth closed. It was Maggie who had slipped up; she had told her mother one morning last week when they had met for tea. Well, there went the plans for surprising everyone. Everyone was thrilled, especially Melanie, who had hoped and prayed for a little brother. Rachel and Liam were now more anxious to find out what they were having.

As Amber led them to a table toward the back of the diner, affording them a little more quiet, she asked, "Names? Have you and Michael started arguing over that yet?"

Patrick pulled Amber close to him and gave her a quick kiss on the cheek. "They are going to name him Patrick."

Daniel pulled out a chair for Maggie and helped himself into one. "Uh, wrong, we are going with Daniel."

Maggie started laughing. "Oh stop, you two. Melanie and Michael already decided on a perfect name, and we will announce it on Sunday at dinner."

"What? My favorite little niece better have picked her uncle's name," Daniel said with bravado.

"Yeah, her Uncle Patrick, duh?" Patrick added as he sat down.

Amber playfully slapped his arm. "Leave Maggie alone. Gosh, you guys act like children when you are together." She turned her attention to Maggie. "I'm excited to find out the name on Sunday."

"Oh yeah, Amber, are you free on Saturday?" Maggie asked hopefully.

"Sure, what's up?" Her brow twitched with

concern.

"I wanted to see if you and Rachel can come over and help me get that dang nursery in order. I'm running out of time."

"That would be fun. Just call me later and tell me what time."

Maggie smiled. "Thanks. I will call Rachel later too."

"Great," Amber responded before she threw her hands on her thick, jean-clad hips and faced Patrick. "So the usual for you?"

"Bring me what whatever you want me to eat." Maggie watched as Patrick gave Amber a sinful grin accompanied with a wink. *Gross.*

Amber turned a pretty shade of pink as she quickly asked, "You, Daniel? Anything special today?"

"Nah, I'll take the patty melt," he answered, completely oblivious to the naughty, but thankfully brief, interaction.

Amber's cheeks were still flushed with embarrassment as she faced Maggie. "How about you, Maggie? Does your lil man want anything special?"

She considered for a moment and rubbed her belly and felt him shift, stretching in his tight quarters. Maggie quietly asked her son—*her son.*

Chapter Eight

Daniel

Daniel held the phone in his hands, his gut twisting with nerves. Why was he worried? Hannah had said she would go out with him. What if she changed her mind? He had been avoiding this call. It had been almost two weeks since he had enjoyed her delicious blueberry pie, since they'd laughed so hard together, so why was he worried? He wanted this, right?

He swallowed hard and waited as he heard the line ring. After a moment, he heard her sweet voice answer, "Hello?"

"Hannah?" Daniel asked.

"Daniel. How are you?" There was a pause and some rustling sounds in the background. "I figured I would never hear from you again," Hannah boldly stated.

He ran his free hand through his hair. Now he was worried. Maybe he had upset her by waiting so long to call. "I know. I'm sorry. I have been working, and with back to school, we actually have more work than normal. Last-minute projects that folks want done before fall gets here," Daniel said, trying to explain. He was afraid she would see right through his excuses.

"I see. Well, you're calling now. So, what's up?" Her voice was still sweet, but there was a sassy undertone which told him she could easily call his bluff, but she was too polite to actually do it.

"I wanted to see if you were free tomorrow. I thought it might be fun to go to breakfast. What do you think?" Daniel suggested. He could think of a million things he'd like to do with her, but his brain was frozen in fear and his thoughts were a jumbled mess.

"Hmm, breakfast? I have a better idea. Why don't you come over here? I'll make breakfast."

"You sure? That doesn't sound like much of a date," Daniel stated.

He could hear her sigh. "Well, if you'd rather not."

"No, Hannah, that's not what I meant. I was trying to say…"

Hannah interrupted him with such speed he was taken a little off guard. "Daniel, I know what you meant. I'm offering you breakfast, and then we can maybe go do something. I just like cooking for you, and you haven't had my huckleberry pancakes yet." She laughed. The sound was angelic and beyond comforting to his ears.

Relieved and starting to feel his nerves calm, he responded eagerly, "That sounds really good."

"Of course it does, silly. We are talking about

huckleberry pancakes." He couldn't argue with her there. Huckleberries were worth their weight in gold, especially this time of the year. The delicious berry was well sought after high into the mountains, where pickers brave enough to get them sometimes had run-ins with bears, who equally enjoyed the tiny fruit.

"Can I bring anything?" Daniel asked, feeling completely at ease with her now.

"Just yourself."

***

Hannah

When she'd answered the phone and heard Daniel O'Brien's voice, she'd nearly dropped the basket of fresh laundry she had been carrying. Hannah had figured the afternoon they had spent laughing together over pie was a fluke, him just being polite, her just being overlooked as usual. But now she knew otherwise, and she felt a little nervous as her tummy twisted in queasy knots. She hoped she had played it off well, trying desperately to sound cool. Hannah didn't want him to think she'd been sitting by that darn phone for nearly two weeks in sick anticipation, like she actually had. She'd kept hoping that it would ring and she'd hear his voice, the one she dreamed about.

As Hannah readied for bed, brushing her teeth, her mind was completely occupied with thoughts of Daniel. She loved his eyes, but all the O'Brien kids had been known for those windows of green, deep and soulful, but Daniel's held a different hint of something special. He was different than the rest of his brothers. Not that Patrick or Liam weren't attractive men; the whole town of Birch Valley would have no problem defending that fact. Yet there was a unique light that came from Daniel. She had felt it the first time she had seen him working at her family's farm. He seemed to radiate good-natured joy; something that seemed rare in people these days. He wasn't moody like Patrick, who had a darkness about him, a shadow which drove a little fear into Hannah when she had met him the first time. She knew he was widowed. The storm that hovered over him, she recognized it all too well in her father—grief.

Hannah exhaled as she pulled the lilac-colored sheets back and fluffed her pillow before climbing into bed. She had a game plan for tomorrow morning. She wanted to impress Daniel with her breakfast-making skills. Hannah considered how her father might feel about this man being brought into their home, so she had decided to ask him over dinner that evening, just loud enough so that Nina could hear. She wanted to be clear that she was inviting Daniel over to eat with them. Nina had acted cold and aloof, but Hannah worried that it did bother her sister. Her father's reaction had been indifferent; he'd grunted his response and had continued to eat his meal. He probably wasn't thinking she had any hopes of this being the start of a relationship with Daniel. Little did either of them know, Hannah had been carrying a secret crush since the very moment she had seen him. It had nearly tore her heart to shreds when Nina went in for the kill. As Hannah muttered the last of her prayers, feeling her mind tire and her eyes grow heavy, she thanked God for this second chance.

***

The bacon sizzled in the cast iron skillet on the stove, filling the kitchen with its glorious smell as she stirred huckleberries slowly into her batter. Hannah looked out the window. Even though it was early, the sun was shining brightly, and fluffy cotton ball clouds hung near the rolling hills. Today was going to be beautiful, and she felt positive that it would be, in more ways than one.

"Did you make coffee yet?" Nina appeared, rumpled from sleep, her pale hair in a loose and untidy bun on top of her head.

"Yeah, I just made it." Hannah grabbed a mug out of the cupboard and filled it with the dark liquid, steam rising from it in magical circles. "Here you go," Hannah said as she handed the mug to Nina.

"Do we have any creamer? I don't like it black," Nina complained. Hannah was already grabbing the plastic container with the sweet milky mix out of the fridge. "How much longer until Daniel is here?"

Not a thank you or anything. Why was Hannah ever surprised at her sister's lack of manners?

"I told him to come a little after nine." Hannah eyed the kitchen clock mounted on the opposite wall. It was after eight.

"So, like, what? Are you guys dating now?" Nina sipped her coffee and glared harshly at her.

107

Hannah flipped the bacon and shrugged. "I don't know about that." She felt a sneaky smile grow on her lips. Hannah wished she could say that, but this was simply a matter of testing the waters, and she hoped that Nina would keep her distance.

"So why would you invite him here to eat? Gosh, that's like all he thinks about too. You guys are probably perfect for each other."

Her words sliced through Hannah, cutting her deep. Hannah was nearly as thin as Nina, just shorter and stockier. Nina's build had always been a source of envy. She wished her frame was long and lean, but she had inherited a completely different makeup. Nina had height, perfect cheekbones, and long legs. She was willowy and looked as though she could conquer any runway. Her pale blonde hair, sun-kissed skin, and blue eyes only magnified her beauty. Nina had always described Hannah as homely, and Hannah didn't see herself as much better than that. Her hair was a heavy golden blonde, like a mix of wheat with sun-bleached bits from working outside. Her skin was fair but smattered with freckles. Hannah's limbs were not willowy nor graceful, but they were strong and created for hard work. She hadn't bothered with makeup. What was the point? She feared that masking her plainness would only make it worse somehow. Besides, when she was out milking the goats or feeding the chickens, makeup was not part of the job requirement.

She decided not to answer Nina and started to warm the griddle for the pancakes. Nina leaned against the counter, watching her work. Hannah turned to face her and asked, "Want to help make pancakes? I can show you how to make these, if you'd like?"

"Uh, no thanks." Nina continued to stare silently as she drank her coffee.

"You know, someday you are going to need to learn to cook, Nina."

Nina exhaled a laugh. "Why, you got plans to leave?"

Ignoring the rude comment, Hannah let it roll off of her. "What about you? Don't you plan to get married someday, have a family to care for?"

"God, no. I want to leave Birch Valley, but I have no desire to play up the role of domestic goddess. No thanks."

Hannah pouted. She figured all women wanted to have families. It had always been a fantasy of hers. "So you don't ever want kids?"

"I have no desire to change diapers or have some sticky gross kid on me."

"Wow, that's kind of sad, actually. What about a man to love and spend your life with?" Hannah almost felt as though she were grasping at straws. Her sister obviously wanted nothing to do with kids and the idea of a family repulsed her, which saddened Hannah. She had failed her mother. Perhaps if she had done more, been somehow more loving and motherly towards her sister, then maybe Nina would wouldn't feel this lack of desire.

"A man? I love men. That's not the problem. It's the husband part. See, they will expect me to do what you do. Which, Hannah, is fine for you and women like you. You guys enjoy cooking and

109

cleaning, all that crap. Me, nope, not interested in the least." A playful smile showed on her lips as she continued, "I have no problem role-playing, but not in the kitchen."

Hannah was taken aback. "What?"

"Oh come on, don't act surprised. I'm not a virgin, Hannah. I'm twenty-two. Everyone I know, like all my friends, none of them are virgins. You're like the only one." Nina laughed a little too hard.

Was there anything wrong with wanting to wait until she found the right man, the man who would be her husband? Was it so wrong to want to have a special wedding night? Hannah didn't think so. She wanted that happily ever after and the magic that goes with finding the right person, the kind she found in the romantic moves she loved.

"Is that a bad thing?" Hannah asked, setting the large mixing bowl near the griddle. She ladled out some of the pink-tinged batter. It bubbled quickly and Hannah flipped it over. The smell was incredible and filling the kitchen. Nina huffed.

"Well, kind of. I mean, I get the whole not wanting to be a slut thing, but come on. You are going to be thirty in a couple of years. Aren't you curious?"

Of course she was. Hannah wasn't a nun, and she even suspected they may be curious. But what it came down to was that Hannah was sticking to her guns. There was very little in this world that a person had control over or a choice about, but this was her choice. It was a virtue she had decided to uphold early on. It wasn't completely influenced by her mother or religion, though those were factors. It was actually the romantic notion of falling in love and being with someone she could trust, to give a gift of herself in such a complete way. Well, in her mind that was the ultimate bond. Then, there was also the fear. The fear of being pregnant, unwed, or unloved. It outweighed any curiosity.

Hannah continued to pour batter and flip it. She removed the perfect circles off the griddle. Nina was bored and left her mug on the counter as she exited the kitchen. Hannah worked on the place settings when her father entered.

"Good morning, Hannah. It smells lovely in here." He took off his straw hat and went to the kitchen sink to wash up for breakfast. This was their routine—not much conversation, but a pleasant enough exchange. "So, you invited that Daniel O'Brien here to eat with us?"

Hannah nodded. "I did. He should be here any minute." A knock on the metal screen door indicated she was right. She set down a plate to answer it, but her father dried his hands quickly and stopped her so he could get the door instead.

Her belly tensed up with nerves as she heard her father and Daniel approach the dining area. Her father had a smile, which was not a common sight. Daniel's face lit up when his eyes met hers.

"Good morning, Hannah," Daniel politely said as he sat near her father after he had nodded for him to do so. "Wow, everything looks amazing. Oh and the smell, just wonderful. Mr. Bclsky, you are incredibly lucky."

Hannah began to serve the men. Nina still had not returned from wherever she had run off to. She was probably back in bed and waiting for Daniel to leave. That suited Hannah just fine.

"Thank you," her father replied. Hannah served him two pancakes and went to put some on Daniel's plate next.

"You did too much. I would have been happy to take you to breakfast. You didn't need to go to all this trouble," Daniel rambled as she fetched the coffee pot.

"Dad will tell you, I enjoy it, and this is sort of what I do."

Her father nodded as he applied a pad of butter to his pancakes.

Hannah finally joined them. Their conversation mainly consisted of Daniel chatting about different things. Her father would actually comment or laugh, but those were both things he didn't do too often, and it was lovely seeing him so at ease with Daniel. He almost looked happy. The deep creases near his eyes and mouth were bent in happiness as he chewed his food and listened to Daniel recount another funny tale. Daniel's stories seemed a little larger than life to Hannah, but hearing the excitement and watching how animated he got as he told them had her giggling.

Finally, after they had all stuffed themselves well beyond their fill, her father rose from his seat and started to excuse himself. "Well, Daniel, it would seem a farmer's work is never done. It was great sharing breakfast with you."

Daniel stood and extended his hand and sheepishly said, "Thank you, Mr. Belsky. If it's okay with you, sir, I would love to take your daughter out."

With a curt nod, her father responded, "That would be fine, son." He nodded again, this time at Hannah, who had remained in her spot.

Daniel waited to sit back down until her father was out the door again, with his straw hat in hand. "Hannah, breakfast was so good."

"Thanks." She eyed him cautiously, then asked, "So what's the game plan here, mister?"

Daniel smiled, his eyes twinkling softly. "I'd like to spend some time with you."

"Well, what did you have in mind?" Now she was curious. It was one thing to eat breakfast with her father, but now the two of them were going to be alone.

He looked at her. She could practically see the gears in his brain moving as he tried to come up with an answer. "I have an idea."

***

Daniel

The idea, well, he hoped she'd like it. It would really tell him whether or not their relationship could be pursued any further. Daniel helped Hannah into his truck but had a little difficulty jogging to his side. He was stuffed. Hannah's breakfast had been incredible, and he'd enjoyed that her father was there, acting as a chaperone in a way. Even as much as Daniel would have loved to be alone with Hannah, he felt it was important to connect with family. He wanted to make Mr. Belsky comfortable with him taking Hannah out. Even though they were both nearly thirty, it was still the proper thing to do. People might call him old-fashioned, but that was fine by him. Daniel considered himself a gentleman, and that's why seeing Nina had been difficult. She was looking for the typical bad boy, and Daniel was anything but that.

He started the truck and looked over at Hannah. She smiled shyly at him as she ran her hands along her jean-clad legs. Every time they connected with a swift glance, he was moved by how simply pretty she was. She seem to sparkle in a way he didn't quite understand.

"So where to, Captain?"

Daniel laughed as he headed away from the farm. "Well, you'll find out soon enough."

Hannah frowned and stated firmly, "You have no idea where to go or what to do."

"No, well, I mean..." He found himself stumbling over his own words. He actually had no idea where to take her. Daniel could think of fun outdoorsy stuff, but was that really a first date type of thing to do? He listened to Hannah exhale loudly and was instantly swarmed by nerves. Maybe this had been a bad idea. Daniel feared that maybe Hannah was more like Nina than he realized.

"Daniel, drive me to the grocery store," Hannah ordered.

She would probably try and phone for her father to come get her. How had this ended before it even started? Disappointed, he headed in the direction of the single grocery store in Birch Valley. They drove in silence and as they approached the store, Daniel broke the awkward tension. "I'm sorry. I, uh…"

Hannah wore a confused expression as he pulled into an empty space in front of the grocery store. "What's wrong? We needed to stop here to get stuff for our date."

"Date?"

"Um, that's what we're on. So, let's get what we need and head out." Hannah unbuckled her seat belt and started to open the door.

"Where are we headed?" Daniel asked as he prepared to get out as well.

"We're going fishing," she stated matter-of-factly with huge grin on her face.

Fishing? If he'd had a ring in his pocket, he'd probably propose to her right then and there.

***

After they grabbed a couple things from the deli inside the grocery store and a couple of other odds and ends, they were on the highway headed the way Hannah had told him to go. Daniel was confused and not aware of any good fishing spots in the direction they were headed.

"Are you sure?" Daniel asked again as they traveled further along.

"Yes, positive. Look, there's the road. Turn right."

He did, and they were now on a rough stretch of road riddled with enormous pot holes and rain ruts. His truck crawled over the rough terrain, and they easily continued down the way. Hannah suddenly gave him a confident smirk. "Right there." There it was, glittering under the sun, a small lake nestled around tall grasses. Lily pads floated near the bank and willows mixed with pines surrounded the water. A river otter's home, which was made of sticks and debris, was clearly visible in the center of the dark water. The area was gorgeous.

"Best kept secret, right?" Hannah asked when they starting pulling out the fishing poles and gear he always kept in the bed of the truck.

"Yeah, how do I not know about this place?" Daniel handed her the two poles they were going to use.

"Well, first, it's a place where Russians hang out, so I'm pretty sure that's one reason. Two, well, it's the same as the first." Hannah led Daniel to a shady spot under a weeping willow that had started turning a golden color, its long branches sweeping the ground. "This is perfect."

"It sure is." He was still stunned he hadn't known about this lake. He also could tell it was probably loaded with fish. He'd kill to take his boat out to the middle of the water. He would bet there was bass out that way.

They sat their poles down and went back to the truck to lug an ice chest filled with the impromptu items Hannah had grabbed at the store. When they returned, Daniel watched Hannah, her golden hair flowing in the slight breeze. She was staring out at the lake with her hands on her hips and a happy smile perched on her face. She must be pretty darn proud of herself because he sure was. Never in a million years would he have guessed she'd want to go fishing. Talk about a perfect date.

"Well, I'm not hungry yet. Why don't we see if they're biting?" Hannah suggested.

"Sounds great." Daniel started to fix up their poles. Hannah placed a hand on his arm.

"I can do mine." She grabbed a fat worm from the white plastic container Daniel had just opened.

"You sure?" He eyed her curiously.

"Yes, I can bait my own hook." She stuck the worm quick, looping and securely it in an expert fashion. Daniel was in awe. "Ye of little faith, I told ya I could take care of mine. You better hurry."

Hannah raced to the edge of the shore. Daniel watched as she kicked off her shoes and went into the water. She pulled her pole back and whipped the line out far into the water. Daniel grinned. He just might believe in love at first sight.

He soon stood next to her, launching his own line out. The sun was warm but not harsh as it sat high in the brilliant blue sky. Birds chirped as the two of them waited quietly.

"I had no idea you liked fishing," Daniel finally said as he reeled his line in.

"There's a lot you don't know about me and vice versa. That's the beauty of first dates."

Daniel cast the line back into the water and said, "Yeah, but it's pretty awesome you like to fish."

"It's one of my favorite things to do. I can't explain it, but just being outside and near the water, it's the best feeling in the world."

"I couldn't agree more."

They discussed everything under the sun, literally. Daniel learned a lot about Hannah and found himself more enthralled by each passing second. She was nothing like he had imagined. She was perfect. They took a brief break to eat the snacks they'd purchased, and then they headed back into the water. Hannah insisted that Daniel roll up his jeans and join her.

"Oh, I think I got one." Hannah yanked hard. Daniel put his pole down carefully, anchoring it in the sandy shore.

"Here, let me help." Daniel reached for the pole, his arms circling around her. The closeness sent a spark through him. She must have felt it too, because she tensed.

Daniel felt himself starting to lose his footing, and before he realized it, he was down in the water and soaked. He wasn't the only one, because he apparently had brought Hannah down with him. He could hear her angelic laugh, the sun casting a near halo around her as it sat low in the now late afternoon sky. She had changed from pretty to downright beautiful in that instant. Daniel grabbed her, bringing her closer to him, and stared at her rosebud soft lips. Before Daniel's brain could catch up to what he was doing, he kissed her. There it was. That spark that he knew existed but hadn't felt with Nina or any other girl he'd ever kissed before. Now he knew what people meant when they said there would be fireworks. He looked into her shocked eyes as he moved away from her tender mouth. As they stayed partially submerged in the cold water, Hannah wrapped her arms around his neck, clinging to him. She kissed him. There it was again—that spark.

Chapter Nine

Maggie

"I think that looks good there, don't you?" Maggie asked Amber, who was nailing up a picture in the now fully transformed nursery.

Rachel sat in the corner on a wide, sliding rocking chair. "It looks so cute in here. Oh, I can't wait to get started on their room," Rachel commented as she rubbed her large belly.

"Thank you both for coming over today and helping me. Now I just need those curtains from Hannah, and it's all set."

"You are really going all out with this theme." Amber held up a blue, stuffed monkey. "I mean, this is a lot of blue."

"Gosh, what if they are wrong, Maggie?" Rachel asked, the sound of slight panic in her voice.

Maggie hadn't really considered that. She and Michael were so thrilled at the prospect of having a boy, they'd sort of went a little crazy. They had been buying everything in blue: sheets, blankets,

119

clothes. Just about anything they needed was in some pretty shade of blue. Looking at the room now she could see how she may have went a bit overboard.

"I mean, blue can be used for a girl too," Maggie defended as she folded a fuzzy, pastel-blue blanket.

Amber looked at Rachel. "Well, maybe, if it turns out that it's a girl, maybe one of Rachel's will be a boy."

"Hey, speaking of which, when are you guys going in for your next ultrasound? You guys wanted to find out the gender, right?" Maggie asked, attempting to redirect the conversation. She didn't want to think about the possibility of her not having a boy. She rubbed her belly, willing the squirming little baby to be a boy.

"We go in next week, actually. Liam is super excited to find out. He thinks we are probably having one of each."

"What do you think?" Maggie asked, lowering herself onto the carpet to sit. Amber joined her, and they both looked at Rachel. Maggie loved how well the three of them got along, and knowing Patrick's secret, she couldn't help but feel a little closer to Amber.

Rachel sighed. "I don't know. I had a dream that they were girls, but they each looked so different."

"Girls, huh? They say when you dream about the gender that's what you are having," Maggie responded. She stretched her legs out in front of her.

"Nope. I dreamt that Dylan was this gorgeous little girl, but that didn't quite happen." Amber laughed.

"There's still time," Maggie said.

Amber gave her a curious look. "Yeah, that's doubtful. I mean, it's not out of the realm of possibility, but I'm getting a little old, and well…" Amber trailed off and looked away. "Oh, never mind."

"No. What?" Maggie insisted, poking Amber gently.

"Nothing." Amber smiled and started to pick at the carpet.

"Oh, come on. Spill it. You preggers?" Rachel didn't beat around the bush.

Amber shook her head. "No, but not that I'd mind."

"So, what then? You're acting weird." Rachel moved forward in the rocking chair and rested her hands on her round belly.

"I think I love Patrick."

Maggie couldn't help but laugh. Did Patrick and Amber think they were concealing some huge secret? Of course they were in love; everyone could see it as clear as day.

"Why are you laughing?" Amber had an unsure look in her eyes.

"Nothing. You and Patrick, I swear." Maggie attempted to get up off the floor. Amber saw her struggling and quickly popped up to help. "Thanks," Maggie said once she was up.

"Hey, I heard that Daniel was going over to see Hannah. What's that all about?" Rachel asked, leaning back in her chair, letting it gently glide. "I need one of these for sure."

"I love that chair. When I had Melanie, I'd rock

her to sleep and pass out right along with her." Maggie could remember the long nights she'd spent alone and tired. She shivered at the memory and was thankful that this time around would be different. Michael was a wonderful father; he'd always had the potential to be, but when she'd had Melanie, his priorities were screwed up. That was no longer a problem, however, and as Maggie stood there with her sister-in-law and soon-to-be sister-in-law, she knew Michael was taking Melanie out for ice cream, being the perfect dad.

"So what's the deal with Hannah? You guys know anything about this?" Rachel asked again, readjusting her position in her chair, snuggling deeper into it.

"Well, my mom says that he was going over for breakfast." Maggie shrugged. She honestly had no idea.

"Wasn't Daniel seeing that awful Nina girl?" Amber asked with a scowl.

"I think that's over. Isn't it? But who knows? Maybe that's why he's going over there," Rachel offered with a frown and unhappy stare.

"Nah, I think we have seen the last of her. Mom says she talked to Daniel, and it sounds like that is dead and buried."

"Liam said the same thing after he went fishing with him, but you know how guys are. Especially if they get a taste of something like Nina," Rachel said, seemingly trying to make a point.

Maggie knew Rachel could be right, but she just hoped she wasn't.

Amber piped in, "Well, I know that Daniel didn't

sleep with her, if that's what you mean."

Maggie felt her mouth open, and Rachel wore a shocked expression. "How do you know?"

"Patrick, of course. He actually asked Daniel," Amber replied as she started to straighten a stack of diapers on shelf below the changing table. "He did say that Daniel acted really weird about the entire thing."

"I mean, I wouldn't want to talk to my brother, Ethan, about my sex life with Liam or anyone else," Rachel explained.

"Yeah, I know, me neither, but you know how men are." Maggie folded a tiny onesie, which was a deep navy blue, and added it a pile of freshly laundered clothes. "I'd just like to know what he's doing with Hannah."

"She's quite sweet. I like her. Would it be so bad if he ended up with her instead?" Amber asked.

"Yeah, I mean, at least we'd be rid of Nina. Amber's right. Hannah is lovely, completely the opposite of her sister."

Maggie blinked. An idea swarmed in her mind. "It wouldn't be bad at all. In fact, I think we need to try and help Daniel out."

"Oh no, I'm not getting involved. Nope." Rachel hefted herself out of the chair and waved her hands in defense. "Remember last time? Oh dear, Patrick was furious."

"What happened?" Amber's face lit up with curiosity.

"Well, as you know, Patrick hadn't dated since Beth died," Maggie started to explain.

"So our girl here thought going behind his back

and making him an online dating profile was a foolproof plan." Rachel gave Maggie a smirk before continuing, "Patrick found out and nearly disowned her."

"Oh, wow, really? Hmm, he never mentioned that, just said that you had been in his business. I suppose that's what he meant," Amber responded.

"Well, Patrick is difficult. I mean, no offense. You just declared your love for him, so you probably think he's like the best thing ever, and he is, to a degree. But I was just trying to help. Daniel, however, is the complete opposite and he would totally appreciate the help," Maggie said confidently, then looked down at the floor. "I think."

Amber and Rachel looked at Maggie as she started to devise a plan. At least she wouldn't have to go online and search for a girl. They already had found the perfect one for Daniel. They just needed to convince him of that.

***

Patrick

"You want another beer?" Patrick offered Liam as he got up to get another one for himself. The twins were playing in the yard, and Patrick and Liam enjoyed sitting in the shade. Amber and Rachel were helping Maggie with the baby's room, and that gave Patrick a lazy afternoon and some much-needed time with Liam.

"Sure, thanks."

Patrick handed him a cold bottle sweating with condensation and took his seat. "So did Daniel or Maggie tell you yet?" He wouldn't be surprised if they had. The excitement and desire to share the news with him would've been more than they could bear. He wanted to include Liam as well, but it just so happened he felt the need to make a point right then at the shop. Patrick was touched by how moved his siblings were, and they were beyond happy for him.

"No, what?" Concern laced Liam's voice. He sat his beer down on the small patio table between them and eyed Patrick with worry. "Is everything okay?"

"Yes. Great, in fact."

"Okay, well, that's a relief. So what's up?" Liam retrieved his beer and took a swig from the brown bottle.

Patrick exhaled and got up from his seat again. "I'll be right back." He quickly returned with the little velvet box. He dropped it in Liam's lap as he took his seat and swallowed a cold gulp of beer from his own bottle.

"Holy crap, are you serious?" Liam was wide eyed as he examined the small box, gingerly prying it open. "Wow, Patrick."

"I know."

"Man, I never would have guessed you'd rush into something like this. I mean, I know you care about her and you seem so happy now, but marriage?"

Patrick scowled. Why wasn't Liam as thrilled as Maggie and Daniel had been? But then it dawned on him how much grief he'd given Liam when he'd wanted to propose to Rachel. He recalled how he'd begged Liam to wait, to reconsider jumping into something so quick. Patrick looked at his stunned brother. "I know what I told you. If anything, Liam, you taught me a great deal. You showed me that sometimes how long you know someone isn't a factor in happiness." Patrick took another sip of his beer and continued, "Look at how happy you guys are. You're about to be a dad, and before you married Rachel, I had never seen you more excited or content. I was wrong." Patrick looked out into the yard and watched his two sons chase each other.

"Wrong? Nah, you were just looking out for me," Liam responded, also looking out at the boys playing. "I have always looked up to you—"

Patrick laughed, cutting Liam off. "Well, I am, like, a hair taller."

"You know what I mean. The way you love your sons and what a great dad you are. I really hope I can be like you."

"Liam, you're going to be an incredible dad, and I'm here if you ever need advice or help— anything." Patrick didn't doubt that statement for a moment. His brother was a great guy, always loving and thinking of others. He was an amazing uncle to Finn and Connor. Liam was patient, kind, and, without a doubt, meant to be a father.

This time Liam let out a laugh. "You just said you were wrong. So, I'm kind of wondering if I should steer clear of your advice from now on."

"Take it or leave it, man. Either way, it's always going to be there for you." Patrick turned to face

Liam. "I'll always be there for you."

***

Maggie

"Mom, we're home."

Maggie turned off the faucet and dried her hands on a nearby dishtowel. "You guys have a good time?"

Melanie ran to her, wrapping her little arms around Maggie. Melanie kissed Maggie's belly and whispered something to it, then looked up at Maggie. Looking down at her daughter, Maggie felt her heart swell with love. She smoothed her Melanie's red hair under her hands. She wondered what her son would look like. She hoped he was every bit as sweet as her daughter.

"Hi, hon." Michael kissed her as he walked by. He looked exhausted, but spending the day with a six year old could do that.

"We had so much fun, Mom." Melanie started to recount the entire day, sharing every detail, down to what kind of soap the restroom at the ice cream shop had. Maggie went back to washing vegetables in the sink, half listening to Melanie, who now sat on a barstool by the granite countertop.

"How was your day?" Michael asked, leaning against the kitchen island as Maggie started to work on prepping a salad for dinner.

Instructing Melanie to grab some more carrots from the fridge, she answered, "Productive. We got a lot sorted in that room." Maggie turned to face

Michael, shaking a bright red bell pepper in her hand as she spoke, "But you know, the girls pointed something out today. What if they ultrasound is wrong? What if it's not a boy?"

"It's a boy, Maggie. Trust me."

"Mom, Dad's right. That's my little brother in there." Melanie pointed to Maggie's overwhelmingly round belly.

Maggie smiled at Melanie. "Well, it's just that we pretty much bought everything under the sun in blue."

"But, Mom, blue can be for a girl too. It's my favorite color."

"I know, sweetie." Maggie looked up at Michael, who only shrugged. "It almost makes it harder knowing." He nodded.

"I already knew it was a boy, Mom. I can't wait for Max to be born," Melanie said with amplified enthusiasm.

Max—the name Melanie and Michael had decided would be best suited for their new addition. Maggie wasn't completely sold on the name at first, but the more they tossed it around, the more she got use to the sound of it. They would be telling the family at Sunday dinner tomorrow, and she wondered what their thoughts would be. Maggie had never planned on naming her children something that began with the letter M, but somehow Michael had insisted. He thought it was the coolest thing, stating that no matter what, they'd all at least have one thing in common. Maggie thought it made them a little weird, but she loved the name Melanie and couldn't imagine her precious daughter being named anything else. Picking out the perfect baby name was so difficult. She remembered scouring through books and going online to find one that was just right. Then, one evening, as she and Michael were laying in bed, he said the name. Maggie had instantly known that it was the one.

She smiled at that memory of a magical time when they are pregnant with their first. Maggie looked over at Melanie, who was digging in the fridge for the carrots. It was Melanie who had first thought of the name Max. Michael had quickly agreed it was brilliant, so now they were on the countdown to meet Max. Maybe they'd let her pick the middle name.

***

Liam

"I'm home," Liam called out once he got inside the cabin. He could smell a scent candle burning, but he paused to listen for Rachel. His home was eerily quiet. "Rachel?"

Starting to grow concerned, Liam walked to the kitchen. No light was on, and nothing was being cooked for dinner. He couldn't help but think that was strange. He headed down the hallway toward their bedroom and called out again, "Rachel?" He paused and opened the door to what would be the nursery room. She wasn't there either. Now he was getting worried, moving a little faster by the time he reached their bedroom door. There she was, inside their bedroom.

The room smelled of flowers, light and delicate, like the naked woman laying asleep on their bed. The candlelight flickered and cast a romantic glow. Liam moved in quietly as to not disturb her. She had made this effort for him, and it touched him. He slid slowly next to her on the bed, viewing her in all her unclothed beauty. He couldn't stop himself from touching her, running his finger along her soft skin. He began to trace along her body, starting with the soft curve of her cheek. He smoothed his thumb along her velvety lips. The temptation to kiss her stirred inside him. Liam let his fingers roam down her shoulder, brushing the full swell of her breasts, pausing at her nipples, moving his thumb against them, bringing them to life. Rachel started to wake. She gave him a sleepy smile as her eyes fluttered open.

"You're home."

"I am." He bent down and gingerly placed his lips on hers. He continued to explore her body with his hands, pulling her closer to him.

Liam heard her moan under his kiss. He deepened it and began to feel pent-up urgency course through him.

She latched her naked calf over his leg and nipped at his bottom lip. "I'm glad," Rachel whispered as she looped her arms around his neck, tucking in beside him, eliminating any free space between them.

They stayed there, relishing the warmth of being near each other. Rachel licked his neck, biting gently, her hands doing their own exploring. Her touch was driving him crazy. In a fluid motion and with incredible speed, he shed his clothes, needing to be naked along with his wife. God, how he had missed this. Fear and worry had prevented him from making love to her over the last several weeks. Liam didn't want to do anything that could hurt her or their babies, but the need burned through him, and apparently Rachel too as she moaned again, this time a little louder.

"God, Liam." Rachel hissed as she splayed her hands against his chest as she mounted him with ease.

Gripping her hips, anchoring her to him, he let Rachel choose their pace. As she picked up speed, crying out in sheer ecstasy, he almost lost control. He caught sight of the vision above him as the candlelight washed over her skin, illuminating all the feminine curves and softened lines of her full pregnant body. Liam cherished the moment, capturing a mental picture he hoped to save forever in his mind. This beautiful creature, who he desired in so many ways, was not only his gorgeous wife, but was also the mother of their children.

***

Daniel

Daniel held Hannah's hand as they stood on the porch of her home. The early evening light was muted, and the skies were turning a bruised shade of purple. They had just returned from the day they had spent together.

"I had a wonderful time with you, Daniel."

He looked up at her and didn't want this moment to end. Their date had been the best Daniel had ever been on—even with the unexpected landing in the water, which had only ended in laughter and explosive kissing. He wished there were more hours in the day. He needed to spend more time with Hannah.

"Me too." Daniel stroked her face with his free hand. He noticed her hair was still damp, transforming it into a lovely wheat color with bright hints of gold sparkling in what was left of the sunlight.

She gazed up at him. He couldn't help but stare at the lips he now loved kissing. He ran his thumb across her rosebud pink lips, feeling their softness under his rough, callused skin. Without hesitation, Daniel lowered his mouth on hers and, gently, he claimed her. It was as if the world stopped rotating, that time was stopped and suspended as he connected with Hannah.

He released her slowly, reluctantly, and stared into her eyes. Flecks of amber shot through the mixture of green and blue, a spectacular color that left him wondering, how had he missed this? Why didn't he notice Hannah sooner? This girl, with the spray of freckles on her pink-tinged skin, sun soaked from the day at the lake. This girl, who had waded out into the water without hesitation, hooked her own worm faster than he did his, and made him laugh until he could barely breathe. He had never met anyone like Hannah and he somehow knew he never would again. Daniel knew one thing for sure:

now that he'd found her, he wasn't letting her go.

Chapter Ten

Rays of sunlight streamed into his room, forcing him awake. A smile crept on his face. Daniel had dreamt of Hannah all night. He didn't understand how he could be hit so hard with all of these feelings for her, but he wasn't questioning it. It was as though God had heard him and finally answered his prayers. He'd just wanted what his siblings had found, what his parents had—love.

Daniel stretched and yawned happily. He had invited Hannah over to share Sunday dinner with his family. The idea for the perfect second date had came to him as he was listening to the late-night news. There was going to be a meteor shower later that night. It was his turn to impress her. What could be more romantic than kissing under a night sky filled with shooting stars? He was shocked when she'd led him to what would now be their favorite fishing spot. Daniel could almost still feel the pressure of her lips against his, the memory still fresh.

"Breakfast is ready," Daniel heard his mother

call out. Another perk of living at home was being well fed by Mary O'Brien, but he had a sneaking suspicion that if he were to marry Hannah someday, he'd still be well fed. The thought made him grin.

Daniel padded down the hallway and into the kitchen, barefoot and still in his pajamas. "Morning, Mom."

"Good morning, dear. I have your plate at the table. Coffee or juice, sweetie?" Mary asked as she dished a scoop of fried potatoes onto a plate.

"He can pour his own drink, Mary," Pat commented from the dining room, where he sat and was reading the Sunday newspaper.

"Come sit, my boy," Grandpa Paddy ordered with a curious look. He folded up his section of the paper and waved for Daniel to join him.

After filling his mug with coffee, Daniel sat next to his grandfather. "This looks great, Mom. Thank you," he said as he eyed the plate. It was filled scrambled eggs, fried potatoes, buttery toast, and bacon. His stomach growled as he forked a mouthful of the crispy potatoes into his mouth. Daniel savored the garlic and onion-infused flavors. His mother was one helluva cook.

Mary smiled and sipped her tea quietly, watching her men eat.

"So, lad, your mother says you've invited another lass to supper?" Grandpa Paddy wiggled his white eyebrows, the unmistakable twinkle of mischief in his emerald-green eyes.

"Yes, I want you all to meet Hannah."

His father put the paper down gently and looked over at Daniel. "Now, is Hannah not the girl we met?" He looked at Daniel in confusion.

"No, this is her sister," Daniel replied as he reached for his coffee. *Here come the questions*, he thought as he mentally prepared himself.

"Good for you, my boy," Grandpa Paddy exclaimed, patting Daniel on the shoulder. "Why have one, when you can have two?"

Daniel shook his head, laughing. "No, it's nothing like that. Nina and I, you know, the first sister you met," Daniel explained. He took a swallow of his coffee and continued, "She and I never really hit it off. But her sister, now, Hannah, is the one I should have asked out in the first place."

"Didn't that Nina girl sort of force your hand at taking her out?" Mary asked, prodding gently.

"Kind of."

"So we're meeting her sister, you say?" Pat asked again.

"Yes," Mary and Daniel both answered in unison.

"Just trying to get it straight. What is it that you like about this one?" Pat eyed Daniel curiously.

"Well, for starters, she fishes. Even hooks her own worms," Daniel announced proudly.

Grandpa Paddy and Pat smiled. Daniel had inherited their love of fishing. "Mom, she's an amazing cook. As you know, Nina wasn't too comfortable in the kitchen."

"I suppose that's true," she replied, taking a sip of her tea.

"I'm thinking though, it probably had a lot to do with Maggie," Daniel stated and scooped some eggs into his mouth.

"Your sister is simply looking out for you. I

wasn't too keen on Nina either. Well, neither was Rachel or Amber."

"I don't blame them, to be honest. Nina wasn't all warm and fuzzy around them," Daniel agreed.

"What about the fact that she was eyeing your brother the whole time?" Pat commented as he unfolded the newspaper and starting peering at it. His glasses sat low on the bridge of his narrow nose, his eyes peeking above the rims as he looked at Daniel.

"I know." Daniel hung his head. It was embarrassing how Nina had openly flirted with Patrick. His brother had been oblivious to it, but then again, since the entire town thought he was one of the most handsome guys, he was probably used to it.

"Boy, don't let that one bring you any troubling thoughts. You're bringing home another now. I can't wait to meet the lass," Grandpa Paddy said, obviously trying to make him feel better. Daniel appreciated the support he always got from his grandfather, and sometimes wondered why his own father wasn't more like him.

"I prayed at mass this morning. I think the good Lord will bring you a love you deserve. I can't help but add that I put in a little request for you to marry and give me more grandchildren." Mary giggled sheepishly.

"Mom, you got a grand baby coming at the end of this month, then two more in November. Geez."

"Can't blame your mother. It'll be nearly a year or more before you'd have any babes," Grandpa Paddy added.

"Not you too."

"I'm not getting any younger, my boy. I'd like to hold one of your babes before I pass." Grandpa Paddy winked, but Daniel didn't miss the sheen of glossy tears in his grandfather's eyes.

The thought of Grandpa Paddy dying made Daniel sober up and go silent, as well as the rest of the table. The man wasn't getting any younger, but to imagine him gone made Daniel's heart ache.

***

He was nervous. He shouldn't be, but he was. The last Sunday dinner he had brought a Belsky girl to had not ended well.

"Daniel, it'll be fine. I'm looking forward to getting to know your family." Hannah sat next to him as he drove.

"They're going to love you. It's just, well, you know…"

"I do," she said, but then added with a little less confidence, "but I'm not Nina, and as you and her have both said, it never really was anything, right?"

"True. I just feel a little bad, is all." Daniel did; it was as simple as that. He worried that Hannah possibly felt like she was second best. Little did she know, that when Daniel picked her up from her home and saw her in that sundress, his heart skipped a beat. She looked delicate and incredibly feminine in her pale pink dress which was dotted with the tiniest flowers. Hannah wore a thin white sweater over it, looking every bit respectable and proper. Daniel knew the moment his mother saw her, she

138

was going to love her.

They pulled into the driveway of the O'Brien home. He spotted his sibling's cars and knew everyone was inside. He inhaled deeply as he shut off his truck's engine.

"It's going to be fine. Trust me." Hannah leaned over and kissed him gently on the cheek. Daniel felt his anxiety evaporate as they both got out of the truck.

Once they got inside the home, the smells of a roasted chicken dinner hung heavy in the air. Daniel led Hannah into the kitchen. There, all the O'Brien women waited. He couldn't help but feel like this time it would be different. He had felt like he had tossed Nina to the wolves, but now, as Hannah stood beside him carrying a dish wrapped in foil, he couldn't dismiss the feeling that he was bringing them one of their own.

"Hi, everyone." Hannah smiled as she moved past Daniel, entering the kitchen further. Daniel watched his mother's reaction first.

"Hello, Hannah. Oh my, what have you brought?" Mary eyed the dish that Hannah lifted up for inspection.

"Cheesecake."

"Bless your heart. My favorite."

Daniel released the breath he didn't know he'd been holding. He looked quickly at Maggie and Rachel, who were both grinning from ear to ear. These were all good signs, nothing at all like when he had brought Nina. As he stood there, almost waiting to be excused, he heard Amber compliment her dress.

"Thanks, I actually made it." Hannah then went on to explain her love of sewing. The women all gathered around listening intently. Mary glanced over at him.

"Sweetie, the guys are all in the basement." She gave him a kind smile and a slight nod that basically told him to beat it.

Daniel slowly retreated out of the kitchen with one solid thought: They loved her.

***

Hannah

She had lied. She was terribly nervous. Who wouldn't be? Especially considering they had already met her sister, and God only knew how that went. As Hannah stood there, in the beautiful kitchen in the lovely O'Brien house surrounded by O'Brien women, she tried her best to smile through her nervousness.

Mary's kind smile warmed her and eased her anxiety somewhat, but it was the genuinely happy looks from Maggie and Rachel which made her feel welcomed.

"Also, Maggie, I brought those curtains for you."

"Really? Perfect. We just finished setting up the baby's room yesterday." Maggie looked relieved and started to laugh. "Let me get my purse before I forget. Pregnancy brain, I swear."

"Oh no, please, think of it like a baby shower gift," Hannah said, quickly refusing. "I was happy to make them and I hope you like they way they turned out."

"Um, if they are anything like that fabulous dress, they will be wonderful." Amber kept staring at her dress. "Okay, I love it. You need to teach me how to make one," Amber finally said as she ran her hands along her own sun dress. It was a soft, buttercup yellow and was beautiful against her tan skin.

"I'd love to. I have been sewing since I was little. My mother used to sew dresses and, well, everything really."

"Well, I appreciate you making those curtain for the baby's room." Maggie walked up to Hannah and hugged her, her large belly rubbing up against her. "Sorry, this thing gets in the way."

"You mean my grandson," Mary teased. "Hannah, can I get you something to drink?"

"Yeah, dinner's almost ready, but we can visit for a little bit." Maggie led Hannah to the enormous dining table. Hannah could only imagine how wonderfully loud that room must get when the whole family was together. Her home was quite the opposite, especially after her mother had passed away.

The ladies all sat as Mary poured tea for everyone.

"Thank you, Mrs. O'Brien. This is lovely. Your kitchen is incredible. The whole house is," Hannah stated as she gazed at the ample counter space, easily envisioning herself rolling out dough on that flat surface. To have all that room to work with? She was a tad envious.

"Call me Mary, dear. Thank you, I do love my kitchen," Mary responded as she offered Hannah a slim-looking cookie.

Hannah accepted it, smelling it first. Once she bit into it, the flavor of lemon exploded into her mouth. The cookie was delicious, light and buttery. "Oh my, this is fantastic."

"Says the woman who makes amazing shortbread and pies," Maggie commented as she grabbed a cookie. "These are really good though."

"Daniel tells us you do enjoy cooking and baking," Mary said, naturally leading the conversation. Hannah didn't feel as though she were being interviewed so she could date this woman's son. Mary's inquiry came from the fact that she a fellow cook who shared a passion for food.

"I love it. I always have. It became a necessity once my mother passed away. Who else was going to feed my father and Nina?" Hannah released an awkward laugh and grabbed her tea quickly.

"Bless your heart, love. Your mother would be very pleased that you've taken care of them as well as you have." Mary reached across the table and patted her hand.

Hannah could sense the kindness from Mary and instantly realized this was who Daniel took after. They shared the same coloring, but their eyes were certainly different. Mary's were a darker, almost hazel color, but they shared a reddish hue in their hair and a sweetness which seemed to emit from them like a light. This woman was responsible for Daniel being the wonderful soul he was.

As the ladies continued to chat, Hannah heard loud laughter as the men started to file into the kitchen. They made their way into the adjoining dining room.

"Hannah, let me introduce you to the rest of the family," Daniel said as he pointed at the small herd of O'Brien men. As she looked at them, she noticed how different they all appeared, which made the fact that Daniel took after Mary stand out even more. The oldest of the group was a tall older man with white hair and piercing green eyes—Daniel's eyes. So that's where he got them.

"This is Grandpa Paddy." Daniel pointed to the old man.

"Pleased to meet you, lass." Hannah felt herself falling in love with his Irish accent; she was a sucker for them. The simple words sounded far more romantic, and she was pretty certain Grandpa Paddy knew he had this effect, as he winked at her. Maybe that's where Daniel had gotten his playfulness from after all.

"This is my dad, Pat." The man was a younger version of Grandpa Paddy, tall and lean, his hair not quite white but a mixture of gray and black. One thing she didn't miss was he too had those sparkling eyes.

"Nice to meet you, Hannah." Pat's voice was rough. She felt slightly disappointed, as though she expected to hear an accent as well.

"You remember Patrick, of course," Daniel continued the introductions. She remembered meeting Patrick when he was helping with the job her father had hired them for. He had seemed moody before, but now he appeared happy. Patrick was devilishly handsome, and that was not a fact that was lost by her sister or anyone in town, but

Hannah wasn't quite as impressed by his dark looks. She rather enjoyed Daniel's lighter coloring, but Patrick also bore those green gems.

"Hello, Hannah," Patrick offered politely as he stood next to Daniel. He was noticeably taller.

"Okay, so this guy is Liam." Daniel patted another man's shoulder. This brother was taller as well, but looked more like Daniel. He didn't have dark hair like Patrick. It was a sandy brown that was missing the red Daniel's had. Again, he looked at her with the O'Brien eyes that seem to smile all on their own.

"Great to meet you." Liam moved away from Daniel and headed toward Rachel.

"Last, but definitely not least, my favorite brother-in-law in the world," Daniel exaggerated loudly. "Michael."

"Thanks, Daniel." Michael playfully smirked. The first thought that passed through Hannah's mind was that this man was most definitely not an O'Brien. He was incredibly good-looking, but in a shiny and luxurious way. Hannah doubted he spent much time outdoors. He seemed far too polished and fancy for that. "Hannah, very lovely to meet you." Michael walked toward her, extending his hand politely, which she accepted nervously. Then he went to Maggie, placing a soft kiss on top of her head.

Wow, the O'Briens were certainly not a small family. One thing which stood out to Hannah was the deep, obvious love these people displayed openly for one another. As Hannah took in the names and faces of the people she had just met, the

144

sound of loud giggles and running feet echoed in the room. A little girl with red, bobbed hair came full speed at Maggie. She wrapped her small arms around Maggie's large waist. That must be Melanie, the niece Daniel adored. Then Hannah spied two identical boys who were quite young and had springy, blonde curls. They looked at her with the most brilliant blue eyes. Hannah was confused as to who these darlings belonged to.

"Those are Patrick's boys, Finn and Connor," Daniel announced, almost as if he sensed her confusion.

Hannah looked over at Amber, who smiled as the boys clung to her and Patrick. A taller, older boy entered the kitchen and said, "Gosh, they are so fast." He had brown hair which was a little too long and partially covered his gorgeous sea-colored eyes—Amber's eyes. Hannah tried putting all the pieces together of who was whose child and spouse.

Daniel sat down next to her and took her hand. "I know. There's a lot of us. It's okay if you forget names. It's probably overwhelming."

Hannah shook her head and decided to play it off. Leaning in toward Daniel, she whispered, "Nope. That is Grandpa Paddy, your father, Pat, your lovely mother, Mary." Carefully nodding in the direction of his parents, Hannah continued to name the rest of the family.

Daniel raised his eyebrows in surprise. "I'm impressed. Not everyone can do that."

"Well, I must be special then," Hannah teased.

Daniel leaned in and kissed her lightly, shocking her. As gentle and quick as the kiss was, she felt it to her core. "Yes, you are."

***

Daniel

"Thank you again for a lovely dinner. It was really wonderful meeting you all." Hannah waved as they started to walk out the front door.

Once outside, she felt that the evening air was still slightly warm. Daniel opened the passenger side of the truck for her.

"Gosh, I really love your family," Hannah stated with a huge smile on her face. It was exact opposite reaction Nina had the night she met them.

"Really? It wasn't too much?" He was still worried somehow, even though she had fit in, like a missing puzzle piece. Daniel had spent most of dinner watching her interact with his family. He saw her laugh with them, listen as they spoke, and her sweetness toward each and every one of them had shone brightly. Daniel knew she could easily become one of them, that tonight very well could have been an image from the future.

"Yes, really. Geez." Hannah slapped his arm lightly. "I think they are the most wonderful group of people. Those kids, oh my, so stinkin' cute." Hannah stared out the window at the Daniel's home. "So where to now?"

"I have a special surprise in store for us." Daniel started his truck and slowly pulled out of the driveway. They drove through the neighborhood and out onto the highway. The sky grew darker as night took, banishing the sun.

They chatted until he turned onto a gravel road. The bumpy way dumped them out to a vast and open field. There weren't many trees hoarding the view of the sky. They should be able to view the meteor shower easily from this spot. Being able to gaze at the stars without light pollution was a spectacular thing in eastern Washington. Late summer, usually around August and September, the skies put on the most incredible show. Daniel loved being outside and staring at meteors shooting brightly against the dark backdrop was his favorite way to cap off summer. The moon was nestled behind the mountain range to the east, making the area even darker and better to watch the show.

Hannah looked confused but then jokingly said, "Night fishing?"

"No, silly. There's a meteor shower tonight. I thought we'd see if we can catch some."

"So, meteor fishing? Sounds fun."

Daniel laughed and parked his truck. "Come on," he instructed her as he opened his door to get out.

He rolled out several blankets in the bed of his truck, creating a cushioned place for them to lay and view the sky. He helped her into the back, then climbed up himself. As they lay there under a blanket of twinkling stars, waiting to catch a glimpse of a shooting star, Hannah snuggled next to him.

"Thank you for this. It's gorgeous out here."

"Not as pretty as you." Daniel ran a finger along her cheek, then lowered his mouth to meet hers. He deepened the kiss, savoring the warmth of her and

147

her sweet taste. The softness of her lips, blended with the tender feeling of them against his, sparked a flame inside him. He pulled back, trying to create a bit of space. He needed some air to extinguish that flame before it went into a full blaze.

He rolled over and looked up. Hannah did the same. They were quiet for some time, alone in their thoughts but still very much together. The sounds of nature at night surrounded them: a cricket chirping, frogs croaking in unison, and the occasional hoot of an owl. Daniel inhaled the chilly air, which was scented with pine, and the smell of the river which flowed nearby. This was perfect.

Daniel gazed at the millions of stars and caught sight of one zooming brightly along. "I saw one," he called out.

"Me too," Hannah whispered, taking hold of his hand in hers. "Did you make a wish?"

"I don't need to." Daniel moved to face her, kissing her again. His wish was right there with him.

Chapter Eleven

"So?"

"What?" Daniel knew perfectly well what, but he would just rather not answer. He'd already been through this with Patrick.

"Why do you get all weird? I'm just curious what's going on with you and these sisters." Patrick and Daniel were driving out to a jobsite to give a bid on a small shed that needed to be constructed.

"I don't get all weird," Daniel rebutted defensively, looking out the window as Patrick steered their work truck onto the highway.

"Yes, you do."

Daniel huffed loudly. He shouldn't have to explain himself. What he did, or didn't do for that matter, was his business.

"Hannah seems nice," Patrick finally said after they drove in silence for a while.

"Yeah, I really like her."

"You know, it's going to be cool, someday you getting married and having kids."

Daniel couldn't argue that. Having children was

the one thing he wanted in life more than anything, and he wanted to share that with someone equally excited about having a family and a simple and happy life. That's all he wanted.

"You think she might be the one?" Patrick asked, turning the truck down a narrow road lined with stark white birch trees.

"Maybe. I mean, I've never felt like this about any girl before."

"She probably is then. That's really great, Daniel. You know, it's like with Amber." Patrick slowed the vehicle as they approached a sprawling property, enormous outbuildings sheltering a ranch-style home that could easily swallow the O'Brien home. Patrick paused. "Wow, this place is huge. Anyway, with Amber I got blindsided and sometimes it's like that."

"Yeah, I kind of know what you mean." Daniel couldn't stop thinking about Hannah. She was on his mind when he went to bed. She lived in his dreams and was there when he woke up. He didn't mind it one bit; it somehow made him feel closer to her, like she was with him all the time. "Dumb question, but how long do you wait before asking someone to marry you?"

Patrick blinked hard and seem to choke on the air. "What?"

"Well, I mean, like if you know someone is the one you want to be with, like how long does a person wait to ask?" Daniel asked again.

"Um, I don't know. I mean, you hardly know her. You guys just started dating."

"Yeah, but, if you know, you know, right?"

"Daniel, I think you need to pump the brakes a bit. Get to know each other a bit more." Patrick's shocked face seemed to relax as he parked the truck.

"But you just said…" Daniel started to argue as Patrick raised his hand to stop him.

"No, what I'm saying is that she *might* be the one. Wait it out, see where this goes for a while before you start hearing wedding bells."

"Liam fell in love with Rachel super quick. Then you and Amber, well, there's that."

"Okay, look at Liam for a moment. Now, I adore Rachel. She's great. But consider why they got married." Patrick gave him a knowing look.

"Well, yeah, but Liam was already in love with her, Patrick. He didn't marry her just because she was pregnant."

"How can we be sure? They got pregnant so soon. I think that really was a factor in them getting married. Liam wanted to do the right thing by her," Patrick explained as they sat in the truck. Daniel was growing more agitated and annoyed with his brother as he listened. "That's why, so please be careful. You don't want to be forced into a marriage because of a pregnancy or something, Daniel."

"Trust me, it's not going to happen," Daniel spat, feeling frustrated with Patrick. He hopped out of the truck without another word.

"Daniel…" Patrick called out, but Daniel just kept walking. This was exactly why Daniel didn't like opening up to his oldest brother. He acted too much like their father, always having all the answers, passing judgment without a second thought, and making Daniel feel like he couldn't make a choice on his own. If he were going to talk to anyone about wanting to marry Hannah someday, it would be Liam or maybe his mother. Heck, he'd even discuss it with Maggie. Daniel rolled his eyes. Patrick sure had a lot of nerve, especially since he was carrying around a ring for Amber, someone he had only been dating for a few months. Nothing like the pot calling the kettle black.

***

Hannah

Humming as she pulled the bed sheet from the clothes line, Hannah released the weathered clothes pin and inhaled the sunny smell of the dried sheet. They had a dryer, but sun-dried clothing just felt and smelled different, and helping her mother hang clothes on the line was one of her fondest memories. When she was a little girl, she would clip the clothespins on her fingers, pretending they were long nails. She usually got scolded for snapping the pins in half. What she enjoyed even more was the delicate scent of the laundry soap they had used. It would waft from the linens, filling her nose. These smells were the same now. Hannah inhaled deeply. They took her back to that time from so long ago.

"Hannah, what's for lunch?" Nina called out as she was strolling across the lawn toward her.

"I was going to make some sandwiches after I finished here. What are you up to?"

Nina started to help remove clothes from the line, dropping them into the large plastic basket.

"I'm thinking of heading into town later. You want to come with me?"

Hannah was shocked that Nina wanted her to join her. It was not often the two of them got along as sisters or even friends.

"You know, that might be fun."

Nina smiled. It wasn't one of her usual sinister or wicked grins. This smile was more gentle and kind. "I heard there's a new coffee place that just opened up. I think it's called Birch Valley Brew or something. Might be good."

"Sure, let's check it out," Hannah answered excitedly. Though a tingle of doubt about Nina's intentions troubled her, Hannah tried to push it out of her mind. No use in borrowing trouble. Maybe Nina wanted to spend time with her. Granted, it was an odd request, but Hannah was happy to just go with it.

***

Nina had been quiet during lunch, and Hannah was growing more concerned as they drove into Birch Valley to visit the new coffee shop and maybe do a little window shopping. The weather was perfect for it: not too warm, but sunny without a cloud in the sky.

"Sure is pretty out today," Hannah said, trying to break the silence as they drove. Nina was behind the wheel, focused on the pavement ahead.

Nina found an empty parking spot along Main Street, which was lined with various shops to explore. The normally crowded sidewalks were barren, the summer tourists were gone, and all that was left were the residents of this small community.

Hannah and Nina got out and started in the direction of a small secondhand store. The bay windows of the ancient-looking building were spotless, allowing them to gaze inside before stepping foot in the shop. Hannah spied a couple things that caught her eye. "Let's go inside."

Nina nodded and followed Hannah inside the shop. The smell of aging things, of dust and time, filled the air. Shelves were filled with old treasures; things tossed aside and forgotten. Hannah loved the feeling that she could stumble across something unique and give it a second chance at being valued. After rummaging through several rows of used wares, she picked up a few things she really didn't need but figured she might be able to find some use for. Hannah took them to the register, the items cradled in her arms. After they paid and left with a paper sack that was quite full, Hannah suggested they return it to the car.

"You okay, Nina?"

"Yeah, I'm fine." Hannah could tell she was distracted, a faraway look in her sister's ice-blue eyes. Something was up, and Hannah intended to find out what.

They resumed their walking. Nina kept her arms crossed over her chest.

"You sure? It seems like something's wrong."

Nina paused and stood looking across the street, not meeting Hannah's eyes. "Come on, Nina, you can tell me."

"I can't, actually." Hannah could see tears

forming in her sister's eyes. Something was definitely wrong.

"Why don't we get some tea or something at that new coffee shop you were telling me about?"

***

Daniel

Daniel was sitting on the comfortable leather couch catching a Seattle Mariners baseball game, snacking on a bowl of pretzels and working on his second beer.

"So, are they winning?" Mary asked as she plopped down next to him.

Lowering the beer bottle from his mouth, he shook his head. "Sadly, no. The season is almost over too. Dang Mariners."

"Well, look on the bright side, dear, the Seahawks will be playing soon," Mary added cheerfully.

Daniel nibbled on a salty pretzel, staring blankly at the game. It was the eighth inning and they weren't showing any signs of making a comeback.

"I really like Hannah, dear," Mary started to say, helping herself to a pretzel. "I think we all do."

"That's good, Mom. Hannah liked everyone too."

It seemed like Mary pretended to watch the game for a moment. "But what do you think of her?"

Daniel sighed. He had been thinking about her all day, especially after his disagreement with Patrick earlier. He couldn't help the way he felt.

Maybe Patrick couldn't understand, but considering he was on the verge of proposing to Amber only after months of dating, Daniel thought Patrick of all people would be able to help him sort out these feelings.

"I like her a lot, actually. I think about her all day. She's the first thought I have when I wake up and the last when I go to sleep," Daniel explained and took a sip of his beer, savoring the bitter taste as it slid down his throat, relaxing him.

"She's quite lovely, I have to admit. I hate to compare her to her sister, but, well, they couldn't be more different."

"Tell me about it." Daniel couldn't agree more. The Belsky sisters were like night and day. "Mom, how do you know, like, if she's the *one*?"

"Your heart will tell you. I knew the moment I had met your father that he was my *one*."

"But how? I mean, I don't know about all this love at first sight stuff. Is it for real?"

Mary gave him a knowing and pleased smile. "I think you already know the answer to that."

***

Hannah

She was wrapping plastic wrap over a dish of leftover pork chops when Nina walked into the kitchen. Hannah hadn't figured out much from their afternoon together. She'd tried pulling information out of her sister, but to no avail. Nina insisted everything was fine, but Hannah was smart enough to realize something was up. Nina continued to be quiet and even distant during dinner. Their father hadn't been much better, but he had asked about Daniel. It warmed Hannah, knowing her father might approve of a relationship. They had never really discussed the possibility of Hannah getting married someday or moving out. It was almost as if she were expected to just remain on the farm and take care of them. As each day passed and her feelings for Daniel grew stronger, she started to think more about what the future might hold.

"You headed to bed soon?" Hannah asked Nina, who was fetching herself a glass of water from the faucet.

"Yeah, I'm tired, but I just wanted to thank you for today. It was nice. We really should do it more often."

"I agree. We're sisters and we hardly ever hang out."

Nina frowned. "Yeah, but since Mom died, you sort of became more of a mother to me than a sister."

Hannah scowled. She didn't quite look at it the same way. She was forced to help raise her sister, but she never thought she was mothering her. Maybe she had, and now she wished she could have bonded with her more as a sister. "I never really looked at it like that, Nina. I kind of had no choice but to step up and help out around here, but I always thought of you as my little sister."

"You were always nagging me like a mom, telling me to bathe, to clean my room, and checking my homework. You didn't do anything like a sister does, like get in trouble, sneak out with me, or share secrets. We just don't have that kind of relationship." Nina leaned against the counter, sipping the water slowly from her glass, looking away from Hannah.

"I never meant for it to be like this. I wish you would've said something sooner."

"Me too." Nina straightened herself upright and put the partially drank glass in the sink. "But the past is the past. We can only move forward."

"Wise words. You must have picked that up from your sister," Hannah joked. She moved to Nina and wrapped her arms around her. "I love you, Nina."

"Love you too." Nina's voice cracked, and the simple break made Hannah want to cry. Her sister was going through something. Hannah had no clue what life-defining thing it was, and there was no way she could know, especially if Nina wouldn't open up. There was only one thing Hannah could do, and that was hug her sister tighter.

***

The room was dark when Hannah woke up. She could hear the pitter-patter of rain as it tapped on the metal roof. Hannah rubbed her eyes and glanced over at the small alarm clock on her night stand. It was a little before six. She would need to prepare breakfast for her father, but there were some days when the thought of snuggling deeper in the warmth of her heavy comforter was tempting, especially on days when the sky was swollen with angry gray clouds, when everything was wet and gloomy. Those were the best days for staying in bed and getting lost in a good book or romance movie. Hannah sighed. That day was not today.

She headed to the kitchen. The air was chilly. Fall was definitely arriving. The wood floor was cold under her bare feet as she stood in front of the sink, filling a coffee pot with water. She stared out the large window which provided an ample view of their farm, the flat fields, and the chicken coop. She caught sight of one of their goats, the rain pelting it as it grazed. Hannah shivered at the thought of the cold rain and started the coffee maker. Within minutes the distinct aroma of her favorite blend floated in the air. Hannah poured a cup and savored the rich coffee as she sipped it. She started to prepare a breakfast of eggs and sausage.

As Hannah cooked, her thoughts moved to Daniel; she couldn't help it. He was quickly becoming her real life fairy tale, her own little romantic comedy movie. Her every task or chore somehow looped back to Daniel. She imagined a life with a man she was starting to fall in love with, the simple everyday aspects of what their life could be: preparing meals for him, washing his clothes, raising their children, all the things she wanted. Releasing a deep sigh, Hannah plated the food. Her father had just entered the house. They were in sync; they didn't need to exchange words. Hannah smiled at her father and went to wake Nina.

Her sister's room was down the hall and across from her own. She tapped lightly against the heavy wooden door. "Nina, breakfast is ready." Hannah paused and knocked again. No sound or response. She opened the door slowly in case her sister was still asleep. Hannah scanned the room in confusion as she encountered a perfectly made bed, unslept in by the looks of the tight folding Hannah had done yesterday. "Nina?" Hannah called out, shocked by the panic in her own voice. She moved inside the small room. On the pillow laid a piece of paper. Hannah felt her stomach bottom out. She had watched enough movies to know that a note left behind by anyone was never good news.

She grabbed the sheet of paper and sat on the bed to read what she knew was going to explain all of Nina's strange and odd behavior.

Hannah,

I know this might come as a complete surprise, but I had to go. I just can't live in Birch Valley anymore. There's nothing here for me. I have decided it's time for me to find out what it is I'm meant to do. I know that living on a farm is not it.

I don't want you to worry. I had to borrow the money in your jar. I needed it to buy a ticket out of here. You always wanted me to be happy, and this is a start. Thanks for understanding, Hannah. I will try and call soon. Please don't worry. This is something I needed to do.

Tell Dad I love him. I love you too.

Love,
Nina

Hannah fought the urge to throw up as she clutched the note. What was she going to tell their father? Where had her sister gone? Thoughts and worry swirled in Hannah's mind, causing her to feel dizzy and sick. Gulping in the damp, cold air, Hannah tried to swallow a breath and wrap her brain around the sudden reality of what was happening—Nina was gone.

Chapter Twelve

Daniel

"It will find a way of working itself out," Daniel said, sounding every bit like his mother as he held Hannah's hand. They sat at her dining room table. She had called him that morning, sounding distraught and hoarse from crying. She needed him, and he wasted no time coming to her rescue. He'd even brought donuts.

Hannah sniffled, wiping her tear-stained cheeks. "I know. I just worry about her. This is so unlike her, and what if…"

Daniel stroked the top of her soft hand with his thumb, enjoying the small bit of affection. "Nina can take care of herself. She shouldn't have left like this and put you and your father through this kind of worry."

Hannah nodded. It broke his heart seeing her this upset. It also made him downright furious with Nina. How could she do something so selfish? But was he really surprised? No. Nina was incredibly selfish, and he knew she would figure things out. Granted, California was a great deal different than Birch Valley, so he understood where Hannah's fears stemmed from.

"Daniel, I really appreciate you coming over."

"You're happy I brought donuts. I know my place." Daniel laughed and snuck a quick kiss on her damp cheek.

"Well, the donuts helped. I won't deny that." Hannah picked at a chocolate-covered buttermilk circle of perfection. A slight smile appeared on her pretty face.

Daniel took a bite of his maple bar. Hannah had made them coffee when he had arrived with the donuts, and then she'd burst into tears. He had held her as she cried. They'd stood in her kitchen, the morning light streaming through the large windows, a clean citrus scent in the air, accompanying the sounds of Hannah's despair. As Daniel cradled her in his arms, Mr. Belsky had walked in, his face vacant of any real expression. Daniel couldn't tell if he were upset or sad. There was just no telling. Daniel had brought him a donut as well, figuring that they all could use one. With that gesture, he found he was more like his mother than he had ever realized. Bringing food and the gentle words to soothe, all of that came from his mother. He was even more thankful that Mary O'Brien was his mother. She had taught him very special things: compassion and how to love. The moment Daniel saw Hannah in such a vulnerable state, he realized he did indeed love her. The gears in his head had already put plans into motion. He just prayed she felt the same way.

***

Hannah

As she sat there with Daniel, she realized one thing: this man was special, as was the softness behind his piercing eyes, the concern in his voice when she had called him that morning. When she'd discovered Nina's note, she hadn't known know what to do. Hannah immediately went to their father, who had been washing up for breakfast. He didn't seem at all shocked, but she couldn't dismiss the disappointment and quiet worry in his eyes. She'd expected more of reaction. Hannah, herself, was both livid and frightened. She had no one else to turn to, except Daniel. The moment she dialed his number and he answered, she felt instantly guilty. Why burden him with this trouble? He didn't owe her anything, yet something told her he was the one she wanted to console her. Then he arrived, with donuts no less, and scooped her up in the most comforting hug. His strong arms had been securely wrapped around her as they stood together in her kitchen. She hadn't been able to stop the tears. It was as though being with him, knowing he had her in his arms, somehow made it okay to let the tears flow. He was her rock, her pillar of support, and never in her life had she ever had anyone who was there for in that capacity. When her mother died, she was the rock, the pillar of strength and support for Nina and her father. No one had been there for her. She'd cried alone. When Nina wailed, begging for their mother, it was Hannah who fought back her own tears, wearing a brave mask. No one even considered that she was shattered inside.

"Don't borrow trouble, Hannah. Have some faith." Daniel gently kissed her nose and then returned to eating his maple bar. She could smell the sweetness on his breath, making her want to kiss him so she could taste more.

Hannah sighed. If today taught her anything, it was that the human body could endure a torrent of emotions. One moment she was devastated that her sister had run away, and the next she wanted nothing more than to make out with Daniel. It was a guilty and internal torture. She wondered if he noticed how desperately she battled against it. She silently prayed she was able to wear a mask that hid that too.

"I know what will cheer you up," Daniel said confidently, giving her a crooked smile she found delicious.

"Fishing," they answered in unison.

***

Hannah felt guilty as she unpacked Daniel's truck and headed for the shore of their favorite fishing spot. What if Nina tried calling? Hannah knew her cell phone didn't get the slightest bit of reception at this lake. Mountains surrounded it protectively on all sides. Even knowing that she still glanced her phone, just in case. No service available.

"Here, let me get that," Daniel called out as he noticed her lugging some fishing gear.

"It's fine. I got it."

He frowned at her, and being the gentleman that he was, he gingerly snatched the heavy stuff from her arms. They trudged down to the sandy edge of their favorite fishing spot. The tall grasses had browned, and the water slightly receded. Hannah heard the honking of geese and looked up, noticing a V formation of Canadian geese against the pale blue sky.

"Boy, you can tell fall is about here." Daniel pointed at the yellowing tamarack trees in the distance. The air had a bite to it, not cold, but the slight breeze nipped at her. Hannah was thankful she had wore a hoodie—her favorite, a soft pink camouflage one. Daniel had already teased her, saying that he wasn't so sure what she trying to blend in with, but she'd be hard to find in Candyland. She had laughed. He had a point, but it was still warm and comfortable.

"You want me to bait your hook?" Daniel asked as he started to thread the line and check the reel on one of the poles.

"Haven't we been over this before?"

"Yes, Miss Fisherman, but can't your boyfriend offer?"

Hannah smiled. *Boyfriend.* There it was, finally out in the open. Neither had really said anything before. It was just been quietly assumed, she supposed. The way the word rolled off his tongue was sort of nice. As she moved closer to him, the breeze picked up. She watched ripples move along the dark surface of the lake. Daniel stood near the water as he busied himself with the pole, wearing a well-loved Seattle Mariners baseball cap and gray hoodie. He looked comfortable, and she suddenly, without warning, found him incredibly sexy. Hannah wrapped her arms around his neck. She felt him drop the pole down carefully, his hands landing on her hips. She felt time pause, her ears picking up the sounds of nature, but they were alone in that moment. Her lips sought his, finally tasting the sweetness she knew they'd promised earlier, along with the after hints of coffee and his maple bar. Daniel O'Brien was delicious in more ways than one.

***

Daniel

Driving home from the lake, Daniel looked over to see Hannah asleep. She had been through a lot that day and was probably more than a little exhausted. As he watched her, he saw her eyes were closed, her steady breathing making her chest rise and fall. He felt his heart swell. Seeing her sleeping soundly, he couldn't but help notice how gorgeous and peaceful she looked. The way her eyelashes fanned out almost drew more attention to the spray of freckles across her cheeks and the bridge of her nose. Her lips were slightly swollen, more red than their usual rosebud pink from how much they'd kissed at the lake. Hannah's long, golden-blonde hair was curling near her shoulders. He tried to keep his focus on the road, but found it quite difficult to take his eyes off of her. Daniel felt a strong urge to protect the woman beside him. He knew she was strong. She could milk goats and wasn't afraid of hard work. Hell, she could even bait her own hook, but that didn't stop him from wanting to shelter her. Seeing her so emotional today, that pulled at something inside him. He vowed to himself that he would do everything he could to make her happy, because seeing her smile, that brought him a kind of joy he had never felt before. Hearing her laugh, watching the brilliant blues and greens and flecks of amber of her eyes sparkle when she was amused, all these small things, they were starting to mean the world to Daniel.

"Hannah, we're home," Daniel whispered as he shut off the truck in her driveway.

She stirred slowly, confusion in her eyes until she looked around. "Gosh, I'm sorry. I didn't mean to fall asleep."

"It's okay. You needed it."

"Probably just tired from all that darn crying." Hannah laughed nervously. "Daniel, it means a lot that you came over today."

Daniel slid over closer to her side. "Hannah, I would move mountains if you asked." Staring at her lip, he saw her tongue flick across them, creating a wet sheen. It was too much to resist. He lowered his mouth onto hers, but not delicately. This was a kiss that was deep, hungry, and needy. Daniel felt desire pulse through him, God, he wanted her. What he wanted was something he had never had, never tasted, but he knew he craved it now more than anything. He was starving for Hannah.

***

Hannah

The fireworks that erupted behind her eyes as she felt Daniel kiss her, she couldn't explain the intensity behind it. She just knew that the flood of emotions from everything that had happened and from what she felt for Daniel was all almost too much. It was consuming her. The rawness of this kiss, the primal moan that had escaped Daniel or her, she wasn't sure who, scared her a little. The blaze that was beginning to burn through her was far more wicked now than it had ever been before. She now wanted something she thought was forbidden. She understood what Nina had meant about making love, and she wanted nothing more than to feel closer to Daniel. Maybe waiting to sleep with someone until marriage was overrated. Her brain felt faulty, her reasoning quickly vanishing. If he had taken her right there, she wouldn't have stopped it, but maybe even encouraged it.

She explored the tight muscles of his back with her hands as she pulled him closer. The confines of the truck were beginning to irritate her as her body started to take control. She slipped her hands under his shirt. Feeling his skin was almost her undoing. The desire to shed her clothing and feel the heat of his flesh on her was growing stronger as his tongue explored and teased her mouth.

She felt his hands move under her shirt, cupping

her breasts. Now she wanted to be naked more than anything. All these sensations, all new and wild, were overwhelming, but welcomed.

"God, Hannah." Daniel hissed in her ear as he suddenly pulled back. He practically flung himself back into his seat, his face flushed, the vivid color of his eyes hazy with lust. Daniel rubbed his face. "I'm sorry."

"For what?" Guilt and shame were starting to enter her mind. Had she done something wrong? Was she not what he really wanted? Self-doubt started to burn through her.

He must have sensed her feeling discomfort, because he reached for her. "Oh, babe, it's not you. It's, uh…me."

Hannah felt her heart thump loudly inside her. Panic began to take over. It was him? Was he going to break up with her? She wasn't sure she could take much more. Today had been a roller coaster.

"I, well…" Daniel was avoiding her eyes, embarrassment or something etched on his face. Hannah was beyond confused. For them to go from being tangled up in each other only moments earlier to this awkwardness? What went wrong?

"It's fine. I get it. You aren't interested. I'm not Nina. You shouldn't have to settle for second best," Hannah spat angrily, trying to work the door open. Daniel pushed the lock button and glared at her.

"What? God, no. That's not it at all."

She watched as Daniel swallowed. He seemed to be slowly digesting his thoughts. She could see him trying to figure out how to tell her whatever it was he needed to say. Her stomach started to move in uneasy waves, she felt her bottom lip quiver in anticipation, and the familiar burn of tears were building up in her eyes. "I don't understand then, Daniel. I thought…"

His eyes had an angry hue in them as he spoke, "First off, let me make myself quite clear. I don't want Nina, ever. I want you in ways I can't even begin to tell you. One way that just about happened here in this truck, in front of your house for goodness sakes."

Hannah frowned. "Okay, you have a point there. I'm sorry. I…"

"Stop apologizing." Daniel moved closer and cupped her face. "You didn't do anything wrong. You wanted what I wanted. But I haven't, well…"

"You're a virgin?" Hannah gasped in shock.

"Yes."

She burst out into laughter. Daniel scowled at her in disbelief. "No, no. no. I promise I am not laughing because of what you told me."

"Then why, Hannah? That's not really something you hope someone does when you tell them that." He slid back over to his side of the truck. Tension started to thicken between them. Daniel must have felt it too. He rolled down the window and stared outside.

Boy, she had really done it. She hadn't meant to laugh, but the sensation of the relief that soared through her, well, that was the way it had decided to escape her. "Daniel, I am too," Hannah admitted, placing her hand on his arm, trying to coax him to look at her. "I wanted to wait until I met the man I wanted to marry. I guess it's kind of cheesy, but I wanted it to be special."

Daniel turned to face her. "I don't think it's cheesy. I think it's beautiful." He smiled at her, pausing briefly before he explained, "It's not common for guys to wait, but I wanted to. I always wanted to be with the right woman, someone I would marry and be with for the rest of my life. I wanted it to be something special that I could share with her and something that hopefully she could share with me."

Hannah couldn't believe her ears. How was it that this man just became that much more perfect?

They both sat quietly. Hannah's mind was racing, but one thing she knew was that this was the man she wanted to marry someday. After all the countless romance novels and all the movies with their happy endings, she realized now it was almost as if they had prepared her for something she didn't think existed. But here it was, right next to her.

Chapter Thirteen

It had been a couple of weeks since her sister had left, and Nina had only called once to let them know she had made it to California safe and sound. Why did she have to go there, of all places? Nina had explained over a static telephone line that she had met someone online who had made her grand promises of a career in modeling. Hannah was leery and scared for her sister. She knew Nina could easily become a model. There was no doubt about that. It was Nina's inexperience and naiveté that worried her. She also knew that not everywhere was like Birch Valley. Hannah had been doing a lot of praying, and her one happy distraction had been Daniel.

Hannah stomped out into the soggy morning, the saturated ground squishing under her boots as she headed to the small barn to tend to the goats. She always milked the goats and fed the chickens around this time of morning, right after breakfast and before she started on any other household chores. She cherished this quiet time, alone with her thoughts and her animals. Growing up on a farm was all she knew, but she was happy here, unlike her sister.

As she opened the wide wooden door to the barn, the heady scents of damp hay, earth, and animal hit her. Straw was scattered about, and several goats with full udders waddled around. Hannah reached down to pet a brown and white goat that had nudged her. She found her stool and locked herself a small pen with the animal and set to work on milking. The milk shot hard into to the metal pail, echoing against its sides as she squeezed in a steady rhythm. Hannah was so focused on the task she nearly jumped out of her skin when she heard her father's voice.

"She being good for you?"

Hannah had to catch her breath and plead for her heart to slow down as it hammered against her chest. "Dad, I didn't hear you come in." Hannah stroked the goat she was milking, trying to soothe the small beast.

"Didn't mean to scare you," he said, offering her a smile, which was a rare treat.

Hannah went back to work on milking the animal. "Oh, it's okay. I was just daydreaming."

Her father leaned against the pen, removing his straw hat. He asked, "Wouldn't be daydreaming about Daniel, now would you?"

Guilty. "Well, him and Nina."

"Yeah, your sister left us in quite a pickle, didn't she? You know, I called your Aunt Olga to come to stay and help us around here."

"Oh, Dad, that wasn't necessary." Hannah

groaned internally at the thought of her strict aunt. The woman had lived in America for decades, yet she was set in the old country ways.

"It is. You are doing far too much here. Besides, I don't think you will be on the farm for too much longer."

Hannah was puzzled. "What do you mean?"

He cocked his head at her. "Hannah, please, we both know."

"I'm not following you, Dad." Hannah looked into his eyes searchingly. They were same icy blue as her sister's, but they were unforgiving and cold, despite the warmth in his voice.

"Daniel."

Now she understood. As much as she fantasized about marrying Daniel, she knew her father needed her here, especially with Nina gone. "Dad, I don't plan on going anywhere."

"Love has a funny way of changing promises we try to make. Hannah, do you love this boy?"

Boy? Daniel was nearly thirty years old, like her. He was anything but a boy. When they were together, the thoughts that entered her mind were slightly wicked and completely unfounded, and she didn't know why these feelings surged inside her. She felt like a ticking time bomb, wanting to explore these urges, especially when Daniel kissed her.

Hannah exhaled loudly. "I think so, Dad. He's just so wonderful."

Her father nodded. "As long as you are happy, that's all I really care about."

Hannah rose up from the stool, wiping her hands

on the backside of her jeans, and went to hug her father. She clung to him, dismissing the awkwardness of embracing the man who stood rigid against her.

*****

Daniel

"I just wanted to ask your permission, sir." Daniel stood as straight as he could. His stance was respectful, but he wanted to show his strength, that he was indeed good enough. Good enough to court Hannah Belsky, the girl he had every intention of marrying.

Daniel had been spending a lot of time over at the Belsky farm, especially since Nina had run off to California. During that time he had grown to fall even more in love with Hannah, seeing how tender she was with her father. He saw her sweetness radiate in everything she did. Daniel knew that it was old-fashioned to ask a father permission to court his daughter, but there was something old-fashioned about their relationship—a timeless kind of romance.

"Well, son, I appreciate you coming to me. It's not every day that you young people think of us elders with such respect. I happily give you my blessing," Mr. Belsky replied as he started to hammer the nail into the post Daniel was holding. "I really appreciate your help, Daniel. You are a good man."

"Thank you, Mr. Belsky." Daniel was relieved it

had gone well. Even though Mr. Belsky's thick accent was sometimes hard to understand, Daniel had gotten his point across. He made it quite clear he had every intent to ask for Hannah's hand in marriage. Mr. Belsky nodded and smiled, and that had been enough for Daniel.

***

Hannah

As she stirred the mashed potatoes, adding more butter, salt, and pepper to it, she spied Daniel and her father sitting at the dining room table. This was becoming their evening routine. Daniel would stop by after work, help her father out, and then stay for dinner. They were beginning to feel like a family, in a way. After sharing a meal, her father would usually retire to his room, leaving Daniel and Hannah alone. It was those quiet times, when it was just the two of them, whether they were sitting on the porch or cuddled on the couch watching a movie, that Hannah felt as close as one could be. Her body responded to every touch, every kiss, even accidental grazes against her skin. He drove her wild. It had been a couple weeks since Daniel and her unveiled that they were both virgins. He had been careful to keep some physical space between them. There were no more heavy make out sessions, though Hannah could see desire burning brightly in his eyes every time they met with hers.

"You wanna watch a movie after dinner?" Daniel came up behind Hannah as she finished with the potatoes. He nuzzled her neck. His simple kisses sent thrilling shivers down her spine and into her core. The scruff of his unshaven jaw was almost her undoing. She couldn't explain why, but she was losing her resolve.

Daniel dipped his index finger into the potatoes, scooping it quickly and slipping it into his mouth. Hannah snuck a look at his lips. They were inviting, and there was no resisting. She dove for him, taking him by complete surprise. She ignored the shock in his eyes, closing her own. Hannah kissed him hard. The salty taste of the potatoes lingered in his mouth as she enjoyed the flavor of what was completely Daniel O'Brien, mixed with the side dish for dinner.

His hands went to her hips, grasping them and tugging her closer to him. It was as though she was fighting some invisible barrier, an impenetrable force field which kept her from feeling like she was close enough to him.

Daniel stepped back, almost losing his balance. "Damn, Hannah."

"I know." She completely understood how he felt as she tried to cool down.

Just then her father reentered the kitchen, and instantly, Hannah felt embarrassed. What if he had seen them?

"Dinner's ready, D-Dad," Hannah stuttered.

"It smells good." Her father started for the dining room again. Daniel followed him, his cheeks rosy, a dead giveaway. Hannah knew her face probably didn't look much different. In a feeble attempt to remove her blush from that explosive kiss, Hannah splashed some cool water on her face and gently patted it dry with a nearby dish towel. She picked up a large platter of fried chicken. God help her. She didn't know how long she could go on like this.

***

Daniel

Keeping his hands and mouth off her was becoming increasingly difficult, but he wasn't the only one who was battling temptation. He'd witnessed first hand the desire Hannah struggled with. Granted, not that he minded her rushing him and kissing the daylights out of him, but it made him want her with every fiber of his being. He wondered just how much longer could they go on resisting what they both wanted.

After dinner, Daniel helped Hannah with the dishes. He watched as the suds clung to her hands. Unsure why he did it, he reached in and scooped some of the soap and flung it at her. The surprised look on her face quickly changed into one of someone ready to meet his challenge.

"You think you're funny, Mr. Daniel O'Brien?" Hannah asked as she threw a wad of bubbles at him.

"I think I'm quite hilarious, thank you." With a palm full of suds, he plopped them on top of her head and left a dollop on her nose.

"You are such a brat!" Hannah squealed as she playfully slapped some of the white bubbles onto his face, but stopped as her fingers glided over his cheek, and slid across his lips. The temptation kept teasing the both of them.

179

He took his hand and tilted her chin up toward him. They were wet from the bubble fight, and sparkly suds reflected the light from the kitchen. Hannah looked almost magical—simply beautiful. Daniel pressed his lips against hers and could hear her moan against him. When would he learn that kissing her was only making the forbidden need worse?

***

"There he is," Patrick called as Daniel entered the shop the next morning.

"Morning, Daniel," Maggie said from the front counter, where she and Patrick stood eyeing him. His sister looked like she was ready to pop. She was due in less than a week, if he remembered correctly.

"Mags, what you doing here? You should be home."

"Why?" She shrugged and tossed him an annoyed look. "Why, because I'm the size of small house and it feels like Max is going to plop out any second?"

Maybe the annoyed look wasn't for him. "Just saying, you shouldn't be on your feet."

"Thanks for the concern, but I'm fine."

"Besides, she has so much to do before she leaves us," Patrick added matter-of-factly.

"He has a point. Patrick, have you considered asking Amber if she can maybe help out?"

Patrick smiled. "I sort of did, but she is being difficult about it."

"Why?" Now Patrick was on the receiving end

of Maggie's irritation. *Pregnancy hormones moved fast*, Daniel thought to himself.

"She isn't sure she wants to work with me." Patrick frowned.

"Well, she's probably right. I can hardly stand working with either of you," Maggie teased as she started to sort some mail that was on the counter.

"You adore us," Patrick rebutted without hesitation. "You wouldn't know what to do without us."

She rolled her eyes, but she smiled. "You're probably right. Where else could I find this kind of entertainment?" Maggie grinned at Daniel. "Like that one, he just cracks me up. You, Patrick, you annoy me." Her hormones were like a game of ping pong, bouncing back and forth. Daniel winced as Maggie threw Patrick a sour look.

"I'm not so sure I will miss her, Daniel. She's pretty annoying herself." Patrick smirked.

"Maggie, for the record, I will miss you. You make far better coffee than Patrick," Daniel added as he poured some inside his stainless steel travel mug.

***

Hannah

The credits started, and Hannah wiped the tears from her eyes. She set her knitting needles down and hit stop on her DVD player. She had been working on baby caps for Maggie and Rachel, so she'd watched a terribly happy movie, something

181

sappy and purely romantic. Hannah released a content sigh. Maybe it had to do with being in love, because Hannah could say without a doubt she was in love with Daniel. Lost her in thoughts and daydreaming about a happy future, she almost hadn't heard the knock at the door. Getting up from the couch, she went to see who would be visiting.

Hannah was surprised to open the door and see Mary O'Brien standing at the other side of the threshold.

"Mary, how lovely to see you."

"Hello, dear, I hope you don't mind me stopping by." Mary offered her an apologetic smile.

"Oh no, please come inside. This is a welcome surprise visit." Hannah led Mary into the kitchen. "Can I offer you some tea?"

"That would be wonderful." Mary unwrapped her light scarf and removed her coat.

The weather had turned brisk almost overnight, leaving a slick wet frost over the fields today. Hannah noticed how frigid the air was when she went to feed her chickens and milk the goats. Summer was only a memory now. The days were shorter and colder. Her father had started a fire in their wood stove this morning. Hannah had tended to it all day, bringing in more firewood, and the inside of the Belsky home was toasty.

"I also made some lemon and berry scones."

"Well, I can't quite say no to that offer." Mary laughed and took a seat at the dining table.

After starting a kettle of water on the stove, Hannah joined Mary, waiting for the water to heat. "So, how are you?"

"Great, dear. I have come by to ask for your help."

"Oh, really? Absolutely. What is it that you need?" Hannah was curious, but it didn't matter what Mary had in mind. Hannah would gladly help.

"Cider Fest is next weekend. Maggie was going to help, but with the baby being due anytime now she isn't so sure she even wants to go. I was hoping that perhaps you would consider helping me."

"Oh, do you have a booth there at the festival?"

Mary nodded. "Yes, I run it to raise money for my church. We usually sell baked goodies and little homemade things. Now, I realize this is short notice…"

Hannah stopped her. "Mary, I would love to help. Do you need me to bake anything?"

The smile that appeared on Mary's face warmed Hannah. The woman, who had not only raised a fantastic son, was an incredible baker in Birch Valley, and it would be an honor to cook with her.

Then Hannah spotted it, a tiny spark of mischief danced in Mary's eyes. Mary looked away quickly.

"Oh, dear, I think that's the kettle," Mary announced.

Hannah didn't hear a whistle coming from the kettle, and she became a tad suspicious as she watched Mary fidget in her seat. She now realized there was a reason behind this visit; it was more than Mary needing Hannah to help bake and work the booth. Something was definitely up.

Chapter Fourteen

Rachel

"Do I really have to have a baby shower? You know, that means my mother will be coming up, Chelsea too."

"Rachel, babe, we have been through this. Yes, you told my mom and sister that you'd let them throw you one." Liam looked at her over his newspaper.

They were in the dining room, seated across from each other in the breakfast nook. Rachel found herself barely fitting, her large pregnant belly rubbing against the oak table. She looked out the window, thankful that the weekend had arrived. School was wearing her out, but not nearly as much as Karen and Mary were with this darn baby shower. It wasn't that Rachel was opposed to a fun little get together. She was thrilled about Chelsea coming to visit, but her mother, not so much. She had seen her a couple months ago for the wedding, and it had gone surprisingly well. It was the phone calls which had followed in the last month or so that had Rachel concerned. Her mother had insisted that the baby shower be held in California, but Rachel knew with her job and carrying twins, it was safer to have the shower here. Her mother had finally agreed and now wanted a date.

"Are you nervous about today?" Rachel fiddled with her spoon, plunging it into her bowl of oatmeal.

"What do you think?" Liam grinned happily at her. Today they were going to find out the genders of the twins Rachel was carting around inside her. "The beauty of it is that once we know, then you can plan the baby shower a little better, right?"

"I guess so." Rachel couldn't help be less than thrilled at having another celebration, especially so soon after having survived her impromptu wedding shower. "What's your guess, Liam?"

He shrugged and folded the newspaper. "Hard to say. It's really a fifty-fifty kind of gamble here, but I will be happy with either, or both. Just as long as they are healthy and look like their mother."

Rolling her eyes, Rachel asked, "So once we know, how do we announce it to the world?"

"You mean the family?"

"Same difference." Rachel laughed and spooned a mouthful of the blueberry oatmeal into her mouth.

"Well, do you want to do something special?"

"Like is that standard protocol, or do we just tell them once we know?"

Liam picked up his mug of coffee. "Hon, that is really up to you. I think it might be nice to announce it in some fun way, but we don't need to go all crazy."

"Well, guess what? Once we know, you get to decide," Rachel teased. "Your mom mentioned something about Cider Fest this weekend. She said she we sort of have to go."

"You'll like it. The town basically gorges on everything *apple*. I mean, you name it, cider, pie, candy, literally a celebration of apples," Liam explained.

"But it's called Cider Fest, so wouldn't it just be about cider?"

"Nope. They pull out this really neat cider press, and they make fresh cider right there. It's, like, the best." Rachel watched as Liam's face lit up as he continued to describe the difference between cold and hot cider, and all the booths, live music, and overall fun to be had. It sounded like a good time and now Rachel found herself looking forward to it.

***

Liam

Liam was beyond nervous, and he wasn't quite sure why. As they sat in the waiting room at the clinic, Rachel tapped her foot against the carpet. He could sense her anxiety. He didn't really understand why either of them felt this way. They knew they were pregnant with twins, and they were here to figure out the gender. This should be the fun part.

"What do you think we're having?"

"Rachel, we already went through that this morning. You asked me at lunch. I have no idea what we are having. Does it really matter?" After breakfast that morning, Rachel had been quiet on the way to the school. Then at lunch she was back at pestering him, asking what he thought, like he could magically see through her belly or had some sort of insight she didn't.

"Gosh, what are we going to name them?" A worried expression crossed her face. Liam hated seeing Rachel this way. She was so unlike herself. This pregnancy was taking its toll on her, and on him. How were they going to be when the babies actually arrived in less than two months? Best not to borrow trouble, that's what his mother always said, and he couldn't think of anything truer.

A nurse with a wide smile came out and announced Rachel's name. Liam trailed behind Rachel as she waddled behind the nurse. He wasn't sure how much larger Rachel would grow in two more months, and he knew she was uncomfortable as it was. All of a sudden Liam realized he was quite thankful to be a man.

"It's going to be a little cold, okay?" The nurse squirted some gel out of a clear tube onto Rachel's enormous belly. He saw her wince.

The grainy screen showed the quick flutter of two hearts, as well as oblong, round shapes that looked like full-sized babies. "There they are. It's getting tight in there," the nurse commented as she rolled the ultrasound wand over Rachel's belly. She started typing numbers into a keyboard. Only the quick sound of the tapping of the keys filled the room. "I will get Dr. Salinger and be right back."

Once the woman left, Liam reached for Rachel's hand. "You doing okay?"

"Yeah, I just want everything to be okay. I always get nervous when they enter information in that darn computer and not say a word."

"Well, I don't think they are allowed to. Besides I'd rather Dr. Salinger tell us if anything was wrong."

"You think there might be something wrong?" Rachel's voice got louder, and panic seared her blue eyes.

"No, I don't think so at all. I'm just saying…"

A soft knock interrupted Liam. He couldn't dismiss his instant relief as Dr. Salinger opened the door and entered the room.

"Hi, guys." Her black hair was in a tight bun on top of her head, and her overly large mouth offered them a kind smile. "How are we feeling?" She looked slowly from Liam to Rachel as she washed her hands at the small sink.

"I feel okay," Rachel managed to say. Liam could hear her voice crack. He knew how worried she was and how miserable she was starting to become.

"Just okay? Well, let me take a look." Dr. Salinger took a seat on the small stool near the ultrasound machine. "Did the nurse tell you what you are having yet?" she asked as she put the wand back on Rachel's belly.

"No, not yet," Rachel answered.

"Oh goody, I get to tell you." Dr. Salinger gifted them both with an extra large grin. "Oh, I know what you're having!"

Liam watched as Rachel's eyes grew wide with anticipation. "Really?"

Dr. Salinger nodded. "Oh yeah, they're both being very good right now and showing off." Dr. Salinger removed the wand and started typing. In large letters on the monitor, where both Rachel and Liam could clearly see, it read, *Say hello to your daughters!*

Rachel turned to face Liam, tears in her eyes. He felt his eyes burn as he tried to hold back his own tears. They were having girls.

***

Rachel

Daughters. Rachel was still wrapping her mind around the fact she was going to be a mom, but now to two girls. It sort of frightened her, yet the excitement she felt was incredible. She couldn't help but think of her mother and the not-so-cozy mother-daughter relationship they shared. Would it be like that with these girls? Rachel really had believed she was carrying boys, and she had been getting used the idea, so much so that she had even started to think of boy names. After bonding with Patrick's boys, Finn and Connor, she just assumed she would be having boys too, but the thoughts of dresses, bows, pink, lots and lots of pretty pink, well, they put a smile on her face.

"Can you believe it?" Rachel asked again, switching the phone to her other ear.

"Oh my God, Rachel, it's perfect. Oh, I can't wait." Chelsea squealed on the other end of the line.

Rachel had had to tell someone, and Liam

insisted on doing something fun to tell the family. Rachel also planned on calling her mother later, but right now, she wanted to share this with her best friend.

"I know, right? I thought for sure I was having boys."

"Even if you were, that would still be amazing. I won't lie. I'm thrilled they're girls." Rachel could hear Chelsea's happiness from over fifteen hundred miles away. "So, baby shower? When is this happening? I'm ready to shop and come up for it."

Rachel rolled her eyes. Yes, the dreaded shower. But now she was looking forward to it, and of course seeing Chelsea. "Well, we are going to tell Liam's family tomorrow or sometime this week. He wants to do something special to announce their gender."

"Oh that's fun."

"I know, and his mom has been after me to plan this shower, so I'm thinking probably mid-October, maybe?"

"That works. Maybe I will fly up with your mom," Chelsea suggested.

"Up to you, I was thinking maybe you could come up before and help in the girls' room." Just saying it out loud made it all seem more real. Rachel was going to be giving birth in less than two months to two girls.

"Have you and Liam discussed names yet?"

"Well, we tossed around a few. It's a lot harder than you would think. I mean, I try to think, do I need to name them after someone? I try to consider if it rhymes with something awful, and if they will get made fun of in school. I don't want them to hate it either. I always sort of hated Rachel."

"Really? I like your name."

Rachel groaned. "I don't. It always sounded so blah. My dad wanted something with an R to match his name, since my mom did that with Ethan. They didn't put a whole lot of thought into it."

"I still like it. After all, it is the name of my very best friend in the entire world."

***

"I'm so glad Hannah helped us with these, but do you think she told Daniel?" Rachel was worried as she carried the tray of cupcakes. Inside each perfect chocolate pastry was bright pink strawberry filling.

Liam was about to open the door to his parents' house, but he paused, answering her as they stood on the porch, "I don't think so. She is coming tonight, right?"

Rachel nodded. "Yes, Daniel is suppose to bring her over. I really like her, Liam."

"I think she's wonderful for him," Liam agreed as he took the tray of cupcakes from Rachel.

"Thanks. Are you nervous at all?" Rachel asked.

"Nah, this is the fun part. Why, are you?" Concern grew in his radiant eyes.

"Well, maybe nervous isn't the right word. It's more like I'm overly excited, and then I worry, what if Dr. Salinger is wrong and we're having boys?" Rachel shrugged. "I told Maggie I worried the same for her, especially after she just went nuts with all the blue in Max's baby room. Watch, I'll go crazy with pink." Rachel loved the name that Maggie and Michael had picked out—another little M name. Liam and Rachel were finding it to be more of a challenge and were planning to ask the family to help come up with some ideas tonight.

"You worry too much." Liam bent down and kissed her.

"Isn't that how you two got into that trouble to begin with?" someone asked in a thick Irish accent. Rachel's cheeks burned with embarrassment as she saw Grandpa Paddy standing by the now open front door. He motioned for them to come in and winked at her as she passed him. "What treats have you brought?" Grandpa Paddy looked curiously at the tray.

"Just some cupcakes for dessert," Liam quickly answered.

"Maybe I should sneak one then. I would hate to be too full from supper." Grandpa Paddy went to reach for one, but Liam pulled them back.

"Best not, Grandpa Paddy, Mom will have your hide."

"She wouldn't need to know. Be a good lad and let your granddad have one," Grandpa Paddy pleaded. Rachel nearly felt sorry for him and almost handed him one, but Liam shot her a reminding glance.

Rachel entwined her arm through Grandpa Paddy's, guiding him to the living room while Liam started for the kitchen. "Maybe dinner is ready and then we can get to those cupcakes."

Everyone was in the dining room when Rachel and Liam entered. It was loud and bursting with activity. This one of the reasons why Rachel had fallen in love with the O'Brien family. She was now a part of this, and her daughters were going to be as well. She couldn't think of a better family to be surrounded by.

"Here, let me take those." Mary entered in the room looking partially frazzled, but stopped long enough to plant a kiss on Liam's cheek. She then moved to Rachel, giving her the same kiss. "How are you feeling, love?"

"Great." Rachel kept her answers short. She was worried she would blurt everything out.

"You baked cupcakes?" Mary raised an eyebrow. "This will be quite a welcome treat. Thank you, dear."

Liam watched her. She could feel him willing her to keep quiet. Mary took the tray into the kitchen, where the rest of women were hiding out. Rachel greeted them. She was given hugs, and asked genuine questions about how she was feeling. She felt so loved and accepted by this group of women and couldn't wait to share her exciting news. There would be more O'Brien women, girls who would learn to bake and cook with their grandmother and aunts. Rachel felt herself on the verge of tears. It was all so moving and emotional. Nine months ago she never would have thought this would be her life what her life was like, and she was so thankful it had turned out this way.

Rachel managed to focus on her food as she danced around several pregnancy questions. She took this time to really evaluate the O'Brien family. They all had become so dear and special to her.

Michael made Melanie giggle quite a bit. He was such an amazing father to that precious little girl. Maggie looked uncomfortable and just ready to be done with her pregnancy. Daniel and Hannah seemed lost in their own little world. Patrick and Amber weren't much different, except how motherly Amber acted toward the twins, and her own teenage boy seem to fit right in. Everyone always seem to fit right in with the O'Brien family. They had accepted her and made her one of them long before she accepted the fact she was terribly head over heels in love with Liam. Mary was quick to clear the table, as their plates weren't fully emptied, which resulted in a chorus of complaints. Rachel was a little a confused by her anxiousness.

Mary returned to the table with the tray of cupcakes, wasting no time passing them out. Hannah glanced over at Rachel but acted completely casual. She eagerly accepted a cupcake when Mary handed her one.

"Well, my son just told me how important these cupcakes were," Mary began to explain. Everyone started to examine their cupcake carefully, inspecting it with a seriousness Rachel didn't quite expect. She looked over at Liam. He blushed. Here he was, so worried she was going to spill the beans.

Liam stood up, gently holding a cupcake in his hand. "Everyone, inside this cupcake is something special. We went to our ultrasound appointment the other day, and we now know what Rachel and I are having. Please bite into your cupcake now," Liam instructed the family. Everyone's shocked faces were suddenly full of cupcake as they dove into the pastries. The sounds of delight, squeals of happiness and congratulations, caused tears to flow from Rachel. To see how joyful everyone was, to feel that amount of love, was overpowering and incredible.

Mary went to Rachel, taking her into her plump arms. "I'm so happy for you both. See, Rachel, I told you that you were a blessing to this family." She squeezed her again.

"Better get to buying everything in pink," Maggie called to Rachel from across the table.

After the dust settled from the news the men all departed, leaving the women alone.

"Have you guys thought of names?" Maggie inquired, leaning back in her chair, rubbing her large belly.

"It's not so easy," Rachel answered and subconsciously found herself rubbing her own belly.

"Told you. Everyone thinks it is, but there is so much to consider, right?"

"Absolutely. Liam has some ideas, but I want some that are cute and classic." Rachel had been considering so many names since the ultrasound. She turned her attention to Hannah, who sat quietly among the ladies. "Hannah, thanks again for helping me out. The cupcakes were amazing, by the way. You and Mary really need to open a bakery."

"Wait, you knew?" Maggie tossed a look at Hannah then back at Rachel.

They both nodded, and Rachel answered, "You didn't think I could bake something that good, did you?"

"I suppose you're right. They were really good."

Maggie laughed.

"I'm just so happy. I will be having a grandson next week, and then two granddaughters in a little over a month." Mary's eyes shone with joy, tears peeking out from them. "We need to plan that shower soon."

"You'll be proud of me, Mary. I was just telling Chelsea that I thought maybe early or mid October."

"Oh, good. You will need to call your mother. We need to start planning."

"Maggie, are you getting nervous? I mean, we're talking like any day now, right?" Rachel asked and searched Maggie's face.

"I'm ready to meet Max. We have everything ready to go. We just need him now."

"We can't wait to meet that precious little guy," Amber said with longing in her eyes. Rachel knew from talking to Liam that Patrick was planning on proposing, but that had been discussed a couple weeks ago and hadn't been mentioned since. Had something changed?

"I can't wait to start a family, it just seems so wonderful. You both are gorgeous," Hannah spoke up. She too had longing in her eyes.

"Thank you, that means so much. I feel like a fat cow." Maggie groaned and then spoke directly to her belly. "Anytime, Max, anytime."

Rachel could relate to feeling large and unattractive. She appreciated Hannah's compliments, but that didn't stop her from hating her changing body. It wasn't that she was vain, and it wasn't even the stretch marks which mapped her body that bothered her. It was the weight of the two princesses inside her and feeling as large as a castle to house them.

"Max needs to stay inside until after Cider Fest," Mary reminded Maggie.

"Mom, I can't guarantee anything."

"Well, I will be praying he just stays put until after this weekend."

Maggie rolled her eyes as the others laughed. She spoke to her belly again, "You hear that, Max? Grams says to stay put. No coming until after her precious apple extravaganza." More giggles erupted from Amber, Hannah, and even Mary.

It was just so comfortable, sitting at the table enjoying laughs like this with them. Rachel hoped that Amber and Hannah would become members of the family as well. They already felt like sisters to her, and she knew they loved the O'Brien men they had been saddled with. As she said a silent prayer, Rachel caught Maggie looking her way. They must have been thinking the very same thing, and they gave each other a knowing smile.

Chapter Fifteen

Daniel

To say he was nervous was an understatement. He toyed with the ring in his pocket. Cider Fest was in full swing, and the city park was decorated with large apple-shaped garlands mounted on various posts. Twinkling white and red lights were strung in the trees, and booths were lined up in neat rows. A band played music as the residents of Birch Valley sampled various baked goods, visited with neighbors, and children ran through some of the fallen leaves. Cider Fest had started early in the morning, and he should know. He had been there when the sun was barely up, helping his mother set up the church booth she ran, selling baked goods to raise money for several of their programs. But now the sun was setting below the apricot and lavender sky, and the air was turning chilly, making it the perfect the time to sip on some warm cider.

Daniel was walking to the booth he had helped set up earlier. It was almost time. He wanted to wait until the lights in the trees were glowing more. He wanted this to be perfect, because she was perfect. When he arrived at the small white-tented booth, Daniel's mother smiled at him, giving him an encouraging nod. Hannah was busy sorting out what baked items they hadn't sold. Maggie sat in a canvas chair looking miserable, as Max had not decided to come yet. Rachel and Liam were standing only feet away, arms entwined and swaying to the beat of the live music. Patrick and Amber sat on a large quilt on the grass, Finn and Connor cuddled in their laps. Dylan was nearby chatting with friends, looking every bit a Birch Valley teenager. Michael and Melanie were returning back to the booth, ice cream cones in hand and enormous grins on their faces. Grandpa Paddy and his father sat in canvas chairs staring out at all the activity. Everyone was here, and Daniel couldn't think of better time or place to ask Hannah to join their family. He stood and watched her for a moment, trying to hush the sick twirling inside his guts. She fit in so perfectly, but it was more than that. He had never felt this way about someone before. Hannah had become his everything in such a short time. There were no words to truly describe the feelings in his heart, but he was sure going to give it a try.

***

Hannah

She inhaled the rich scents of apples, apple cider,

apple pies, apple everything. The spicy fragrance of cinnamon clung to the light breeze, drifting throughout the park. Hannah loved every minute of it. The lights flickering in the trees looked almost like fireflies, delicate and simply romantic. The flurry of activity was finally winding down, and Hannah was exhausted but couldn't recall having a better time. The day, as hectic as it was, had been shared with some of the best people—the O'Brien family.

Hannah had been under that tent since dawn, bumping into Maggie, Mary, Rachel, and Amber. The small quarters had afforded them a chance to bond even more. She had never laughed so much in her life, well, except when she was with Daniel. He had been scarce most of the day, helping take care of the children with Michael, Liam, and Patrick. When she saw him twirling the little twin boys around in the grass, carrying Melanie on his shoulders to see the magician who had performed earlier, Hannah realized he was a natural father and it made maternal needs stir inside of her.

"Hannah." Daniel's voice was low as he approached. He ran his hand over his beard nervously.

"Hey, you're back. You having fun?" Hannah reached up and kissed him on his cheek. He blushed instantly. She loved that about him. He wore his emotions so clearly on his face.

Mary hovered nearby. Hannah could feel her eyes on them, and Maggie was looking over at them. In fact, all the O'Briens were looking at them through the early evening darkness. Hannah grew concerned. The lighting was terrible, but she could tell Daniel was fiddling with something. He seemed different, nervous or on edge.

"You okay?"

He nodded, his wide smile obviously attempting to hide something else.

"You sure? You're acting weird." It wasn't a question. It was a factual statement. Hannah could almost swear she see could see some beads of sweat on his brow.

"Yes, never better."

"If you say so. You seem weird, though," Hannah countered, reaching to grab his arm, as if she needed to inspect him to fully believe that he was fine.

"Hannah, trust me. I'm okay." His voice was wobbly.

Now Hannah was growing more concerned and a little annoyed with him. She could feel the stares of the family, which only added to the tension that mounted inside that tiny booth. "Daniel, I'm serious."

He released a long sigh and tilted his head up toward the canvas covering over the booth. Hannah looked over to Mary, who smiled back, beaming. Something was up, and now Hannah felt far more confused than concerned.

"Hannah…"

She watched Daniel reach behind him and withdraw a glass apple, but it was when he started to lower himself, kneeling, that she felt dizzy with the realization of what was happening. Hannah started to tremble. She could sense the family watching and waiting, but not moving. Time froze, quiet. She didn't hear the music of the band, or the children squealing as they played. There was no sound in this moment. Life was suspended as Daniel started to speak.

"Hannah, you are the most incredible person I have ever met. You are kind and simply beautiful." Daniel paused, wiping his eyes. Hannah felt her heart beat hard against her chest with anticipation. Daniel's eyes were bright, even in the darkening tent. He swallowed and began to speak again, "You can bait a hook like no other and know some incredible fishing spots. You make me laugh so hard, Hannah." His voice was cracking, and Hannah's cheeks were damp as tears started to stream down.

Grandpa Paddy called out, "Just spit it out, boy." Everyone laughed through their own muffled tears.

Daniel grinned wide, looking up at her. He held out the glass apple. "You keep me on my toes, and that's something I want you to do forever. Hannah, will you marry me?"

Fairy tales, they were something that little girls grow up with, something women casted aside when they realized Prince Charming didn't exist. But for Hannah, he did. He was on his knee, right in front of her. She placed her hand on the apple, feeling the weight in her palm. Daniel clasped his hands over hers. Again, time stood still, allowing her to savor this moment. Hannah brought the glass apple, clear with a hint of green and red, close to her chest. Reflecting off the light, hanging off the glass stem, was a gorgeous diamond ring. Simple, but grand in so many ways—much like her prince.

"Yes."

Daniel shot up from the ground, pulling her to him as he slipped the ring onto her finger. Hannah kissed him and didn't care who was watching them. There was the distant sound of clapping and a couple of ear-piercing whistles. Everyone was smiling, but it didn't compare to the happiness that seem to buzz off Daniel. Joy lit up his face, the face of the man she was going to marry, have children with, and grow old with. Realization dawned on Hannah through the magical haze: she was now engaged.

***

Daniel

There was that brief second, that moment of true doubt, the worry she wouldn't say what everyone was hoping and expected her to say. But as Daniel heard her say yes confidently through happy tears, all the anxiety and stress he had attempted to mask all day had floated away. He was now engaged to this amazing woman, someone who understood him, who made him feel complete in so many unexpected ways Whatever emptiness he had was now filled by her and no one else.

"Congrats, you guys!" Maggie exclaimed as she tried to remove herself from the camp chair she had been sitting in.

His mother moved in to hug him and Hannah, her eyes still wet. "I'm so happy for you both." As she looked at Daniel, she said, "Son, you have picked a woman who we all love, and who we know loves you with every inch of her heart." She turned to Hannah, taking her into her arms. "Welcome to this crazy family. Bless you, my sweet girl." They both laughed.

Daniel's brothers, father, and grandfather shook his hand, hugged him, and gave him so many pats on the back he actually started to feel a little pain. Yet it didn't measure to how full his heart felt at the moment. He tossed a glance to his fiancée, who was surrounded by all the O'Brien women, complimenting the ring he had just placed on her finger. Fiancée, wow, he hadn't seen this happening only a few short months ago. It was funny, the journeys life had taken him through. Looking back several months ago, he had felt alone as each of his siblings found their happiness, their soul mates. But now, as he stood there with his family, looking at all of them, he didn't feel alone or envious, because he too had found his other half.

***

The booth was empty, everything packed away, and the entire family had said their good-byes and congratulations only moments ago. Now only Daniel and Hannah remained, the lights in the trees still glowing. The park was quiet. All the attendees were gone. It was just Daniel and Hannah.

Daniel reached for Hannah's hand, and they started walking together. Each quiet and content, but still reeling from the shock and high of everything that had just taken place.

"So, are you happy?" Daniel asked in a near whisper.

"Daniel, you have no idea."

The grass was partially covered in leaves, and as Daniel and Hannah walked, they kicked lightly through them, scattering the brown leaves as they went.

"I know it probably was weird proposing here of all places. Gosh, with, like, everyone there too. I'm sorry."

Hannah stopped and turned to face him. "Daniel, it was perfect. You know what? It all had the same end result. We're engaged now." She stood up on the tips of her toes, her lips meeting his. She whispered, "I love you, Daniel O'Brien." And then she kissed him tenderly and again, it felt as the world had stopped spinning. They were alone, the chill of the fall air nipping at them as their tongues found the warmth of each other's mouths. Even with their eyes closed, romance was all around them. Daniel relished the kiss, feeling it fill him with more want and need, but also with the promise of a future to explore all of those desires. The one thing that he knew for certain was that true love did exist, and he had found it.

***

Hannah

Could this be any more perfect? She highly doubted it. Daniel's lips were on hers, his strong arms covering her as they embraced in the middle of the city park, not another soul there, just them. As Daniel pulled her in deeper, she felt something vibrate hard against her. It was his cell phone.

"Oh, crap," he said, pulling away slowly from her, almost stumbling from the daze of their kiss. "Hello?"

Hannah watched as his face twisted in confusion. "She okay?" He paused and blinked, worry replacing his confusion. "Okay, we're on our way." He turned off his phone and looked at her.

"Everything okay?" Hannah regretted asking as soon as she spoke.

"That was my mom. Maggie's in the hospital."

The baby. "Gosh, is she having the baby?"

"I think so, but it sounds like there is something wrong. I don't know. My mom sounded panicked." Daniel grabbed her by the hand and started to lead them through the empty and dark park. It no longer felt magical or romantic, but scary as fear started to creep in.

Hannah said a silent prayer. She asked God to protect Maggie and Max. She took a moment to thank Him for bringing Daniel into her life. Daniel had been a pillar of strength for her when she'd needed him. She was now going to have her chance to be his. Oddly enough, they were both experiencing worry at the hands of their siblings, though it wasn't necessarily intentional. The thought of siblings made Hannah say another prayer for the safety of Nina. She was still desperately worried about her, but right now, Daniel, her fiancé, needed her.

Even through all her concern for Maggie and Nina, she couldn't help but smile. Today had been one of the most incredible days of her life.

Hannah squeezed Daniel's hand to reassure him. She also knew God was there taking care of Maggie and the soon-to-be-born baby, Max. Hannah had strong, unwavering faith. It had gotten her through so much in her life. It'd kept her sane during the times when things seemed hopeless and bleak, and it grew brighter with the moments that were light and wonderful. God was always there and right now, He was with the O'Brien family.

Chapter Sixteen

Daniel

He drove as quickly as he could to the only hospital in Birch Valley. Once they arrived, he and Hannah raced inside to find his family in the waiting area. They had been in this very room before. Then, the circumstances had been awful, beyond any kind of nightmare he thought possible.

"Mom." Daniel went straight to her. Her eyes were red and raw from crying. Hannah appeared instantly. He hadn't meant to ignore her, but he was riddled with worry for Maggie. Hannah pulled Mary into a hug, and Daniel rubbed his mother's back. He looked at the rest of the family, who were seated nearby. Liam and Rachel were huddled together, sullen looks on both their faces. Patrick was missing, and Daniel realized why. There was no way Patrick could relive this all over again. Daniel's father and grandfather were also missing. "Where is everyone?"

Mary released a sigh. "Well, Patrick and Amber

are watching Melanie. Your father and Grandpa Paddy were here for a little bit, but you know how tired Grandpa Paddy gets. They will come if anything happens." Her lip started to quiver, a floating sea of tears threatening to spill from her eyes.

"Mom, what happened?"

"Oh, Daniel," his mother cried. Hannah reached for her again and cradled Mary against her chest. Hannah frowned, and all Daniel could think was that this must be all very bad. His mother was the solid rock in this family, the one who supported everyone. She was a strong woman, who, for being as sweet as she was, was not made easily vulnerable.

Liam and Rachel stood up. Rachel joined Hannah in soothing his mother, guiding the older woman to one of the uncomfortable seats. Liam grabbed Daniel's shoulder, ushering him away toward a small table which had a coffee pot set up. Daniel remembered the bitter and stale taste of that coffee from a little over four years ago, when Beth was here, when they were all here waiting for news. Daniel searched Liam's eyes, which also had hints of red and were glassy from unshed tears.

"What the hell happened, Liam?" Daniel was growing agitated.

"Well, Mom got the call from the hospital. Michael didn't have any time to call her. He called the ambulance, I guess," Liam began to explain.

Daniel had so many questions. "Why did he have to call an ambulance?" He ran his hands through his hair. No one called an ambulance unless things were very dire.

He could see that Liam was choosing his words carefully, in an attempt to keep from scaring Daniel. Too late for that. He was terrified.

"I guess after they got home, Maggie felt sick, and suddenly there was blood."

"Well, isn't that kind of normal when you are having a baby?"

Liam shook his head and shrugged. "I don't think so, not like that. So Michael called for help and they rushed her here. They ended up taking her back, I think to surgery. She'll be okay though, Daniel."

"Well, why was she bleeding so much then? That doesn't sound good, Liam," Daniel stated firmly. "What about Melanie?"

"Michael dropped her off at Patrick's since he lives right down the street."

"Oh God, I mean, what do you think is going to happen to Maggie…to the baby? Why did this happen?" Daniel started to ramble, but the sound of a doctor coming through two large swinging doors interrupted his next set of questions. Liam and Daniel practically sprinted to see what the man had to say. The one thing that did not go unnoticed, and was absolutely horrifying, was the amount of blood that was on the his light green scrubs.

"Okay, we have some news on Maggie's condition," the doctor started to say. There wasn't anyone else in the waiting room, just the very worried O'Brien family, but the doctor searched the waiting room, almost to verify what was plain to see. There was no else waiting to hear how Maggie was doing. He offered them a weak and tight-lipped smile as he headed slowly toward them, continuing, "Well, first let me tell you all that Maggie is headed back for surgery now. We are going to perform an emergency c-section."

"So what happened?" Daniel blurted out. He was tired of no one explaining anything clearly, and his frustration was getting the better of him. He felt Hannah's eyes on him, urging him to settle down. She was sitting with his mother, their arms looped together. Thank God for her.

"Well, quite frankly, Maggie's placenta became detached. It's something that is called *Placenta abruption.* Even though it's not super common, it can happen."

Daniel wanted to roll his eyes. *Well, obviously it can happen.*

"Will Maggie be okay?" Mary's voice was laced with stringent concern and fear.

"Ma'am, that's our goal here. Luckily, she lives here in town, so they were able to bring her in right away. I'll be back with an update as soon as the c-section is over, or if anything changes." He disappeared behind the swinging doors.

The last part was not necessary, Daniel felt. It felt like hours, but in reality only about forty-five minutes had passed by the time Michael emerged from the doors, dressed in scrubs. He looked exhausted but deliriously happy.

"Max is here!"

Everyone jumped up from their place, except for Rachel. She was having some trouble getting out her chair.

"How's Maggie, dear?" Mary asked, her hands

clasped together. She had been praying nonstop, the rosary she kept in her purse still tangled around her fingers.

"She's fine. They did a c-section, and little Max, who is not so little, was born. They were able to stop the bleeding and get Maggie all taken care of," Michael tried to explain, but it was obvious he was still recovering from shock.

"How big is Max?" Liam asked as he shook Michael's hand and pulled him in for a hug.

"Over nine pounds, if you all can believe it. He's beautiful, you guys." Michael's eyes grew shiny, filling with the beaming pride of having a new baby.

Relief came in another wave as the doctor returned. Michael slipped back to be with Maggie and Max. The doctor went on to explain how they were able to deliver a very healthy baby and that they were able to repair some of the tears in Maggie's uterus. Daniel almost passed out as he tried to listen to the doctor explain the procedure. But what he learned was that his sister was fine, his brand new nephew was a healthy whopper of an infant, and having Hannah there to help with his mother and alleviate his stress made all the difference. Today had been a remarkable day all around and proved to Daniel once again the O'Brien family could get through anything, as long as they were there for each other.

***

Maggie

Morning light infiltrated the room. She was confused for a brief moment, but the searing pain reminded her of what had happened the night before. Maggie looked over and saw a plastic tub, a swaddled and stirring Max inside of it. Michael was in an awkward position on a reclining chair, looking rumpled but still as sexy as ever.

Wincing as she tried to move a little in the hospital bed, Maggie was glad everything had ended well. She had never been so terrified in her entire life. When they had returned home from a lovely day at Cider Fest, she had felt exhausted and almost ill. In all fairness, she really hadn't felt well all day, but after learning her brother was going to be proposing to Hannah, she wanted to be there to witness that special moment. But once they got home, Michael went to get Melanie ready for bed. Maggie had a sip of water, felt the urge to use the bathroom, and noticed she was bleeding profusely. She calmly called for Michael, asking for just him to come in. She didn't want to alarm Melanie, let alone traumatize her, but Maggie had been scared and started praying. Once Michael entered their bathroom, the color drained from his face. He'd turned around and immediately called 911. Not long after, the sound of sirens splintered through their quiet neighborhood. Maggie recalled feeling weak and suddenly tired. The rush of activity at the hospital didn't bother her like it should have.

Looking back at it now, she realized she had lost enough blood to impair her thinking. She barely recalled recovery, Michael standing over her holding something in a stark white blanket or towel.

Maggie wasn't quite sure where she was or what happened, but then she remembered the darkness that followed. Sometime during the night, she wasn't exactly sure when or what time, her mother had been at her bedside. Then Liam and Daniel. No Patrick, but Maggie's brain was able to retrieve that answer for his absence quite easily and with little effort. Hannah and Rachel wore happy, quiet smiles. Then they were all gone. During the middle of the night she'd heard him—Max. Michael quickly snatched him up, trying to soothe the very loud and demanding son of theirs. Maggie felt herself smile, but then sleep came again. Now it was semi-bright in the room. Her senses were still a little muddy, but she knew one thing: Max was here.

***

Rachel

Rachel felt a swift kick from inside her. Her eyes fluttered open and she rubbed her belly, begging whichever daughter it was to settle down in there. She glanced over and caught sight of Liam, his naked torso exposed, their comforter bunched near his waist. Her brain started to replay the events of the night before. It had seemed like a nightmare, and though everything had ended well, Rachel now saw how something explosive affected the O'Brien family. They rallied around each other, but seeing Mary so shattered and distraught, that broke Rachel's heart. Seeing a mother's intense love for one of her children, her daughter, well, it opened

Rachel's eyes to a lot of things. After breakfast she was going to call her mother. Then they would be going to the hospital to visit Maggie and cuddle that precious Max.

She had no idea just how adorable he would be. If she weren't already pregnant, she would demand Liam and her have a baby. She loved the way Max fit into her arms, and the hints of his sweet scent she caught as she hovered above his beanie-covered head. He was pure magic, and Rachel knew without a doubt that motherhood was now something she felt privileged to experience. Her mind wandered to all the fun she and Maggie were going to have with their children, especially with them being so close in age. What Rachel kept forgetting was that she was getting two for the price of one. She was going to have her hands full, but after seeing how excited the family was at the birth of this special little boy, she knew they would be there for her daughters as well.

"What are you doing up?" Liam's voice sounded sleepy and scratchy. He yawned and stretched, revealing even more of his skin.

"Just thinking."

"About what?" He moved to face her, his hand grazing her cheek and moving the hair out of her eyes. Those pesky bangs.

"Just about how last night went. I think I'm in love." Rachel exhaled softly.

"Really?" Liam raised his eyebrow at her with interest.

Rolling her eyes, she playfully slapped at his chest. "Max. And babies in general."

215

"Well, I guess it's a good thing we got you pregnant." He inched closer to her.

"I guess so." Rachel took in her husband's handsome face. Liam's jaw was covered in a rusty brown-colored stubble, his eyes heavy and sleepy but deliciously sexy. At the sight of his nude chest and the tight and smooth muscles of his abdomen, she couldn't resist letting her fingers travel down the length of his torso. He gave her a wicked smirk, one which dared her to move further down. Rachel was up for a challenge.

***

Amber

Patrick was flipping his famous pancakes, and the wonderful smell of the cooking batter filled the kitchen and dining room. Amber started to set plates on the table. Last night had been exhausting, filled with worry and finally relief at the arrival of baby Max entering the world. Melanie was anxious to meet her baby brother, and they would all be going to the hospital after breakfast. The house was filled with more energy than Amber's coffee could keep up with. Finn and Connor were watching cartoons with Melanie in the living room, and Dylan was still asleep like a typical teenager.

Amber crossed back into the kitchen and got the milk and juice out of the fridge. She stared at Patrick, who wore dark forest-green pajama bottoms and a well-loved and faded Seattle Mariners t-shirt.

"You doing okay?" Amber asked Patrick, who seemed lost in his own world, but on auto-pilot as he flipped the golden round circles of perfection. She paused as she reached into the cupboard to get a few cups for the kids.

"Yeah, I'm just glad it all turned out okay, you know?" His face was still covered in creases from the pillow. They hadn't slept much, and the little they got consisted of a lot of tossing and turning. Patrick had called out in his sleep at one point, waking Amber. After that, it had been nearly impossible to fall back asleep. Watching him as he poured some batter, he looked rather worn and disheveled, but he was still sexy in her eyes.

She stretched, trying to reach his cheek to kiss him. "But it did turn out well, and now you get to meet a new nephew today. We should probably bring something fun to Maggie's room since she will be there at least a couple days." Amber started planning out some ideas in her mind: balloons, a bouquet of flowers, and maybe some yummy treats.

"Whatever you think is best." His answers were clipped, and she could tell his mind was miles away.

Grief was something that changed. It never quite left, but eventually it loosened its hold. That was, until something triggered it, giving it permission to seize down again. At least that was how Amber viewed the process of grieving. She should know. She'd wrestled with it until Patrick had entered her life. He'd made her feel alive again. When her husband died, Amber had lost herself, or at least an enormous part of who she was. It had taken her a long time to figure out how to go on with a huge hole in her heart and soul. One thing Amber realized was, that as each day passed, Patrick filled that hole, that horribly empty and sad space. He was now taking up room in her heart and soul. But in moments such as these, where Patrick was distracted and obviously thinking about Beth, grieving those missing bits and chunks of their life together, Amber couldn't help but wonder if she was even filling up his heart and soul. Was Patrick still clinging to the memories of Beth?

***

Hannah

She had faith things would ultimately work out. Granted, that didn't stop her from feeling sick to her stomach as Mary sobbed, as she saw Daniel angry and hurting. When the doctor had appeared, covered in Maggie's blood, she briefly questioned her faith, a split second of doubt, but she'd buried it quickly. The morning sunlight burse through the house, birds chirped and sang cheerfully outside, and the promise of another day unfolded in front of her.

Hannah marched happily with a little more bounce in her step, on the way to feed her chickens. She spied her father coming from the barn. He waved. This morning at breakfast he had explained how Daniel had come to him two different times, one to ask if he could court her, and the second to ask for her hand in marriage. Hannah had been at a loss for words. She hadn't know that Daniel had done that. It warmed her heart, knowing he had considered her father's feelings.

She had just finished feeding and collecting eggs from her chickens, who all seem to be extra feisty today, when she heard the phone inside the house ringing. Hannah hurried inside, to the nearest room with a phone, and picked up the receiver that was in the kitchen.

"Hello?" She could hear some scrambled noises in the background, and what to her ears sounded like sniffling.

"Hannah." It was Nina.

"Nina, my God, where are you? Are you okay?"

There a distinct pause, almost as if Nina weren't quite sure she wanted to make this call, but she finally answered, "Yes, I'm okay. I'm in Spokane, at the bus station."

It couldn't be possible. Her sister had come back. "Do you need me to come get you?'

"Please." Nina's voice sounded harsh, yet weakened with the sound of defeat. But in Hannah's eyes it took guts to come back, and she was thrilled that her sister would be where she could keep an eye on her. Much like the mother hen she just wrassled with to get eggs from, she was always watching and protecting—that was Hannah.

"I'm on my way."

She left immediately after hanging up the phone. Her relief was met with a hidden anger, and the mixture consumed her as she drove the hour to Spokane's bus depot.

Hannah wasn't prepared for what she saw when she arrived to get Nina. Nina looked even thinner, if that were even possible, and the rims of her eyes were pink and raw from crying. Her cheeks were sunken in, and her face wore a mask of sorrow.

Hannah wrapped her arms around her frail sister, all feelings of anger dissipating. She wanted nothing more than to protect Nina.

Chapter Seventeen

Rachel

"So you'll pick up Chelsea and my mom tomorrow, right?"

"Yes, for the thousandth time. Why are you so freaked out?" Liam asked as Rachel stirred the pot on the stove. She was heating some soup for dinner, as she wasn't up for actually cooking anything. Work was driving her crazy. Rachel felt exhausted, and now the baby shower was that coming weekend. It was all too much for her to handle, so a can of soup was tonight's dinner.

"I'm not freaked out, thank you very much. I just have a lot going on."

Liam came up behind her, linking his long arms around her. "Everything will be fine. I know you are worried about your mom coming up." He kissed the back of her exposed neck, sending tiny shivers down her spine. "You need to relax. You're too tense."

"Easy for you to say, she's not *your* mother."

221

"Well, she kind of is now, and trust me, mother-in-laws have a way worse rap."

"Not mine, she's pretty darn amazing."

Liam laughed and kissed her neck again. "I suppose you're right."

***

Liam pulled up the curb. Children were slowly entering the school. He leaned over to kiss Rachel as she undid her seat belt.

"Try not to worry," Liam begged. "I love you."

Rachel looked back as she got out of her silver BMW. "Love you too. Drive safe." He grinned and gave her a wink.

She watched as the silver paint seemed to glitter in the morning sun. Rachel started for the school. She couldn't shake an odd sense of worry or dread. When she'd woken up that morning, the day seemed daunting and she was feeling a great deal of anxiety. Rachel didn't tell Liam. There was no point, as he would just tell her not to worry and try to pacify her feelings. She could only reason that it had to do with her mother's arrival. The upside was that Chelsea was arriving as well. Her best friend would become the buffer. Chelsea had a magical way with Evelyn. There were times when Rachel envied how easily the two got along. Rachel exhaled as she opened one of the double front doors to the school, allowing several children to enter, giving them a happy smile and well wishes for the day.

Karen was talking to a parent but gave Rachel a

slight wave as she headed down the hall to her office. She just felt like hiding in there, her own little cave. It was dark and quiet, and Rachel couldn't help but be tempted to rest her head on her desk and nap. That's all she ever felt like doing anymore. She was just plain exhausted. The gentle knock on her office door alarmed her.

Poking her head inside, Karen had a serious look on her face. "Rachel, Liam's on the phone."

Rachel figured he was still headed to Spokane to pick up her mother and Chelsea. She glanced up at the clock mounted on the wall. There was no way that he would be there yet. "Thanks, Karen, go ahead and transfer it into here, if you would please." Seconds later, a red light blinked on the multi-line phone on her desk. "Hello?"

"Just checking in on you."

"Liam, I'm fine." No, she wasn't. That was a complete lie. She was tired, irritated, and just plain hormonal, but she mainly craved sleep.

"You seemed out of sorts and I wanted to see if you were feeling better." She appreciated his concern, but she was slightly annoyed he could see through her, that he knew her better than she knew herself at times.

"I promise." The bell rang out loudly. "I need to go. I will call you later."

He hesitated before responding, "Okay, I love you."

"Love you too." She did love him, and if she weren't so cranky she would even find his worry and checking up on her adorable. But right now she had to make it through the day while fighting this nagging anxiety, and then she had to mentally prepare herself to deal with her mother.

***

Liam

The highway was nearly vacant as he drove south to Spokane. He turned on the radio, carefully sipped coffee out of his travel mug, and tried to push the thoughts of worry out of his mind. Rachel seemed off that morning. He knew a lot of it had to do with her mother coming, the baby shower, and just being plain worn out. Liam had no idea how women dealt with being pregnant, and he felt it was his job to make Rachel as comfortable as possible. After going through the scare with Maggie, it made him realize how unprepared he was, in so many ways. Mainly, he was unprepared if something were to happen to Rachel.

The sky was bright with vivid hues of blue, and the giant, fluffy, cotton ball-looking clouds seem to hover within arm's reach. Looking ahead, Liam could see the burst of colors on either side of the highway, the trees proudly displaying the splendor of fall. Eastern Washington was gorgeous every season, but autumns were incredible. This was a typical October. The vibrant tones, with varied shades of red, orange, and gold would last until November, sometimes all the way until Thanksgiving. Then the trees would be barren of their magnificent glory.

The drive to Spokane seemed to take forever, but

the scenery kept Liam company. He hadn't felt nervous until now, but he really didn't mind Chelsea or Evelyn. They each loved Rachel and that's all that truly mattered to him. Liam hoped that seeing her best friend would cheer her up, but her mother, not so much. He spied the sprawling city of Spokane ahead in the distance. Liam didn't mind it, but he preferred the quiet community of Birch Valley.

He steered the car into the terminal at the airport, scanning to see if he could locate Evelyn or Chelsea. He noticed Rachel's overly blonde and bubbly friend waving him down, a Louis Vuitton rolling suitcase next to her and a gigantic purse, that she could probably fit into, slung on her thin shoulders. Liam saw Evelyn, posh looking as always, wearing large sunglasses, masking her emotions. She turned and spoke to a man who stood beside her and Chelsea. She pointed in Liam's direction. Liam maneuvered the BMW carefully along the curb, switching on the hazard lights. He got out to greet them.

"Evelyn. Chelsea. How are you guys?" Liam hugged each one as the man watched, making Liam quite uncomfortable.

Evelyn spoke first. "Hello, dear." She turned toward the man, her demeanor aloof as she introduced him, "This is Robert, Rachel's father."

Liam was taken aback. He had not been aware he was coming up, and Liam was pretty sure Rachel had no idea either. He extended his hand to the man with a golden tan, polo shirt, and perfectly stark white teeth. "Hello, sir. I'm Liam."

"Yes, I'm well aware." Robert was cool, hesitating to accept Liam's hand, but he finally shook it, gripping it a little firmer than necessary.

"Pleasure to meet you, Robert."

"I'm sure it's more of a surprise." A smug look paraded across Robert's face.

Liam nodded. He had him there. "It is, but a pleasant one. I'm sure Rachel will be thrilled."

Chelsea seemed to choke on the air, coughing. Evelyn gave her a sour look. "Liam, I assure you this was very last-minute." She glared at Robert hard from even behind her trendy sunglasses. They acted as a mask, but they couldn't hide her irritation with her ex-husband.

Chelsea shot Liam a sympathetic look. "So, how is my best friend?" Liam started loading the luggage into the truck of the car.

"Well, she's exhausted, for one. She is not so keen on this shower either, but I think with you guys being here maybe she will have a change of heart."

Evelyn moved closer to Liam and Chelsea. "We will get her in the spirit for this baby shower. I actually spoke with your mother, Liam. She's quite excited."

"Yes, it's all she's been talking about for the entire week." Liam lifted the heavy designer suitcase into the trunk.

Evelyn started for the front passenger side, but Robert protested quietly. Their squabble was loud enough for Chelsea and Liam to hear.

"Are they always like this?" Liam nodded in Rachel's parents direction.

"Oh, Liam, you have no idea. This is nothing. They aren't all sweet like the O'Briens."

Liam whispered, "Hey, Rachel doesn't know her dad is here. What should we do?"

Chelsea exhaled, then bit her bottom lip. "I know. I wanted to text her, but I know she's stressed. When I arrived at the airport this morning, there he was. I didn't know what to do. Any suggestions?"

"You got me there. I mean, it's her dad. Maybe she will be happy about seeing him." Liam shrugged. He knew that was mostly wishful thinking on his part. He knew very well Rachel was going to freak out. He just wasn't so sure if he should warn her beforehand.

"Well, there isn't a whole lot we can really do about it. The question is where will everyone be staying? There's a hotel in Birch Valley, right?"

Liam nodded. "Yeah. I figured you and your mother would stay at our place. I can stay over at my mom's, or even at Patrick's."

"How is that brother of yours?" A smirk appeared on her face. He wasn't too sure if she was genuinely asking about Patrick or if she was being sarcastic. He was going to go with the latter. When Chelsea had been here for Liam and Rachel's wedding, they tried double dating with Chelsea and Patrick. It had been an unpleasant disaster, to say the least.

"Um, we probably better head out. You guys hungry?" Liam redirected the question awkwardly.

Chelsea rolled her eyes and started to get into the car. No one could agree on a thing: where to eat, the weather, the traffic. Literally everything was up for debate. Liam felt the tension brewing in the car; it was thick and heavy. There was no way Rachel was going to be happy about this. He snuck his phone out and proceeded to send her a text as discreetly as possible.

"Are you texting and driving?" Robert asked in a firm tone.

"Uh, I…uh."

"Isn't that illegal here?" Evelyn started to question. It seemed to be that if one made a comment, the other needed to add to it.

"Oh please, Evelyn, you are the queen of texting and driving," Robert spat.

"Are you serious? You live on your phone. It's always been glued to you."

"I need to be available for my clients. What's your excuse, Evelyn?" Liam caught sight of Robert's perfect tan starting to tinge with red.

"Sorry, I was just letting Rachel know we were on our way," Liam apologized. He looked forward, staying focused on the highway stretched in front of him. He could feel their eyes watching him.

"Wow, Liam, the trees are gorgeous. Is it always like this?" Chelsea asked in an obvious attempt to rescue him.

"Every fall. Lovely, isn't it?" He was thankful because Robert and Evelyn turned their attention to the splendid scenery outside their windows. Yeah, Liam was sure of it. Rachel was not going to be happy one bit.

***

Rachel

Oh God. She had just received a text message from Liam. It was clipped, and there were some misspellings, almost as if he were in a hostage situation. But she got the gist, and she was not thrilled. Angry was a more accurate description. Her father had decided to come up. Why hadn't her mother or Chelsea, especially her, warned Rachel? She couldn't help but wonder what Robert Montgomery wanted. He had refused to come to her wedding. She had kept her distance after that, only responding to the rare email he would send. Her brother, Ethan, had tried to make excuses for him, but ultimately agreed their father was at fault. Rachel understood he may not have agreed with the rushed nuptials and the unplanned pregnancy, and he had been dead set against her moving up to Birch Valley, not because it was so far away, but it wasn't anywhere prestigious enough for him. Should she have chosen Seattle or Portland, anywhere but the sleepy, rural community of Birch Valley, he would have been fine.

A knock on her office door disrupted her thoughts. Karen peeked in. "Your hubby is on the phone."

"Thanks, Karen." Rachel offered her a weak smile. She wasn't happy, not one bit, and it was difficult to try to mask her annoyance. But Karen was kind and sweet, and certainly didn't deserve to have any of Rachel's grief taken out on her.

After Karen carefully closed the door, Rachel reached for the phone on her desk. "Hello?"

"Hey, babe." She could hear the hesitation in his voice, as though he were walking on eggshells.

"So where is he now?"

"Well, we just got back into town. He asked to be dropped off at the motel here, and your mom and Chelsea are actually window shopping."

"Where are you?" Rachel didn't mean to snap at him. It wasn't his fault any of this was happening. Rachel felt dizzy, upset, and almost queasy, something she hadn't felt for almost six months. She was due in less than a month, and her first couple months of pregnancy had been spent near a toilet.

"Rachel, I'm sorry, hon. I know you aren't happy. I was totally surprised. I don't think he likes me much," Liam slowly answered. "I'm over at my brothers' shop."

"Oh, Liam, I'm sorry. I don't mean to bite your head off. I don't feel well, and it's just annoying that he's here. I mean, this is for a baby shower. It would have meant more if he would have come up for our wedding." Rachel felt her throat tighten, her eyes burning with tears begging to be shed.

"I'm sorry, babe. Maybe you guys can work this out somehow?"

Rachel severely doubted that. She glanced up at the clock. School was about to let out. "You coming to pick me up soon?"

"Getting ready to leave here. What do you want to do about dinner? It might be easier to go out?"

"No, I think we will order out, but it's probably best if we handle this is at home, don't you think?"

"Why? Are you going to make a scene?" Liam

teased, but she could hear the seriousness behind it.

"With the way I feel right now, anything is possible." She wasn't lying either. Rachel couldn't explain her swirling emotions, or the twisted knots forming in her stomach. Yet there was a sense of excitement at seeing Chelsea, though she was a little mad with her. At least Liam had the sense to try to warn her. Chelsea could have least sent her a message. What could have Rachel done, stop the plane?

"You know, maybe we should just go to Herrick's?" Liam offered.

Rachel responded harshly, "Why? So that way I'm so embarrassed I can never show my face again? I love Herrick's, but it's my happy place, Liam. I won't let my dad ruin it for me."

"True, you do love their fries."

"I sure do." Rachel could almost taste the homemade golden fried shoestrings of perfection.

"Remind me never to upset you. The thought of you choosing fries over me, well, it's pretty sad."

"Well, I don't need to remind you just how scrumptious Herrick's fries are, do I?"

"I'm not scrumptious?" She could almost picture him pouting.

Rachel let out a laugh, and Liam joined her. She would get through this because she had Liam.

***

Rachel exhaled the breath she had been storing inside her cheeks, her arm looped through Liam's as they walked to the table where her father, mother, and Chelsea were seated. Liam had told them to join them for dinner at the only Mexican restaurant in the whole county, Burrito Borealis. It was so out of place, and it didn't look one bit like a traditional Mexican food place—at least not like the ones in southern California. The decor was woodsy and very Pacific Northwest, with shadowed sculptures of moose and deer on the walls. There was a mural of the aurora borealis on the ceiling. It might not look like a place that would have extraordinary burritos, but they were there, and they even gave the burritos back home a run for their money.

Evelyn and Chelsea hopped out of the seats and ran to her. "Oh my God, you are huge," Chelsea exclaimed, but then seemed to regret her words. "But, like, in a totally awesome way. I mean, you're having twins, Rachel. Oh, I'll just shut up now," Chelsea rambled, laughing as she hugged Rachel tightly.

"I have missed you so much," Rachel replied. She felt the tightness in her chest return as she was overcome with emotion.

"Me too." Chelsea seemed reluctant to let her go. Evelyn pulled Rachel away.

"Let me look at you. Oh wow, you are having twins. But you're positively glowing, Rachel." Her mother squeezed her lightly. "Pregnancy looks fantastic on you."

"Thanks, Mom."

Finally her father approached, almost sizing her up. Well, he looked like he always had, dressed in a crisp polo shirt, his tan set off by the pale, robin-egg blue. He flashed her his perfect Newport Beach smile. "Rachel."

"Dad," Rachel managed. Robert paused. He didn't seem sure if he should hug her, but then decided to very awkwardly and quickly side-hug her.

"Why don't we have a seat?" Liam had sensed her discomfort and guided her to the table.

Looking over the menu, they all debated on what sounded good. Her parents had a small squabble over whether or not the salsa had cilantro or oregano in it. Somehow, they managed to get halfway through their burritos before another argument started to heat up.

"Robert, honestly, you have no idea what you are talking about. You haven't even been here before. Remember when our daughter got married in July and you were too busy?" Evelyn spat, her voice pitched loudly.

"She knows perfectly why I didn't attend." Robert swung a quick glance in her direction. Rachel swallowed, looking to Liam. She saw a muscle tick in his jaw. He was harboring his temper, trying to show restraint, but Rachel knew that, as easygoing as Liam was, he could get upset, especially when it came to protecting those he loved.

Rachel peeked over at Chelsea, who frowned back and stared down at her food. Chelsea had witnessed many fights between her parents. This wasn't anything new, but that didn't change how utterly embarrassing and uncomfortable it was. Rachel felt her head starting to pound as her parents started to both raise their voices. Yes, not going to Herrick's had been wise.

"You have no idea how important it was. She needed you, Robert. You're her father. You should have walked her down the aisle, end of story." Evelyn was fuming, and her milky skin was blotchy with pink patches as the color crawled up her throat.

"Evelyn, you didn't want to go to the wedding either, so quit trying to act like you're the perfect parent." Robert was smug, glaring hard at her mother.

"At least I showed up," Evelyn countered, staring him down. She was not going to relent. This had been a problem for years. Neither of them could compromise, and they would square off, unrelenting, with no one apologizing or backing down.

"Guys, please stop." Rachel felt her back stiffen, a searing pain driving through her. Her brain felt fuzzy, her chest aching. God, was she having a heart attack? Pressure was building fast. It felt as though someone was on top of her. She couldn't breathe. It was as though her lungs were emptying, becoming deflated balloons. The pounding in her head had migrated to her ears, increasing with a piercing ringing of a siren. She could hear someone talking to her, but their words were confusing and muddled. What was happening to her?

***

Liam

"Rachel?" Her eyes had become fixed, her breathing irregular, as if she were gulping for air. Liam gingerly shook her. "Babe, are you okay?"

Liam started to panic. He sent a glare to Rachel's parents. This was their fault.

"Chelsea, call nine-one-one," Liam ordered. He rubbed Rachel's back soothingly, willing her to breathe. She continued to suck in the air, fear present in her blue eyes. Liam had never been so scared as he was in that moment.

"Oh, Rachel," Evelyn cried and then turned to Robert. "This is your fault."

"It's both of yours," Liam shouted back. "Robert, how do you think your daughter feels that you wouldn't come to her wedding, one of the single most important days of her life? And then you just show up now."

Robert started to answer, but Liam shot him a look which told him to hold his tongue. "I understand she's your daughter, but she's my wife and the mother to both of my daughters." Liam glared back at Evelyn. "Evelyn, you know how stressed she is, and this is not helping. We need to figure out what is happening. So just enough with the fighting, okay? Is Robert in the wrong for not being here? Absolutely. But it's in the past and he's here now, hopefully to right things with his daughter." Liam sent Robert a glare.

"You're right, Liam. You love our Rachel, and I can't tell you how much I appreciate you standing up for her." Evelyn got out of her seat, her eyes wet with tears. She started to pat Rachel and kiss the top of her head. She looked to Liam. "Thank you for loving our daughter so much." Evelyn kissed Liam on top of his head, then returned her attention on Rachel.

"Hey, Liam, the ambulance is on its way, okay?" Chelsea called out as she went to Rachel's side. He nodded a curt thanks to her. They all surrounded Rachel, but she was still gasping for air, almost like a fish out of water. Her eyes were wide, and Liam did the only thing his mother had taught him to do when things seemed too far out of control—pray. Praying worked in several ways as far as Liam was concerned. One, it calmed down the person praying, allowing them to focus their worry. Two, asking God to help never hurt, and he wasn't about to risk not asking Him to watch over Rachel and their girls.

Two men with a stretcher entered the restaurant. They worked quickly, taking vitals, trying to gauge what was wrong with Rachel, and to stabilize her for the short ride to the hospital. Liam recognized one of the EMTs, a guy he had grown up with, but he had been a grade or two above him—probably in Patrick's grade.

"Do you know what could be wrong?" Liam asked him, as the man jotted down some numbers onto a notepad.

"You know, hard to say. Panic attack, maybe? Her blood pressure is dangerously high. Did you want to ride in the ambulance with her?"

"I will," Evelyn answered instead. The man looked to Liam for approval, and Liam nodded.

Evelyn hugged Liam before she followed the stretcher out. Chelsea stood next to Liam. Robert was still seated, his face frozen in shock.

"Do you think she will be okay, Liam?" Chelsea asked softly, tears hanging off her eyelashes.

"Well, just pray. Let's head over to the hospital."

Liam walked to Robert, placing his hand firmly on his shoulder. "Do you want to go with us?"

Robert simply nodded. He struggled to speak, but clamped his lips shut. Rising from his seat, he followed Liam.

***

Rachel

Dreams were a funny thing. Sometimes they moved fast, like a flurry of activity she couldn't quite capture. Other times they were vivid and real, but this was not one of those times. The sounds of everything around her were muted and that only confused her more, but dreams were like that. Rachel just didn't recall going to bed. She wracked her brain, begging herself to wake up. Willing herself to not allow the dream to swallow her up, she blinked hard. Pain still traveled around her body, but it settled in her back and chest. She never had felt pain in a dream before. It was so odd, all the sensations she was experiencing, like she was moving, but she was laying down and moving. It didn't make any sense at all, and Rachel gave up trying to figure things out. Her dream went dark, but only briefly.

"Rachel." Rachel could hear now. Sound was present once again, but it seemed distant. She felt her eyes fluttering open to see who was calling for her through the tunnel. She looked up to see Dr. Salinger standing next to her. Blinking hard and trying to shove the fog out of her brain, Rachel tried

237

sitting up. "No, you just lay there, okay?" Dr. Salinger's voice was soothing, but it sounded like it was surrounded by a tin, almost metal echo. Rachel couldn't figure out why her doctor sounded that way, which made her feel even more out of place and worried.

"Rachel, you are here in the hospital." Dr. Salinger spoke slowly, pronouncing each word carefully. "Your babies are fine."

Rachel was shocked Dr. Salinger knew she was going to ask that, and thankful she didn't need to try to construct the sentence. Her mouth was dry and felt slightly numb. What had happened to her? The haze was starting to lift and Rachel could see Liam, with a look of concern she had never seen before. Her mother's eyes were red, and Chelsea's flawless makeup was smudged from crying. All of sudden, Rachel's mind started to fire off the last bits of pictures of where she had been. The Mexican food restaurant. Her father, where was he? She turned and saw him with his head cradled in his hands. She had never seen him look distraught. Again, Rachel pondered what had happened.

Dr. Salinger's soft voice started to explain why Rachel was in that hospital bed, and Rachel was thankful her brain was allowing her to understand what was being said. Though one phrase stuck out more than high blood pressure and severe panic attack—*strict bed rest.*

Chapter Eighteen

Rachel

"I wish you would quit making such a fuss, Liam. Geez, I'm fine now."

Liam frowned. "Look, that was the scariest thing I have been through, so just stop being difficult and let us take care of you."

Rachel huffed. She had only been home from the hospital for two days, and she was done being babied. Of course she had been scared too, as she had no idea what even had happened. She was thankful that her daughters were fine, but with Liam, Chelsea, her mother, and even her father constantly hovering over her, watching her every single movement, every breath she took, it had just become too much. Even the O'Brien family had stopped by to check on her. Then that was met with constant phone calls making sure nothing had changed since the last time they had called, which usually was only a span of twenty or so minutes. She'd had enough.

"Tomorrow is the shower. You excited?" Chelsea asked from across the living room of the cabin. Chelsea was curled into the recliner. She had been playing on her cell phone all afternoon, obviously distracted by something or, rather, someone.

"Well, oddly enough, yes. I think mainly because I'm dying to leave the house."

Liam returned into the living room with a serving tray. He had made tea for all of them. Her mother was out with Mary working on last-minute touches for the baby shower. Her father had stayed for the last two days, and they spent most of their time talking and breaking some ground on the many deep issues they had buried over the years. Liam had driven her father to the airport that morning, and returned in a great mood, not because he was rid of this man, but because they were forming a relationship. Rachel's episode, as she called it, had brought some peace to their family, even if it was temporary.

"Here, babe. It's hot, so be careful." Liam handed her a cup, then gave one to Chelsea.

"Thanks, Liam," Chelsea said, turning her attention back to her phone.

"Okay, I have to ask, who or what are you doing on that phone? You have been like surgically attached to it all flippin' day," Rachel said.

Chelsea rolled her eyes. "Whatever, mother." She laughed and then explained, "Actually, if you must know, it's this guy I am kind of seeing."

"You didn't mention you were dating someone. Details, please."

Liam took that as his cue and carried his tea to the kitchen. "I'm going to go grade some papers. If you need me…" He bent down to kiss the top of her head as he passed the couch.

She stopped him in mid-sentence. "Yes, I know, geez. I'm not an invalid. Go grade papers before your boss fires you."

"Oh, babe, you wouldn't want to do that, then I would be here all the time."

"Good point." Rachel kissed him backed as he leaned over the couch, and then shooed him away. Turning her attention back to Chelsea. "Okay, spill it."

"Well, his name is Ian, and he actually used to live in Spokane," Chelsea started to explain.

"That's sort of cool. So tell me more. What's he like? How did you guys meet?"

"It's funny actually. Do you remember Kimberly?"

"Sort of, wasn't she in your yoga class?"

Chelsea nodded. "Yes, well, her boyfriend plays on the Angels baseball team. So she had some tickets and invited me, and I figured, why not? So we went and it's actually a lot more fun than I realized. And the uniforms, Rachel, my God," Chelsea started to ramble.

"Okay, I got it, you love baseball now. But what does this all have to do with Ian, was it?"

Chelsea sighed and paused briefly, as if composing her thoughts. "Yes, it has everything to do with how I met Ian. So, here we are at this game, suddenly a player hits what I guess is called a homer or something. Well, the ball winds up in my beer cup." Chelsea started laughing, and Rachel joined her. Only something crazy like that would happen to her pal. "So, next thing I know, people are sort of surrounding me, like trying to take the ball. Then this guy, wearing some other team's hat, I think it's a Washington team, but anyway, he sort of protects me and tells everyone to back off."

"Aww, your knight in shining armor, well, baseball cap. I bet it was a Seattle Mariners hat. Liam and Michael love them."

"Yeah, that's the team. So then this guy is like so hot, Rachel, like seriously smoking hot."

"Nice. Boy, you sure know how to find them."

"Oh please, you got yours."

Liam shouted from the kitchen, "I can hear you both, and yes, Chelsea's right, you got yours, so quit drooling."

"Leave us alone and keep grading those papers," Rachel teased back. "Okay, so tell me more about Mr. Mariners-baseball-loving hottie."

"Oh there's so much to tell you." Chelsea was practically bouncing the recliner in excitement. "He introduced himself and told me that he would ignore the fact I had on an Angels shirt and had caught a ball from his team. I noticed a little girl was next to him. She had on the same hat and looked so sad. So I offered her the ball."

"Look at you, being all sweet. Wait, you own an Angels shirt?" Rachel asked, knowing full well that Chelsea pretty much despised children. They were not an accessory she wanted to wear.

"Well, turns out the little girl is his daughter. And, well, Kimberly gave it to me, it's super cute."

"Oh no, deal breaker?" Rachel groaned.

"Hell, Rachel, if you saw this guy, you would understand why I don't care. But anyway, so Ian introduces himself and his little girl, Mackenzie. How adorable is that name?"

Rachel was shocked to see Chelsea so affected by this guy. This was so unlike her.

"So, then we get to talking, and he asks me for my number when the game is over."

"Who won?" Liam called out again from the kitchen.

"I don't know, Liam. I wasn't paying attention," Chelsea shouted back to him.

"Never mind him. Okay, so you guys obviously hit it off. What's his deal?" Rachel asked.

Chelsea rolled her eyes. "Well, get this, his sister owns a modeling agency down in LA. Ian lived in Spokane his entire life. His sister moved, started this business, and eventually convinced him to sign on with her."

"What? He's a model?" Rachel choked on her tea. "Chelsea, show me a picture of this guy."

"Yes, he's a model. But he does some other job. I think like a motorcycle mechanic or something. But he's a model, Rachel," Chelsea emphasized.

"So, like, the perfect abs and all sexy and stuff?"

Chelsea nodded and handed Rachel her phone. "Look for yourself."

Rachel couldn't believe what she was looking at, and she had grown up around beautiful people her entire life. To say this guy was gorgeous was an understatement, from his muscular physique to the sexy smile and perfectly white teeth, he was a beautiful specimen of a man.

"Wow, Chelsea."

"I know, right?" Chelsea grabbed her phone back and went back into the recliner. "The thing is, he is so nice."

"What's the deal with the little girl?"

"Her mom and her actually live in Spokane, or maybe it's somewhere else. I'm not too sure. He flies her down once a month, and then has her, like, during the summers," Chelsea explained.

"How long have you known him for?" Rachel was curious why Chelsea hadn't bothered to mention Ian or his daughter, Mackenzie, until now.

"Gosh, I think the game was last month. It's still really new."

"That's so cool, Chelsea. I'm thrilled you met someone. Hopefully things get a little more serious, you know?"

Chelsea swatted at her playfully and shrugged as she said, "Rachel, I wouldn't go that far. I am just thrilled to have landed a model. He even had me come to one of his shoots they were doing for a book cover, so hot."

"You just never know." Rachel took a sip of her tea and eyed Chelsea, who had already started to go back on her phone. *Yeah, it isn't serious at all*, Rachel thought. *You're just completely infatuated.*

***

Mary and her mother had done an incredible job. They had used the cafeteria to host the shower, and Rachel honestly couldn't recall having more fun.

They played games, snacked on all sorts of delicious treats, and there were presents—tons and tons of presents. But the one thing that stood out, above all the pink streamers and balloons, was how nicely her mother and Mary got along. They almost seemed like old friends, and they were inseparable the entire time. It made Rachel sad that her mother would be leaving in the morning.

"Rachel, where do you want me to put these extra diapers? The changing table basket is full," her mother asked as they sorted all the gifts into the nursery, which her mother had magically transformed into an organized and beautiful space during her visit.

"In the closet is fine, Mom." Rachel rocked in her new gliding chair, a gift from Maggie, who obviously took notice of how much Rachel loved hers. "Mom, thank you so much."

"Oh, sweetie, I'm happy to help. I wish I could be here for the birth of those precious girls."

"I know. I'm sad you're leaving tomorrow."

Chelsea was leaving as well. She seemed eager to get back to explore her new relationship with Ian, and Rachel was excited for her. They'd discussed her coming up to visit the babies over the holidays, and Chelsea loved the idea of coming up for Christmas. Rachel's mother had promised to try to come up as well, but she wanted Rachel to get into the swing of things before bombarding her.

"Well, I think I will aim for the holidays. It would be wonderful to be here for their first Christmas," Evelyn commented as she emptied a shiny pink gift bag, separating the contents.

"I never realized you needed so much baby stuff."

"The truth of it is you won't use half of this, or they will grow too fast before they can wear all these outfits. People just can't help themselves." Her mother giggled as she held up two glittery pink dresses she had bought for the girls. "Like these, you make sure they wear these at least once, and send me a picture."

"Oh, I will." Rachel started to feel herself grow emotional. "Mom, I'm going to miss you."

Evelyn went to Rachel, wrapping her arms around her. "Me too, sweetheart. You, my beautiful girl, you are going to be an amazing mother. Far better than me, I can tell you that." Evelyn's eyes were shiny with tears.

Rachel tried to swallow past the lump forming in her throat. "Mom, you are a good mother, and though we have had some rough times, I'm glad you're my mom. But you will be an incredible grandmother because you already are."

***

Hannah

Liam had asked her to stop by the cabin to check on Rachel. She could only imagine how annoyed she must feel, constantly being watched. Hannah decided to make this fun, and as she knocked on the door to Liam and Rachel's home, she waited and continued to work out the details of her plan.

Rachel finally opened the door. Her sour

expression told Hannah she was none too pleased to see her or be bothered. "Liam sent you?"

"Yeah, I'm sorry."

"It's not your fault. I'm sorry for being grumpy."

Rachel looked exhausted. The skin under her eyes had a purplish hue. She was wearing an oversized shirt and gray sweatpants, not the most flattering outfit, but the poor woman was also pregnant with twins and due anytime. She was also a prisoner of her own home.

"It's okay. I can only imagine how rough this is," Hannah commented as she followed Rachel inside. Rachel promptly lowered herself back onto the couch.

"Have you eaten yet?" It was a little after one and Hannah was hopeful that Rachel would be hungry.

"I did, but I can always eat. That's all I do now: eat, sleep, pee, repeat. Just keep this in mind, Hannah, when that brother-in-law of mine starts asking for babies. Is this really what you want to become?" Rachel questioned, tilting her head, motioning to her large belly.

"I can't wait." Hannah laughed. "I had an idea, if you're willing."

Rachel agreed, but she didn't seem completely sold on Hannah's idea, which was having a picnic outside. She figured the fresh air could only be good for Rachel.

"You made all of this?" Rachel's eyes were wide as looked at the feast that was arranged on the glass patio table on the deck.

"Yep, a little bit of everything." Hannah started

to name off and point at all the treats she had brought. "There's enough that you could have leftovers for dinner with Liam."

Rachel started to bite into a chocolate-covered strawberry. "Oh, he's on his own. Actually, no, he can have some since he asked you to come over. I really do appreciate you going to all this trouble. You shouldn't have."

They both were seated, and Hannah poured some sparkling grape juice into two tall plastic champagne glasses she had packed. She wanted to make this seem special. Luckily, the weather was cooperating and the sun was shining, casting a warm glow on them as they dined on the deck.

"I wanted to do this. I know it has to be terrible, being cooped up in the house. It won't be too much longer."

"Less than a month, but Dr. Salinger says anytime from here on out is okay. But the longer they are in there, the better."

"So you think before Thanksgiving then?"

Rachel popped a large purple grape into her mouth. "Way before then. My due date is like around the tenth or so."

"Wow, so not much longer. Halloween is coming up soon."

"I know. I'm bummed. I wanted to take the twins and Mel out for trick or treating. I love Halloween and this was my first one here in Birch Valley."

Hannah felt awful for bringing up things that Rachel couldn't participate in. She kept putting her dang foot in her mouth, but Rachel was taking it all in stride. "Hannah, it's okay. This will pass, and

248

next year, for all we know, you could be preggers." The thought warmed Hannah. She would love to be carrying Daniel's child, to experience motherhood. They continued to gorge themselves, not leaving much in the way of leftovers. Hannah enjoyed the rest of the afternoon with Rachel. Keeping her company had been almost more good for her. They laughed and shared details about growing up. Hannah learned so much about Rachel, things she never would have guessed, and found herself truly wanting to be not only her sister-in-law, but her friend.

***

"Oh my God," Hannah heard Daniel call out, and other loud shouts followed. Mary looked at Hannah. They dropped the spoons they were using on last night's dinner, and both darted in the direction of the noise. Mary led the way, which took them to the den. It was foggy, and the smell of tobacco hung in the air. Liam, Patrick, and Daniel were all gathered around their grandfather, each of their faces were in varied shades of shock.

"What is the matter, boys?" Mary demanded.

Grandpa Paddy, who was sitting in a tattered recliner, looked up at Mary, his eyes bright and glistening with wetness. "I've won the lottery, lass."

"For Pete's sake, the lottery?" Mary seemed confused at first, then frowned. "You mean, those awful scratcher tickets that leave their shavings all over?"

"No, Mom, he bought a ticket," Daniel explained.

"Oh dear." She raised her hand to cover her mouth, and the color drained from her face.

Hannah looked over at Daniel for him to explain. She didn't know too much about gambling, other than her father had frowned upon it. He said it wasn't worth it for a man to spend his days chasing after the impossible.

Daniel stepped over to Hannah and said, "See, Grandpa Paddy has been playing the lottery for years, mainly scratcher tickets, but he's been buying the state lotto and even playing Powerball, and, well, he likes to sit and watch them draw the numbers. Liam, Patrick, and I just happened to be in here when they announced the numbers." Daniel paused, clearly getting choked up. He looked over at his grandfather. "The old man finally did it. He had all the numbers tonight, Hannah. It was his lucky day."

"That's incredible." She was speechless. The man shook. His eyes were watery and wide with disbelief that he had won such a large sum of money. Hannah watched Grandpa Paddy grasp the sliver of paper. He just stared down at it, looking at the numbers that had forever changed his life and the lives of this family.

"Isn't it? It's the most wonderful thing for him, well, for the family." Daniel exclaimed as he wrapped his arm around her shoulders. Hannah looked at Mary, who seemed to be trying to digest the good news.

The entire family, still reeling from the excitement, now gathered around the large wooden table where they had shared Sunday meals for years, where bouts of contagious laughter were heard, miserable tears of sorrow shed, and where many prayers were whispered and ultimately answered. This slab of wood, polished with their memories, good and bad, was now adding another layer of finish, one of incredible good fortune. The luck of the Irish was with the O'Brien Family on that lovely Sunday evening, just as it had always been.

Chapter Nineteen

Patrick

"God, Patrick, that was incredible," Amber exclaimed, her voice winded, and her face flushed.

He stared at her. She was gorgeous, especially after making love. Patrick leaned over and kissed her exposed collarbone, traveling to her shoulder. "You're incredible."

"Oh stop." Amber laughed, and he watched her eyes sparkle. They were the color of the Caribbean sea, a blend of green and blue, and simply breathtaking.

"It's true." Patrick couldn't stop touching her, his fingers exploring the softness of her skin under the white sheet which twisted around them. He doubted he could ever be satisfied. He was always hungry for Amber, and Patrick yearned to feel the warmth of her.

Patrick watched as her eyes closed. Her breathing grew quiet. Seeing her fall asleep made his heart fill with a flood of emotion—pure love.

He rolled over carefully, not wanting to wake her, and reached into the drawer of his night stand. This was the perfect moment he had waited for. Patrick slid closer to Amber, her dark hair fanned out on the pillow. She looked majestic, and he felt need stirring inside him again. Taking her hand in his, he slipped the ring onto her finger, then kissed her gingerly on her full lips. Amber stirred and her eyes fluttered open, confusion sweeping across her face. She smiled up at Patrick. His face close to hers, he lowered his mouth to kiss her again, needing to drink her up, a feeble attempt at quenching his longing.

"Hey, you. I must have fallen asleep." Amber's voice was raspy with sleep and deliciously sexy. Patrick squeezed her hand in his. He stared at her, giving her a moment to figure out that there was now a diamond on her finger.

He had no intention of asking her. He didn't want to risk her saying no. Patrick knew he wanted her, and he was certain Amber loved him too. He knew she loved his sons and the rest of the O'Brien family. Patrick wasn't sure he would have ever found another woman to become his wife again. He had lived under a terribly dark and stormy cloud for nearly four years, but then Amber came into his life, a bolt of light, intense and fierce, completely shattering the wall he had callously been built around his heart and soul. She had melted all the cold and despair. He found her to be amazing. She too had been given the burden of a spouse passing away, yet she was far stronger than he was. Her ability to find the silver lining in all the darkness, to have the sense to know that behind the gray clouds the sky was still blue and the sun was still shining, made him proud. What she didn't realize was that she was his sun, his moon, his beam of light to guide his path, which he had strayed from for so long. She was his *everything*.

As Patrick watched her expression change, he noticed tears pool in her eyes. She understood what he was asking. There was no exchange of words, and her bottom lip quivered as she bit down on it. Patrick hovered over her, cupping her head with his hand, to hold his precious treasure. With Patrick's promise fulfilled, he felt open to the future, their future together. He gazed into her eyes, catching a glimpse of her beautiful soul. Their lips met, and the power of unspoken words bound them in a moment that they would always remember.

***

Amber

She couldn't feel herself breathe, but she didn't need to. It was as though time froze. An intense surge of emotion was transferring between Patrick's mouth into her soul. He was her oxygen, her breath.

This was the most non-traditional proposal she could imagine, but yet it was perfect. Her mind was moving in so many directions. She had no idea he had been thinking about marriage, as they hadn't really discussed it. If anything, Amber was certain Patrick was too afraid to ever embark on another journey of matrimony. The risk was too great. He had said he wasn't sure he could survive another experience like Beth's passing. But as Amber felt the metal of her engagement ring against her skin, it hushed all her fears and doubts. He was rising above his fears as well, and that spoke volumes of the love he must feel for her.

Patrick brushed his mouth along her neck, and she welcomed the weight of his body on top of her as she linked her legs around him, securing Patrick tightly to her. She couldn't get close enough. It was as though they were trying to merge into one being, when suddenly a tidal wave of lust washed over them both. A current of desire and primal need pulled them into an undertow, again. Amber couldn't feel herself breathe. She let herself sink down into this oblivion of unrestrained rapture.

Amber's body was happily numb and spent from the beautiful love they had just made, but it had been different this time. It was a mating of souls. Again, no words were spoken—there had only been touch. It was though Patrick was laying claim, as was Amber, searing an invisible mark on each other. Patrick brought her to his chest, spooning and protectively covering her with his arm.

***

Maggie

"You want to help me change Max?" Maggie asked Melanie, who was staring down at a very cranky and stinky Max.

"He smells, Mom." Melanie pinched her nose

close dramatically.

"Well, yes, Mel, he's poopie. He doesn't mean to be such a stinker, does he?" Maggie cooed to Max. He was on the changing table kicking his legs, his face growing red as he cried, starting to demand a clean diaper. "Hang on mister."

"Here, Mom." Melanie handed her the wipes and a new diaper. "He sure is cute." Max stared at the sound of his sister's voice. "Max likes me."

"Mel, he loves you. You're his big sister, and you are such a great helper too." Maggie smiled at her daughter, quickly changing Max then re-buttoning his onesie. She couldn't resist kissing his naked little feet. Her heart swelled with love and joy as she spent time with her two children. She looked at her growing daughter, a beautiful young girl. She was smart, helpful, and athletic. Melanie was so many things Maggie was not. Her outgoing spirit was so much more Michael, and she had the mischief of an O'Brien. But Melanie was also uniquely her own person, and Maggie was so grateful to be her mother.

Max was so new to the world, his needs simple, but he let them all know there was a large personality swaddled in the pale blue blanket Maggie carried to the rocking chair. This little boy, who was not even a month old, quickly had everyone wrapped around his tiny little finger, and was already ruling the Trembley house. His hair was black, and his eyes were beginning to change from slate blue to a green, an all-too-familiar green. He had the O'Brien eyes.

Maggie didn't know it was possible to feel this

content, even with the sleepless nights and mountain of laundry begging to be done. Her heart felt as though it was had expanded to at least double its size, and she had never been happier. Her marriage was stronger than ever, they had healthy children, and their home was bursting with love.

As she glided slowly and steadily in her chair, lulling Max into a milky slumber, she heard the phone ring. "Honey, can you bring me the phone?" Melanie ran out of the nursery to answer it.

Returning with speed only a child can possess, she handed Maggie the phone. "It's Aunt Rachel, Mom."

"Thanks, sweetie." Maggie took the phone, cradling it against her neck, moving very little as to not disturb Max. "Hello?"

"Hey, Maggie."

"What's up, Rachel? Everything okay?" Maggie grew concerned. Rachel had recently been put on strict bed rest until the birth of her twins.

"Just bored. I'm so sick of doing nothing," Rachel complained.

"You pack your bag for the hospital yet?" Maggie was trying to think of tasks Rachel could maybe occupy herself with.

"I have packed it, repacked it, and repacked it again."

"Sorry. I know it sucks."

"So how is my precious little Max?" Rachel asked, her voice turning cheerful.

"He's sleeping in my arms as we speak. Hey, Halloween is coming up. I was thinking maybe I will let Michael take Mel out for trick or treating.

Maybe Liam can go with them, then you and I can hang out," Maggie offered.

"Only if Max is coming over," Rachel countered playfully.

"That's a given." Maggie laughed. "I even got him a costume. I just couldn't resist."

"Oh, really, what is he going to be, besides the most adorable little man ever?"

"I'll let it be a surprise. But it's adorable," Maggie promised.

"Well, I'm looking forward to it. I need something to look forward to. I'm so tired of being on bed rest."

"You miss work?"

"Honestly, no. I miss seeing Liam whenever I want. All I do is sleep. Like, literally, my day consists of eating and sleeping. Well, and peeing. That's my existence at the moment. So glamorous."

"Just think, next month those precious little girls will be here. Then you will still be peeing a lot, and you'll be sleep deprived. Yay!" Maggie exclaimed sarcastically.

"Calling you was a terrible idea," Rachel joked.

"Hey, what are sisters for?"

"Maggie, I really do appreciate you, you know that, right?"

"Oh, Rachel, of course. You will get through this, and if you need anything just call me."

"Thanks. I'm getting sleepy again, so I'm going to nap before dinner."

Maggie knew that feeling all too well. Her own eyes were growing heavy, and she was envious of her tiny sleeping bundle. "Me and Max will see you this weekend, okay?"

"I can't wait. Love you, Maggie."

"Hang in there, Rachel. Love you too."

***

Michael

"I'm home."

Melanie ran toward him, her chubby finger on her mouth. "Quiet, Daddy, you'll wake Max."

Michael nodded. He understood all too well how difficult it was to get their little boy back to sleep. After hugging Melanie, Michael put his briefcase away and made his way to the nursery. There he saw the most beautiful image: Maggie's eyes were closed, and Max was nestled in her arms, his little face peaceful in a delightful slumber. Maggie's chestnut hair was scooped up into a light knot on top of her head. Several long silky strands had escaped, tempting Michael to twirl them around his fingers. His wife was tired, but still simply beautiful. He tip-toed out of the room, going back toward the kitchen.

"Mel, want to help me make dinner?"

"Sure." She was such an eager helper. Melanie went to wash her hands while Michael stood in front of the pantry looking to see what he could conjure up for dinner. After grabbing a couple odds and ends, he concocted a simple meal with the help of his daughter, who truly knew her way around the kitchen.

"Was Max good today?" Michael asked as he

used a wooden spoon to stir a sauce he was heating.

"Max is always good, Dad. He's a baby," Melanie explained. He knew how much his daughter adored their new addition to their family. She defended him so easily and always wanted to help with him.

"You help change any yucky diapers?" Michael teased her. That was where Mel drew the line with her precious baby brother. She didn't like stinky diapers, not one bit.

Melanie shook her head. "We should potty train him soon."

Michael laughed. "Yeah, that's still a ways away, sweetie. But I wish we could too. We'll ask your mom."

He didn't hear her come into the kitchen, because he was too busy making Melanie giggle, taunting her with the veggies for their salad.

"It smells good in here." Maggie yawned. Michael turned around, trying to quickly remove the two carrots he had in his mouth that were acting as fangs. He found he enjoyed being more silly since they moved to Birch Valley. The lack of stress had made such a huge difference for him. Things weren't taken so seriously here in town, and everyone was friendly and kind. He regretted not moving their family here sooner. Still feeling a bit goofy, he decided to leave the thin carrot sticks lodged in his mouth and play Dracula by going for Maggie's neck.

Maggie squealed and tried to run from him, but allowed him to capture her far too easily. It was moments like these, completely unplanned, silly, and ridiculously unlike Michael, that he found were the best. Their life was different with Max now born, and everything felt whole. They were where they should be, no question. Michael had been content with their life back in Seattle, but never truly happy. He knew that providing for Maggie and Melanie was his first priority, but he had missed out on moments like this, the sheer abandonment of fun, laughter, and love. When Maggie had left their home in Seattle that spring, it'd rocked his world, but he was too stubborn to admit she was right. She had been all along. Maggie's marriage to him had meant everything to her, and he just hadn't been able to see past what he thought was important in their marriage. Michael working those insane hours, pushing to make partner, not being there for events and things that mattered most in their lives, these were the moments he would never get back. That was part of the change in their lives, realizing that family always came first, and he now knew total happiness. His only regret was not being open to it sooner.

***

Liam

"Do you need anything, babe?"

"To not be on bed rest anymore." Rachel groaned.

Liam stared at Rachel stretched out on the couch, looking every bit as bored as she sounded. The scare from only a little over week ago was enough to shake them both up. Rachel survived the baby shower, and she'd even had a little fun. She'd also mended things with her father, and that pleased Liam a great deal. Family was so important to him, and he wanted Rachel's family to be included in their lives and the lives of their precious girls, who were due in only a few short weeks.

Rachel was now being closely monitored. The only time she was allowed to leave the house was to go in for stress tests to make sure the girls were doing okay. *The girls.* Liam loved the sound of that. They still were undecided on their actual names, as they couldn't seem to agree on just the right ones. Rachel finally told Liam they were going to wait until the girls were born, then after they looked at them, they would choose then. Liam thought that was actually a good plan and was anxious for their arrival, but he wasn't nearly as eager as Rachel was.

"Not much longer until the girls are here, then you will be begging for bed rest. Gosh, we are going to be so exhausted," Liam stated as he sat down on the couch, lifting Rachel's legs and placing them on his lap. He started to massage her calves, causing her to moan softly.

"You're right. I'm just so bored. I'm used to doing stuff and living, you know?"

"I do, but every time you start 'living' you get all dizzy and your blood pressure raises. So, no living," Liam teased, working his hands up and down her leg muscles, wrapping them around her thin ankles.

"I think that whole 'not living' thing could become a problem, don't you?" Rachel laughed. God, he loved that sound.

"You know what I mean," he said.

Rachel stared at him with an intense longing for a moment. They had both learned just how easily life could change, and that they were so bound to one another. They had known they loved each other, but that frightful experience revealed just how much, and now their love just continued to grow.

Liam held her gaze, falling more in love with her right then. "I love you, you know."

Rachel smiled. "I love you more."

***

Rachel

How did she, of all people, get so lucky? To find a guy as great and loving as Liam, it was beyond her. She looked over at him, his sandy brown hair still a tad too long. His strong jaw was outlined in a light beard he insisted was part of his autumn ritual, but she knew he really just hated shaving. But his eyes were what she loved most, those brilliant green eyes which had burned into her so deeply the first time she gazed into them. Eyes she prayed their daughters would inherit.

Liam and her had been through quite a bit in such a short time. Even though they still had only known each other since the start of the year, a little over ten months, they had grown to love each other in ways Rachel was convinced was only for cheesy romance movies. It was the typical case of girl meets boy, girl gets angry with boy, then boy makes the most incredible love to her, then boy creates a ton of unexpected emotions in girl that she can't quite cope with, then girl learns she does love boy more than she ever thought possible, then girl learns she is having twins, then boy and girl get married under a shower of fireworks. Okay, so it wasn't the typical case, but it was their love story. It was one that had been met with frustration, annoyance, pure desire, and ultimately, had the best happily ever after.

Now if she could just survive the last few weeks of this bed rest, she would be okay. Liam had been waiting on her, not allowing her to do much of anything, and it was driving her crazy. He had sent his mother over while he was at work, and his father, and even Grandpa Paddy, had come over to keep her company. She actually enjoyed visiting with him a great deal, and Grandpa Paddy would even allow her to get up and make them both tea. The stories he would share with Rachel had her laughing, crying, and falling even more in love with this truly remarkable family. As Rachel rubbed her belly, feeling a Braxton Hicks contraction and one of their girls pounding against her womb, she couldn't help but think how lucky these precious babies were going to be. They would know a love far greater than she did growing up. They would have a family here in Birch Valley that would shower them with affection, support, and pure unconditional love. These sweet little babies would also have the newly developed love from their grandparents in Newport Beach, and they would be spoiled without a doubt. Then there was their Aunt Chelsea, who was beyond excited for their arrival, and already had made so many plans for them, including their first trip to Disneyland, their first time seeing the ocean, where they would build their first sandcastle. Chelsea also stressed that she wanted to be there for when the time of boys and fashion became important in their lives. Rachel couldn't help but giggle at the thought of Chelsea of all people giving romantic advice, but her best friend had been right about Liam. Rachel may have been blind to it all or just too darn stubborn to realize that it was possible to fall for someone so quickly. She would love Liam for the rest of her life, and Chelsea was partially to thank for that.

***

Daniel

"God, their coffee is so good." Hannah sighed as she set down her jumbo mug. They were seated inside the new coffee shop, Birch Valley Brew. It was cozy, the lighting low and romantic, and today there were only a few other customers seated at the various tables. The shop had an eclectic feel to it, with hodgepodge decor and mismatched chairs. The scent of espresso hung heavy in the air.

"I know. But this cookie is like the best thing ever." Daniel held up a half-eaten double chocolate chip cookie.

Hannah scowled at him. "Is that so?"

Daniel swallowed and answered cautiously, "Well, I mean…"

Then Hannah erupted into a loud giggle. "Sorry,

I couldn't keep up the angry act."

Daniel was confused and didn't quit follow. "Huh?"

"I made those cookies." She pointed at what was left of the delicious cookie.

"Wait, what?"

"Yeah, I started selling them some of my stuff. I even convinced your mother to sell some of her amazing muffins too."

"Whoa, how did you manage that?"

"Manage what? Selling the cookies?" Hannah asked as she sipped from her enormous mug.

"Managed to get my mom to sell her muffins. Rachel tried convincing her. Hell, we all have," Daniel explained as he brushed off the crumbs on his shirt.

"I think because her and I are sort of the same. We bake for the simple joy of it."

"Hmm, I think it's more than that. Amber bakes. She is like you and Mom, and she couldn't get Mom to sell them even at Herrick's."

"Well…okay, you caught me." Hannah smiled coyly at him. "I told her it was to raise money for our wedding and to buy a home we could fill with lots of grandchildren for her."

Daniel laughed. "So that's how you did it? Clever girl." He stretched over and kissed her quickly on the cheek, making a rush of pink color her face.

***

Hannah

Sitting there with him, feeling comfortable and content, Hannah wouldn't have imagined this happening only a few short months ago. Life was funny like that. You think you are on a path, certain that direction is the one you are meant to travel. Hannah's had been a lonely one, and she figured that was what life had decided for her. Then Daniel O'Brien, in all his jovial goofiness, had stumbled into her life, but it was a different route that life intended for them to take before it allowed them to travel on the same road together.

To think that Daniel had briefly dated her sister, Nina, and to watch her not appreciate the kind and gentle man that he was, was not a huge surprise. The shocker was finding herself dating Daniel and falling hopelessly in love with him in only a matter of moments, but perhaps that was because she had loved him from the second he stepped foot on their farm. He had become her best friend, a man who stirred many wild and new sensations inside her, and someone that would protect her with all of his being. She was now engaged to this man, who made her laugh and kissed the daylights out of her. Hannah was eager to be his wife in every sense.

Hannah, a fan of all things romantic, was now experiencing a real life romance, something far better than anything she could read about in her books or watch in her favorite movies. As everything was righting itself in her life, her sister had returned home with a different view and appreciation for her family and Birch Valley. Nina had even started to take a few community college classes, and it was doing her a world of good. Her father seemed happier than he had in years, mostly thanks to Daniel, who was spending time with him, helping him around the farm, and even taking him fishing, just the two of them.

Hannah stared at him as he drank his coffee. Daniel looked around the coffee shop, unaware that she was devouring his handsome face with her eyes, drinking him in. She was savoring every morsel of Daniel, his casual kindness, how his face was always full of life, and the smile he readily gave out to anyone he crossed paths with. Hannah leaned in closer to him, smelling the spicy hints of his aftershave, feeling the softness of the green sweater he wore rub against her cheek. She sighed. He was special, and he was all hers.

Some might say that she was wrong, and possibly foolish to believe that life can could resemble a magical fairy tale, but here she was, living proof that fairy tales do happen, and happily-ever-afters did exist. They just so happened to be simple. There was no grand castle, yet, but she could picture them living on a beautiful piece of land in Birch Valley. Nor was Daniel riding on a white steed to sweep Hannah off her feet or driving a great pumpkin carriage to carry her off to a ball, but his truck, which was always covered in mud, was just fine. No, this wasn't what a lot of people would consider a traditional fairy tale. It was just two people who loved to fish and loved each other with all their hearts, and wasn't *true love* the best kind of fairy tale?

"I love you, Mr. O'Brien."

He looked over her, a funny expression twinkling in his emerald green eyes. "I love you too, future Mrs. O'Brien."

Chapter Twenty

Liam

"Trick or treat!" Liam could hear young voices shouting it over and over again as he made his way to the front door. They lived several miles from the heart of town, where tons of children were in costumes and begging for candy.

"Boo!" Liam exclaimed, wearing a werewolf mask and absolutely terrifying his nephews and niece. Finn and Connor started to cry, and Melanie, after recovering from the scare, giggled.

"Thanks, Liam," Patrick complained as he tried to hush Finn, who was masked as the Hulk. Connor, dressed as Captain America, was being soothed by Amber.

"Everyone, come on in. Aunt Rachel made you guys some fun treats," Liam said, trying to ease the stress of the loud sobbing.

"Happy Halloween, Uncle Liam," Melanie said. She was wearing a glittery set of wings and looked to be some kind of fairy.

"Happy Halloween to you too. You look very pretty."

Melanie blushed and then ran past him to find Rachel. Maggie and Michael entered, Michael carrying a newly awakened Max, who was dressed as a devil. He even had a little mustache drawn on him. His beanie had plastic horns, and he wore a little cape.

Once everyone was inside, Rachel came out to join the children and visit with all the adults. Rachel wanted to make fun of how enormous she felt she was and was proudly wearing a pumpkin costume, her thin legs were covered in green leggings. Liam thought it was a bit much, but she looked adorable.

"Hi, everyone. Happy Halloween." Rachel greeted everyone. Finn and Connor ran up to her and wanted to feel the stuffing of her pumpkin costume. They kept poking her and laughing. She reached down to hug the boys, and gave them each a goody bag filled with an assortments of miniature candy bars, small toys, and suckers. Melanie stood next to Rachel, holding onto the special bag that Rachel had made for her. It also had candy, but it contained new pencils and erasers for school, and a few other odds and ends Rachel thought a six year old might enjoy.

"Oh let me look at him." Rachel cooed as she spotted Max. "My God, Maggie, he's adorable. Can I?" Rachel asked, holding her arms out to hold him. Maggie smiled and happily handed her son over. "Liam, you see this little mister?" Rachel cradled Max, showering him with kisses.

After a couple minutes, Liam said, "Well, time to

gather these ghouls and terrorize the neighborhood."

"Uncle Liam, we're just going trick or treating," Melanie argued with a large grin that showed a few missing teeth. Liam wanted to say she looked like a jack-o-lantern, but thought better of it.

"Well, same difference, kiddo. You ready to go? Remember, you have to give your uncle like at least a fifteen percent cut of your loot."

Melanie shook her head and suggested he just buy his own candy, since he was grown up. Everyone laughed. It was worth a shot, Liam figured. He gathered Michael, Melanie, and himself inside their car. The twins got loaded inside Patrick's SUV, and Amber and Maggie stayed behind to keep Rachel company. Liam smiled as he backed the car out of the driveway. This time next year his two daughters would be nearly a year old and would be celebrating their very first Halloween.

***

Daniel

"You sure you don't want to go trick or treating with your family? They are only little for so long, Daniel," Hannah said.

"No, I wanted us to go out, just the two of us." Daniel wanted to spend some much-needed alone time with Hannah. He had been working a lot at the shop, and with the recent excitement of Grandpa Paddy winning the lottery, things had been chaotic, and right now he just needed to be with Hannah,

272

alone.

Daniel helped Hannah inside the truck. He wanted them to have a romantic dinner, then maybe go for a drive. He honestly couldn't care less what they did or where they went, as long as they were together.

"Italian? Mexican? What are you in the mood for?" Daniel asked as he started up the truck. It rumbled loudly and shook. He turned up the heat inside the cab. It was getting colder each night, and they would be soon expecting snow.

"Well, I have an idea."

"Sure, what do you have in mind?" Daniel started driving in the direction of town. Overhead, the sky was a deep, rich navy blue. Stars speckled across it, and there wasn't a cloud in sight, which also indicated it was going to be downright cold.

Hannah instructed Daniel to go to grocery store. This scene seemed all too familiar, but he went along with it. She hurried to the deli counter and ordered several things. As they waited for their order to get filled, Daniel asked, "You don't want to go out?"

"We are," Hannah replied.

"No, like to restaurant or somewhere."

"Nope, you'll see."

Hannah thanked the clerk behind the counter, and they set off to go back to the truck. Once inside, Daniel asked, "So where to?"

"You really don't know by now?" Hannah giggled.

Daniel looked over at her, her face smiling in the darkness of the cab. He knew exactly where she wanted them to go, and this was one of the very reasons why he loved her.

"Ah, you know now?"

"Yes, I just feel bad. I feel like I need to take you out, like somewhere where we can sit and eat."

"Daniel, as long as I'm with you, I don't care where we are. If you'd rather we sit inside somewhere, we can. I just figured you would like to go somewhere we both know we'd enjoy. Our spot," Hannah explained.

Their spot was gorgeous, and Daniel knew that it would always be theirs.

***

Rachel

November arrived full of rain, sleet, and wind. It was turning out to be an extremely nasty month. Rachel stood looking outside their large window, watching the angry rain relentlessly splat against the glass. It was dreary and miserable outside, but in their home it was toasty and cozy. Liam had started the fireplace and carried in enough wood to last Rachel for the day while he was at work. Rachel eyed the bright digital clock on the microwave. School would be getting out soon, and she was thankful that Liam would soon be back. She couldn't shake the anxiety she had felt clawing away at her all day. Rachel had attempted to put it at rest by napping, but she'd found herself tossing and turning. Finally, after waging war in bed with her sleeplessness, she surrendered and got up. She

274

heated up a can of soup and cup of tea and watched as the rain pelted the ground and bounced off their lake.

Without warning, Rachel felt a sharp sting run through her. It came fast and made her gasp. She felt her belly tighten as another pain, this one more dull, settled deep into her back. Rachel waited for the pain to subside, but it seemed to remain, not easing its hold on her. Was this ever going to pass? Should she call someone? Questions stormed her mind, running around chaotically. She couldn't focus and the pain was increasing, almost to the point of blinding her. Then it dawned on her. Was she in labor?

***

Liam

"So, class, can anyone tell me what the phrase 'magnetic pull' means?" Liam held up two giant magnets in front of his fourth grade class. The telephone inside his room buzzed. "Everyone turn to page thirty-six in your science book and read the definition."

Liam grabbed the phone and answered, "Mr. O'Brien's room."

"Liam, sorry to interrupt your class period." Karen paused and then explained, "Rachel just called. She said for you not to worry, but she had called your mother and is having her take her to the hospital. She thinks she might be in labor."

"Are you serious?" Liam felt panic and

excitement surge through him.

"She asked that you just finish class, which is like ten minutes. But, hon, I am happy to come and fill in, if you want to go," Karen offered.

"You don't mind?" There was no way he was going to be able to finish class.

He could hear the sound of Karen's smile in her voice. "Of course not. It's not every day someone becomes a father, and to twins no less."

"Thank you so much, Karen. I appreciate it. I'll see you in a couple minutes." Liam hung up and explained to the class that Ms. Karen would be coming in to watch them finish up, and that they were to be on their very best behavior. He started to gather his things, but felt completely out of sorts and scatterbrained when Karen appeared and greeted the class. Everyone adored the school secretary, who had been there since Liam was a student. She was sweet and kind, but she also meant business.

"You get on outta here. Good luck, and have your mother call me." Karen ushered him out his door. He got into his truck, started it up, and realized, this was it, his daughters were coming into the world. He was officially going to be a dad, something he didn't know he wanted until Rachel had told him she was pregnant. Ever since then, the desire to meet the little people growing inside his wife had grown. Liam was thrilled. He sped to the hospital, which was only a few blocks down the road. Time to meet his girls.

***

Okay, so babies didn't just arrive in a matter of minutes. No, they take their sweet time. Liam had figured that by the time he'd arrived at the hospital it wouldn't be long before his girls arrived. He couldn't be more wrong. Rachel agonized through hours and hours of intense labor, and it wasn't until the next day in the early morning hours that they welcomed two healthy and very pink baby girls.

It had been two days, and now he and Rachel were staying in a balloon and flower-filled room. Ethan, Rachel's brother, had the most incredible gifts sent to her. The family had each spent time helping them get through the process of labor. They brought snacks, gifts, and their support.

"God, they are so beautiful." Liam cradled one of his daughters. Rachel held the other, and they just stared at their creations.

"I can't stop looking at their faces and their tiny fingers." Rachel started to get weepy again. They both had cried. In fact, everyone who had visited them became a little teary eyed. Liam supposed that happened when you hold an angel in your arms, something so precious, that smelled of heaven and life.

"They look just like you, Rachel," Liam stated. These girls were gorgeous, with perfect rosebud lips. They had Rachel's cute, slightly upturned nose, but their hair was a whole different matter. Each baby had a wild crown of red hair, so vibrant and fiery. Liam hoped it wasn't a sign of their tempers. The crimson color helped Rachel and Liam determine their names fairly easily, and once they said them out loud, it was as though those names had always been the perfect names. Rose and Ruby O'Brien, two nearly eight-pound girls. They were identical in almost every sense, except Ruby had a tiny birthmark on her rear, the size of a thumbprint. His mother noticed it right away and said that God had done that, that it was His thumbprint. Either way, Liam found it to be adorable, and had kissed the birthmark several times.

"We did it, babe," Rachel whispered to him.

Liam rose carefully, not wanting to disturb the sleeping beauty in his arms. He went to the side of the hospital bed and said, "No, you did this. You carried these princesses inside you, you protected them, and then you bravely gave birth. I didn't think it was possible, but I love you even more."

"Oh, Liam, I'm so happy. I never truly realized how much I needed them and you in my life. This is all I could ever ask for."

He leaned down and kissed her.

Their newborns were a reflection of their passion and love, two tiny souls that now made them into a family. Liam smiled down at the sleeping and swaddled precious little beings. Not only did Rachel have his heart, but now so did their daughters.

***

Mary

"The bird is almost done and then we can start getting everyone ready to be seated," Mary announced as she basted the golden turkey in her over.

Today was Thanksgiving, and she couldn't be happier or more thankful. Their home was bustling with activity. All of her grandchildren were there. Melanie was playing blocks with Finn and Connor, and there was little Max, sporting the famed O'Brien eyes and handsome black Irish features of his grandfathers and Uncle Patrick. Rose and Ruby, the cutest set of red-headed babies, were already showing a hint of the emerald O'Brien green in their newborn eyes. And there was Dylan, not her grandson by blood, but simply by love.

All of her children were there, happily partnered with the best people. Even she couldn't have found them better matches.

Liam, her easygoing son, was the one who never took life too seriously or engaged in confrontation. Then Rachel came into her son's life, turning it upside down. It had been almost comical, seeing the two deny their feelings, when everyone could plainly see how much fire blazed between the two of them. It took another shake up to finally get them to see reason, Mary had prayed hard for them, and her prayers had been heard. Rachel was now an incredible daughter-in-law, Mary knew she would be the moment she'd met her. What she hadn't known was what an amazing wife and mother Rachel would become.

Maggie, Mary's only daughter, was the one who was also so strong and independent. She was the one who'd needed to spread her wings and leave Birch Valley, only to find that home is truly where the heart is. Mary adored Michael and could see how much he loved her daughter, and their beautiful children. He just needed a little guidance. Mary had prayed a great deal for them. Their marriage had endured a great deal of pain, but ultimately Mary's prayers had been heard as well.

Patrick, her oldest son, was the man who had experienced something even she hadn't. Becoming a widower, with two brand new babies, had broken him, and her as well. Mary and all of the family had prayed for him to find happiness once again. Those prayers were also heard. It took another, who shared the same grief, to reach her boy. Amber was an incredible light that was able to brighten even the darkest corners of her son. Mary would always treasure her for bringing her son back to life.

Daniel, her sweetest boy, was the one child that was most like her. His kind and gentle nature always had separated him from the others. She had seen the sadness and loneliness take a hold of Daniel when each of his siblings had found their special someone. Mary's heart ached for him, knowing that he deserved a good woman. In his desire just to find someone to love, he'd almost wound up with the wrong woman. But again, Mary had prayed, and her prayers had been heard. Now, Hannah, a woman worthy of her son's love, was going to be joining the family. Hannah reminded Mary of herself, and she knew that Daniel, her special boy, would always be loved and taken care of.

"Anything I can do to help?" Hannah asked, breaking into Mary's thoughts.

Mary smiled at her. The sweet girl didn't realize she had already done more than enough. "You can take these yams to the table, dear."

The family gathered around the old kitchen table, marred from the many meals that had been shared. They all clasped their hands in prayer as they sat surrounding the delicious feast on the beautifully decorated table. Mary sat down and looked at the people who surrounded her. Her husband, though growing grayer, was as handsome as when they first met, and he had given her all these precious children. Grandpa Paddy was always one to make mischief, but it was his lively spirit that filled this house, and Mary would always love him dearly, no matter how much he tried to get under her skin.

Liam, Maggie, Patrick, and Daniel were her very reason for living, for being the best mother she could be. She had moments of doubt, when she thought that perhaps she had failed them in some way, but seeing them now, all happy in their lives, she realized she did one thing right: she loved them with all of her being.

***

Daniel

"God, I'm stuffed. I can barely move," Daniel stated as he and Hannah walked to his truck, each carrying an armload of Tupperware filled with leftovers.

"But it was incredible. I have never experienced a Thanksgiving like that. We never really celebrated it."

Daniel took the containers from Hannah and

loaded them inside the truck. They each managed to get inside, and sat for a moment. "Turkey coma setting in?" Daniel teased.

"Actually, I have a surprise for you." Hannah's voice was nervous. She seemed unsure.

"Okay…"

"Take us to our spot," Hannah ordered softly.

Daniel started the truck, wondering if something were wrong. Fear started to breed inside him. Maybe Hannah had changed her mind about him. Had he done something to upset her? Daniel couldn't think. She'd seemed fine during dinner, perhaps a little quiet, but that was normal when there were so many O'Briens grouped together. Daniel felt his worry grow. It festered into an enormous monster within him. Hannah was silent during the drive, looking outside her window. He couldn't imagine she would break things off, not on Thanksgiving. They arrived at their spot. The gravel road had been freshly laid, which Daniel thought was odd.

He continued to cruise slowly up the way. Then, as he neared the water, he saw it. Daniel's mind spun. He glanced over at Hannah. Her hand covered the smile she had obviously been trying to hide the entire car ride.

They both hopped out of the truck's cab quickly. Daniel grabbed her hand, and they walked toward a wooden sign with large and bold letters which read: *Sold.* The sign had been planted near a large tree, a few feet from the shore. Metallic balloons were floating and bouncing against the slight breeze.

"Surprise!"

Daniel scooped her up into arms, bringing her tightly against his chest. He kissed her more passionately than before. He had been sick with worry that she was going to end their relationship, but here she had done something remarkable and special.

When he pulled away, her lips were red and swollen, her cheeks were the prettiest shade of blush. As she tried to speak, he almost kissed her again, but she raised her hand to stop him. "Remember when I said that I was selling cookies to that coffee shop?"

"Yes, my little Girl Scout."

Hannah playfully slapped him, "Oh stop." She turned and looked toward the sign. "I was saving for this."

"But I don't understand, I didn't think this land was for sale," Daniel questioned, searching her eyes for answers.

"Well, it wasn't. I had to track down who owned the actual land. I just knew this place would be perfect for our wedding."

"It is kind of our spot," Daniel agreed, but that didn't explain the sold sign.

"Daniel, I feel like we started our relationship here, and I want us to start our life here. So I put a down payment on the land."

"Are you serious?"

She nodded. "I mean, you own a construction business, so I kind of figured."

Daniel pulled her against him again as they both laughed, and he kissed her again. They linked their arms together, watching the light wind send ripples across the lake. The late afternoon sky revealed white clouds which were laced with ribbons of gray, that now had started to spill delicate snowflakes. He couldn't help but think, as they stood there alone, without a soul for miles around, with the first snow of the season falling around them, that he needed to build their dream house as soon as possible, because he needed to marry this wonderful woman. Several perfect icy flakes landed on Hannah's beautiful face, and Daniel was tempted to brush them off, but decided to kiss them away instead. They both looked out the land that was now the building site of their future home, the altar where their nuptials would take place; the place where they would raise their children and grow old together.

The End...or is it?

Epilogue

She stood there, snow falling lightly from the night sky, landing all over her, getting on her clothes, in her hair, and just everywhere. It was dark, and the moonlight was tucked behind heavy storm clouds, the filtered light illuminating the icy, white flakes that were coming down faster as each minute passed.

God, it was freezing here. She could feel the tears starting to build up again. She swallowed hard against the enormous lump that had been remaining in her throat. Her eyes felt raw and sore. She was still in shock as she stood in front of that door. The branches of the trees that surrounded the home were weighed down with heavy layers of snow. Giant piles of glittering white stretched out along the ground like a winter comforter, full and thick. Why had she come here? Because in actuality she had nowhere to go. She really didn't want to bother them. That's why she hadn't called. She had acted purely on instinct. She hadn't paused for a moment, not thinking, but she'd known this place was safe.

She had packed what she could, then just left.

Her life was in complete disarray. Never in all her years would she have thought this would have happened. Maybe it could happen other people, but definitely not her. Inhaling the sharp, chilly air, feeling it burn her lungs, she tried to calm the tears that threatened. She wiped her face, knowing full well her mascara was smeared, her eyeliner smudged. She knew looked like an awful mess. There was nothing pretty about her or the situation she now found herself in.

Gathering all the strength she had left to knock, she closed her hand into a weak fist, and rapped her knuckles against the heavy wooden door. She waited. Silence, that was all that was out here. No sound at all, just stillness. It made her uncomfortable. She felt vulnerable and exposed out there. She knocked at the door again and waited. Her ears picked up on the sound of someone coming to answer, steady and fast footsteps headed for the door. The tears came. There was no more holding them back. They unleashed an ugly flood down her cheeks. Her nose was cold, numb, and dripping.

The door opened slightly, allowing enough space for her eyes to connect with the one person she knew she could count on. Eyes filled with intense confusion stared back at her. "Chelsea?"

About the Author

I was born and raised in southern California and relocated to beautiful eastern Washington state. The rural small towns that speckle this vast area have inspired my ideal setting for most of the stories I write. The pine and tamarack trees covering the towering mountains, the shimmering lakes and rivers, the abundant wildlife and a feeling of a time forgotten, stirs so many of my creative juices. I can't thank my parents enough for dragging this city kid on long roadtrips up to this rugged foreign area, because now it is my home and I truly love my life here.

Reading was something that spurred me to begin writing at a young age. I enjoyed creating characters, different settings, and describing anything and everything. Storytelling, I have found is something I have inherited from both of my parents. I love attention to detail, using words to fully bring the picture alive, that is something I got from my dad. Creating characters and figuring out their story and how to achieve their happy ending comes from my mom. Then there is the smell of a book, new or old, the weight of it in your hands as you balance it open, seeing all those beautifully typed words spun and woven into sentences, this was created by a writer. I knew that was what I wanted to be when I grew up.

Over the years I fiddled with a story here and there, but it wasn't until 2015 that I realized it was time. Time to get those dreams down on paper (or my laptop) and so The Cloverleaf Series was born. Coming from a family that is focused on being involved in each other's lives as much as possible created a great deal of inspiration and ideas for The Cloverleaf Series. My family is one that has weathered several terrible storms and still somehow keeps propelling forward. During those sunny times we can be seen gathered around, eating good food, sharing memories, and laughing until we can't catch our breath. We fight hard and love hard.

Romance, I simply love it, that's why I write it. I remember my mom giving me my very first paperback romance novel. It was a pretty exciting one filled with suspense and an overall excellent storyline, she had just read it and she felt it was suitable for my teenage eyes. That was it, I was hooked. I began to devour these romance stories that varied over the years from sweet to sultry, I consumed thousands of books and stories over the years. Each time I finished reading a novel, the desire to write my own grew stronger. As ideas for books swirled in my mind, it always had a romantic element to it, and I suppose it always will. What is there not to love about falling in love and finding that special person to share your life with? Who doesn't wish for passion, butterflies in your stomach, and that happily ever after?

As a reader, I can't even begin to thank all of the writers that have created so many emotions for me, falling in love with characters, mourning their loss, sighing as I close the final chapter or smiling when everyone lives happily ever after. As a writer, I just want to do the same.

Facebook:
http://facebook.com/authorgloriaherrmann

Twitter:
http://www.twitter.com/@gloriaiswriting

Website:
http://www.gloriaherrmann.com/

Goodreads:
https://www.goodreads.com/authorgloriaherrmann

Instagram:
http://www.instagram.com/authorgloriaherrmann